INTO THE VORTEX

The glowing mist coalesced, thickening into a long scar of brilliant white energy. To the villagers it seemed that the phenomenon was somehow rushing forward across a great distance. As if through the fissure they could see into a sky beyond their own, a window into what was coming. The torrent of wind heralded its imminent arrival. Something titanic. Something never before known to Earth.

The ground trembled and shook. The crackle of live electricity, the roar of an immense fire, the clamor of exploding bombs, these and more mixed into a reverberating echo, and with one final, violent flash of light the arrival was upon them.

No one ran—there was nowhere to go . . .

VOR™

THE MAELSTROM

INTO THE MAELSTROM

LOREN L. COLEMAN

ASPECT®

WARNER BOOKS

A Time Warner Company

WARNER BOOKS EDITION

Cover design by Don Puckey
Cover illustration by Donato
Cover logo design by Jim Nelson

Warner Books, Inc.
1271 Avenue of the Americas
New York, NY 10020

Visit our Web site at
www.twbookmark.com

A Time Warner Company

Printed in the United States of America

First Printing: December 1999

10 9 8 7 6 5 4 3 2 1

For Mike Nielsen, who started a fun adventure
and was never too busy for one more question.

The author would like to thank the following people for their support and assistance over the course of this novel:

Mike Nielsen, for reasons already stated. Jim Nelson, who also fielded phone calls.

Donna Ippolito and Annalise Raziq, at FASA, for their efforts in helping meet a tight deadline. Jaime Levine, who handled everything on Warner Books' end.

Always, Dean Wesley Smith and Kristine Kathryn Rusch for continued support in this business.

Lisa Smedman, Dean Smith—again—and Jerry Oltion, who are helping flesh out the universe and provided a few neat story tie-ins.

Russell Loveday, science and technology consultant. Allen and Amy Mattila, Irina Busenbark and Alex Okhapkin for the assistance with Russian languages, history, and customs.

My wife, Heather, and my three wonderful children, Talon, Conner, and Alexia, for unswerving and loving support. Thank you.

VOR™
THE MAELSTROM

INTO THE MAELSTROM

EARTHFALL

1

The waning moon hung low over the horizon, a sliver of white, dimmed now and again by wisps of trailing clouds. The waters of the Atlantic shimmered in its silvery light, the gentle swells gleaming like burnished steel, sweeping in against Angola's coastline. The rolling surf crested and washed up onto a steep, shallow beach, then fell back whispering the promise of its next surge. Even here, near the water's edge, the land knew little relief from Africa's long days. Late into the night the sun's heat continued to seep from the blistered ground, barely stirred by a sluggish and intermittent breeze.

Here the Maelstrom would first taste of the Earth.

A dozen fishing skiffs had been dragged well above the high-tide mark and lashed to supports sunk deeply to prevent a rogue wave from claiming one of the small boats. No harbor, no docks. Local people thought of Novo Cocarada as a fishing village because half the families relied on the Atlantic's fickle waters to survive. The rest depended on what little they could grow in the sun-baked dirt, the few scrawny cattle and goats grazing on sparse grasses and shrub, and the generosity of village fishermen.

In a century of *supposed* progress, Novo Cocarada had changed little. A small collection of ramshackle buildings formed its entirety, the whole village built from warped planks, corrugated tin, and what little fiberboard had been scrounged from nearby Covelo and Lobito. A single window left open to the outside cast flickering lamplight onto a garbage-strewn road.

Novo Cocarada was no more than a small dot on some map, a narrow stretch of flatland, caught between the Atlantic and the sharp-edged foothills rising sharply into the Serra Cambonda range to the south and east. It fell beneath the military attentions of both the Union and the Neo-Soviet empire, and contributed perhaps one soldier every decade to the defense of United Africa. The global buildup of arms and increased conflict had done nothing to relieve the Earth's poverty. The constant skirmishes had, in fact, only created more such places. That Novo Cocarada would soon be a site of infamous renown was not a distinction the villagers would live to know.

The winds struck first, without warning, smashing down from higher atmosphere to chop the ocean swells and whip up an instant storm of dust and debris over the village. Window coverings of light plastic and loose wooden slats ripped free. Hard gusts smashed lean-tos and rickety sheds into kindling. Cattle lowed their distress, and the goats bleated shrilly. The burning lamp that lit one window toppled, spilling an instant oil fire across the floor. Another dilapidated shack collapsed under the sudden onslaught. Screams of fright were lost to the winds as lightning split the sky and thunder shook the ground. A suddenly angry surf pounded the coast, the waves now rushing farther up the shore.

More lightning, twin forks that slashed across the sky and then broke into whiplike tendrils. Only this time the darkness did not return completely. A glowing fissure split the heavens, a narrow chasm filled with luminescent mist cutting across the sky, running from out over the ocean inland to the Serra Cambondas. Lightning played along its edges, to the accompaniment of thunderous noise. Over the Atlantic the mist brightened, a pulse that quickly traveled the fissure's length. The fingernail moon paled and was lost to an artificial daylight as the strange glow bathed the land.

A few villagers had stumbled from their homes, worried over their boats or livestock. They now stood transfixed by the wounded night, their dark skins washed gray in the unearthly illumination, their eyes tearing from the dust storm. The winds poured down from the fissure above, smashing into an unsuspecting Earth before rushing outward in a furious howl. A large sheet of tin tore from the roof of one shanty, then sailed away on the gale. Whipped by the gusts, the lamp fire leapt up the walls of one house and now threatened another, the flames reaching out as they crackled and snapped their anger. Novo Cocarada was dying, and no one moved to save it. No one knew where to begin.

The driving surf continued to punish the beach. Waves lapped up against the grounded skiffs. One comber curled up to immense height, walking up the steep beach to smash two small launches and tear another from its mooring before spending itself. Thousands of liters of seawater swept into the village in a shallow flood—knocking two villagers off their feet, carrying them along several hundred meters before finally letting go. Where water hit the burning house it extinguished the lower flames, but failed to staunch the full inferno.

The wash of seawater broke the paralysis that had seized the villagers. Shaking off the shock, they began to move with something akin to purpose. One rushed to check the boats, and others to help rescue people trapped beneath the collapsed building. Their eyes were diverted from the alien sky for only a few seconds.

In that brief instant, they missed the end of Novo Cocarada.

The glowing mist coalesced, thickening into a long scar of brilliant white energy. There was no indication of actual movement, though to the villagers still distracted by the sky it seemed that the phenomenon was somehow rushing forward across a great distance. As if through the fissure they could see into a sky beyond their own, a window into what was coming. The torrent of wind heralded its imminent arrival. Something titanic in size. Something never before known to Earth. And, in the eyes of the villagers, something evil.

The ground trembled and shook, knocking them all from their feet as a new noise assailed their senses. Not a true thunderclap, like those heard so far. The crackle of live electricity and the roar of an immense fire. The clamor of a series of exploding bombs. These and more mixed into a reverberating echo, and then, with one final, violent flash of light, the arrival was upon them.

The fissure cracked, and a long tendril of blazing energy tens of kilometers long and easily a full kilometer across fell from the sky over Angola's coast. It struck into the Atlantic first, far to sea, pushing the water back in great columns and building twin tidal waves that rushed off north and south. The line continued to descend, plowing the ocean and raining lightning over the land.

No one ran—there was nowhere to go, to hide, no safe haven. Some prayed. A few were mercifully shocked past any ability to think clearly. Most expected a wash of heat or burning energy to incinerate them, having for decades understood the very real threat of a nuclear end. Neo-Soviet forces had demonstrated time and again their penchant for such weapons, though never on African soil.

But as the tendril fell over the village, the touch of energy did not burn, and was not comprised of true light. The villagers' final sensations before death claimed them were of cold, and darkness.

The wall of energy stood several kilometers out to sea, running southeast to Angola's coast and over the site where Novo Cocarada had once been. It stretched up into the Serra Cambonda range, filling valleys and stretching over peaks until overlapping with the Catumbella River.

Nearly half a kilometer high, it remained for several long seconds—exactly as much time as it had taken to fall from the sky. Then, as though with casual indifference, the tendril rose slowly back into that sky, tearing up the Earth as it left. The land came away with a terrible cracking and grinding, as if an immense hand had gouged into the ground and torn it away. Several hundred meters deep at the coast—over a full kilometer where the crackling energy had pooled into Cambonda valleys and now uprooted entire mountains—and several kilometers wide. And with a final shattering of the sky with violent lightning and deep, roaring explosions, the tendril was washed over in a blurry field of energies that widened the fissure. The arm of blazing energies slipped back through, pulling the stolen land with it.

Surrounding territory continued to shake with violent quakes, the Earth stressed from the sudden loss of mass and the pounding as the Atlantic waters rushed in to fill the deep void. The roar and boom of a thousand waterfalls thundered in the night, a terrifying discord heard as far away as Covelo. A new rush of wind scoured the arid lands as air was displaced by ocean. Quickly undercut by the raging torrent rushing inland, large swaths of coastal land slid into the chasm, widening the newly made bay. Millions of liters of seawater rushed by the headland every second, pushing a great wave farther into the interior of Angola. That wave finally burst and washed up over sea level some twenty-two minutes and seventeen kilometers later. The deep bowl continued to wash and flood, fighting to establish itself with the Atlantic.

The canyon ripped through the Serra Cambonda range would never be filled, the majority of it being above sea level. Cliffsides collapsed and slid into the canyon, barely denting such an immense evacuation. The Catumbella River diverted its course to fall into the deep gorge, leaving dry the Angola towns of Benguela and Lobito along its original bed. Eventually the river would trace a path through the gigantic canyon, reaching Cocarada Bay to begin its fight to establish a freshwater basin. By then news of the incident would have reached the Union and Neo-Soviet intelligence communities. United Africa would have its first inspectors on-site, who could do little but make inconclusive reports. The fissure had already closed, leaving behind no evidence of what had caused such devastation. Gentle swells again moved easily toward Angola's coast.

And a thumbnail moon continued to rise in the African night sky.

2

Night cloaked the waters of Karskoye More, the darkness guarding the Union Army's infiltration of Neo-Soviet territory. Colonel Raymond Sainz, commander of the Seventy-first Assault Group, stood on the observation deck of the lead Leviathan antigravity vessel, holding tight to the safety rail. Ahead lay more darkness occasionally lit by the flicker of distant lightning. At his back the immense vessel's open bay held a dozen Hydra ag transports and several support vehicles awaiting off-load to the northern shore of Siberia. All but a few soldiers—scouts mostly, unused to tight confines—remained canned.

Through the light squall of freezing rain Sainz could barely make out the other two vessels carrying the rest of his command, though all three Leviathans were running at close quarters. Water beaded and ran off his camouflaged foul-weather gear, a few drops finding a seam at his neck and dripping icy fingers along one shoulder. Sainz was a big man, standing 1.9 meters tall, and with a touch of natural bronze to his skin hinting at his Mexican-Union birth. His broad face pinched into a frown as he studied sea and sky.

"What do you think, Colonel?" The vessel's captain, Jorgen Fredriksson, stepped from the protective alcove that led to his enclosed bridge. Tall even for a Scand, he was the only man aboard who forced the colonel to look upward. Despite the weather, he wore only a thick sweater under his standard uniform, as if the cold and rain dared not bother him.

"These aren't my home waters, Jorgie." Sainz pronounced the captain's name *Yorgie*, his polyglot skills giving him familiarity with the Scandinavian tongue. "But born and raised in Matamoros, I never saw water behave like this except once in the eye of a hurricane."

He gestured out to where nearby swells ran at odds with one another, as if tide and current and wind no longer affected them. A set joined together for a moment, pitching upward high enough to slam the side of the antigrav vessel and shoving a hard jog into its glide path. Sainz gripped the rail even tighter. In the open bay soldiers cursed as they tumbled to the deck or were thrown up against one of the Hydras. Too late the Leviathan's terrain-compensation circuitry kicked in, raising the huge craft another few meters only to settle back to an efficient glide when no further large waves were detected.

Captain Fredriksson held his footing with a wide-legged stance, needing no extra support. "Ya, well, there's no hurricane about. I've run missions over northern waters for fifteen years, and never seen anything like this. And it looks like we're heading into much worse." He nodded forward, past the bow and toward the distant light show. The flickering glow of heavy lightning jumped over a fair arc, and for a brief second lit up several degrees of the southern horizon. "That looks to be centered just east of the city of Dikson. We'll skirt it by fifty kilometers or better, but I'm still betting we catch hell trying to make Taymyr Bay."

Sainz wouldn't presume to debate the captain. It was Fredriksson's knowledge that had convinced Union brass to risk three Leviathans on this insertion rather than the more easily detected Navy amphibian transports. The Scand officer had known just how close they could skirt the northern defense post Novaya Zemlya without detection, and could identify any stretch of Neo-Sov northern coastline at a glance. He also guaranteed full withdrawal of the Leviathans before the four hours of northern night ended.

Sainz's brown eyes locked onto the captain's frosty blues. Both men blinked water from their vision. "Are you saying the insertion is in danger?"

Fredriksson laughed, his deep voice a hint of thunder itself. "No Scand would worry about a little storm while in command of this monster." He slapped a metal bulkhead. "The sea's no match for a Leviathan. Not even as strange a sea as this one."

He paused and studied the horizon. "A tidal wave *might* flip us," he said, his tone a touch more cautious. "Heard one wiped out Lagos in Nigeria last week, after some disturbance near Angola. You think we have a similar problem?"

Sainz considered the several ways he might answer that question. Fredriksson was obviously fishing for information, and in a way that didn't *exactly* violate secrecy orders.

Sainz appreciated the captain's desire for more information. It came with accepting command and responsibility for the lives of others. But the final truth of the matter was that Sainz didn't really know. And any discussion, no matter how vague, still impinged on the oath he'd taken as a Union officer. In twenty-three years of service, Raymond Sainz had managed to avoid any compromise of his personal honor. One of the major ways, he believed, the Union differed from the Neo-Soviet empire. One of the differences he fought to protect.

"Get us to shore, Jorgie." He broke from the captain's wintry gaze, again searching the darkness as if he might detect any hidden threat to his command. "Just get us to shore."

Clouds rolled away on a sharp northerly wind, opening the sky back up to a brilliant field of stars. The early dawn of extreme northern lands was still a good hour away, touching the southeastern horizon with only the dimmest light. The bulk of the Seventy-first Assault Group, unofficially known as Raymond's Rangers for their CO's former career in special forces, was drawn into its two columns awaiting orders to move. Pickets established a safety perimeter at two kilometers. Nearby, a small wooded stand grew up from a shallow, bowl-shaped depression, probably fed and kept alive by a hot springs. Everywhere else, one saw arctic plains and low, rolling hills covered by scrub and short, straw-colored grasses. Nothing to indicate trouble.

You think we have a similar problem?

Fredriksson's question continued to haunt Sainz, the more so as scouts sent to recon the deployment zone reported back their *qualified* "all clears." No Neo-Sov forces. No remote-detection equipment. The huge Leviathans had departed after depositing their charges on the north Siberian tundra, removing the greatest risk for accidental detection of his command. And topside brass had promised a window in the coverage by Neo-Soviet internal-security satellites. It should have left him feeling as secure as he might be in enemy territory.

What had him uneasy was the specimen he held in his hands and the oddity he was kneeling next to. One of the scouts had brought him this sample of petrified scrub. Though neither botanist nor geologist, Sainz still recognized its inexplicable nature. This was not a sample of vegetation turned rock over centuries of fossilization. Its twisted length was fully intact, from evergreen needles to a full root system, as if turned to stone in an instant's time. Dirt still clung between petrified tendrils of the rootstock. The pathfinder had reported finding an entire field of them, as had other scouts. One also claimed to have seen a plant that looked spun from glass, though it had shattered at his touch.

Sainz preferred to believe the latter another manifestation of this strange petrifaction process. He had enough of the bizarre to deal with already in that the stones he knelt over also defied immediate explanation. Salted over the ground for hundreds of meters, glossy smooth like obsidian, they glowed with a lustrous emerald sheen. Pebbles to the size of a man's head. Slightly warm to the touch. At first the Union troops had worried over intense radiation or some new chemical threat—CBR was always a primary concern—but the unit's ChemBioRad experts quickly confirmed that the area was clean. Or as clean as one could expect in Neo-Soviet territory. No reason to worry.

Still, they *had* taken samples for later study. And Sainz

remembered the footnote attached to the Eyes Only report from United Africa—the strange mineral deposits and "unexplained biological damage" noted by investigators at the Novo Cocarada site. It left him with concerns of his own for the safety of his people.

Footsteps scuffed the ground behind him. "I have the juniors assembled at the trailer," said Major Rebecca Howard, his XO. Her voice was rough from years of shouting commands but not altogether unpleasant. Short and compact, she wore her long, wheat-colored hair in a single braid sealed in place with a special wrap when on duty. She toed at one of the glowing stones with the rough tread of her combat boot, flipping it over. It had rested in a slight depression, as a natural stone would, but came away clean of any earth.

"Not still worried about these rad-stones, are you?" she asked.

"They're not rad-stones," Sainz told her.

Howard shrugged uneasily, then breathed on her ungloved hands to warm her fingers against the Siberian chill. "Then why did the CBR boys make a point of bagging them in lined satchels?" She flicked the bulge made by the personal dosimeter sewn into a pocket of her fatigues, a passive detector that would be read after the mission to estimate her personal radiation dosage.

"We'll know later, of course, but I'll bet we're off combat duty for a year after this one. And I've read of similar effects. The Neo-Sovs pasted a lot of real estate with neutron bombs over the last century—I hear some rocks in China are still glowing, even from the sites hit back in ought-nine."

Sainz ran a hand back through his short dark hair. "Sure, sometimes we see a glow of white or even reddish orange. But never *green.*" He shook his head. "And never this far north. Why aim a strike up here?" He gestured to the open tundra.

"No," he said, rising to his feet, "this is something else. Except for when they flattened Novosibirsk to put an end to General Matirov's four-hour rebellion, they never walked a neutron device north of Sayan Khrebet." Seeing Rebecca's frown, he gave her the translated name of *Sayan Mountain Range.*

Her frown deepened. Sainz knew that some officers resented his mastery of languages, which included several dialects of Russian.

"So a power-plant meltdown, then," she said. "They've enough of those in the region. Or maybe it's something new. Will you allow it to hold up the mission? *Sir*?" She blinked rapidly, then looked down at one of the glowing emerald green stones on the ground.

Sainz smiled thinly at the implied rebuke. Rebecca Howard was as good an exec as he could hope for, and usually she kept her animosity buried. Her home state of Texas was, after all, a reluctant member of the Union. Texas supported the old American states above all, tolerating the Canadians but looking down on the equal status given Mexico. Many Texans barely concealed their hostility when speaking to those they considered inferior. In four years and eleven combat assignments, Major Howard had never allowed that bias to interfere with her duty. That it did now revealed her nervousness, whether or not she would admit to it. The colonel let her challenge slide. Everyone's nerves were stretched taut.

"This mission won't be held up, Major Howard. For anything. Let's hit the trailer and put on our show for the juniors."

His nod got her going, but Sainz remained a moment

longer, still holding the piece of petrified scrub amid the field of glowing stones. He looked around him at this disturbing place one last time, then knew he had to be on his way as well. He hadn't revealed to Howard the changes he was making to the mission's deployment. He would save that for the trailer.

And that would save any *discussion* for much later.

The Hades command glider was the unit's most advanced vehicle. It was smaller than the Hydra troop transport, packed with an incredible amount of communications and sensor equipment as well as a turret-mounted light rail gun. Its angular body, like that of the Hydra, incorporated a healthy measure of stealth capability, especially when charged with the signal-dampening field. Antigravity fields were stronger, allowing it to run smoothly over very rough ground, and it packed an improved thrust-to-weight ratio. Able to outrun any other vehicle deployed by the Seventy-first, it was still referred to as the *trailer* because Union tactical doctrine always placed command transports near the rear of any column. A dozen men and women gathered around the grounded Hades, waiting for their commanding officers. Waiting for the show.

The show was part procedure, part superstition—like most military traditions and protocols, Sainz suspected. The Seventy-first had been well briefed before departure, of course. But operational guidelines recommended a refresh for junior officers and senior enlisted personnel once a unit hit its deployment zone. It was crucial that everyone set the same foot forward when leaving the DZ. Sainz and Howard had, over four years together, honed their routine to a fine edge. Each knew which questions to field and how to play off the other's comments.

The assembled soldiers came to attention, saluting as

Howard and Sainz walked up to the command vehicle. All faced Colonel Sainz as they did so, except for one sergeant who turned away just enough to hint at a rebelliousness without being called on improper honors.

The two officers stopped just short of the group, and Sainz flipped a quick salute back to the assemblage for the both of them. Rebecca Howard nodded, and said, "Stand easy." The seven junior officers relaxed, arms folded across chests or leaning up against the Hades. The senior sergeants present fell into easy parade-rest stance, except for one of them who slouched back against the command vehicle.

Howard led off. "You know the drill. Intel has placed a Neo-Sov weapons facility in the plateau region southeast of our DZ. It's our one and only target this run."

"Chernaya Gora—the *Black Mountain*—is not turning out standard arms," Sainz said, giving the Neo-Soviet name, and its translation, for the facility. "We aren't worried about another few thousand chem-sprayers or Kalashnikov rifles. Black Mountain has its own liquid-metal fast-breeder reactor and is fully capable of nuclear-weapons production. Very likely it houses facilities for chemical and biological weapons, as well as any prototype weapons of mass destruction."

"Like the Angola blast device, Colonel-sir?" This from Sergeant Tom Tousley, the senior sergeant leaning casually against the command transport. Carefully disrespectful, as his earlier salute had also been. "That *is* why we're here, isn't it, Colonel-*sir*?" Tom Tousley was a Texan like Rebecca Howard, but he was everything she was not when it came to proper conduct. Tousley was the one who had dubbed the Seventy-first the *wetback brigade* the day Sainz formally accepted command. *That* comment had cost him a rocker stripe, administrative punishment, and his position as command master sergeant.

Sainz might have bounced him all the way back to the Union Army Replacement Department, except for Howard's personal intervention *and* the sergeant's record. The fact remained that Tousley, for his one major fault, possessed skills Raymond Sainz needed. He was a man willing to do whatever it took to get the job done.

Fortunately for the continued preservation of Tousley's rank, Howard did an excellent job of reining him in and keeping any discipline unofficial and off the record.

"I don't want to hear chow-hall rumors about what may or may not have happened in Angola," she told the group, "and how that might influence our mission. Or whether it does. Or whether it should. United Africa released its statement, basically explaining nothing. The press printed some slanted supposition, but even less in the way of fact. So, end of file. We're here," she said harshly, giving Tousley a hard stare, "to end a very real threat to the Union." She waited until Tousley dropped his gaze, conceding the point.

Sainz nodded support for his exec. He also had an idea of what victory might mean in the larger scheme of things, though he couldn't share such thoughts, not even with Howard. The Siberian lowlands were considered the Neo-Soviets' greatest weakness. It was an immense, sparsely populated territory, through which an enemy army could hope to move undetected. Which was exactly what the Seventy-first proposed to do. An army that could gain access to the Kirghiz Steppe could then swing south of the Urals, with all of the empire's southwest lowlands left wide-open. Take out or hold Moscow, Kiev, and Donetsk, disrupt or destroy Gorki, Kuybyshev, and Sverdlovsk, and you paralyzed the Neo-Soviet empire. China breaks away first, likely followed by what was left of Korea and then Japan. Sainz had heard it called the *Siberian gutshot.*

"Chernaya Gora should be in or around Gory Putorana," he said, returning to the briefing and identifying the mountainous region they would be searching. "This puts us in the neighborhood of Noril'sk. That city's our biggest threat, since the Neo-Soviets maintain three decent task forces there under competent commanders. If even one takes the field against us, we'll know we've been in a fight."

"The Putorana area," Rebecca Howard said, stumbling only slightly over the unfamiliar name, "is not too unlike the Four Corners region, if a bit smaller and taiga versus high desert. Still, I expect our training on the Colorado Plateau should pay off. You'll see similarities. A good variation of temperatures between night and day, though this time of year it shouldn't dip into freezing. There are forested areas that can hide us from the Neo-Sovs. And a lot of deep canyons where the Black Mountain facility can hide from us."

Staring off slightly south of east, Sainz estimated by the brightening sky that less than thirty minutes remained before the north's long day began. Time to broach the changes, and get the Seventy-first's twin columns moving. He drew a deep breath of the chill air.

"Because we've already seen a few minor surprises," he said, alluding to the curious discoveries made by the scouts, "every pathfinder patrol will be backed by a combat squad." Howard hid her surprise well. Only a slight tensing of the shoulders gave her away, though the semirigid padding of her field uniform hid most of that. "I want our people covered."

Only Sergeant Tousley looked ready to take issue with

the idea. Sainz had expected as much—the change meant combat squads would be pulling extra duty.

Howard headed off any problems by saying, "You give the pathfinders room to operate. Don't crowd. You're there for support, *in* case things go wrong. Not to make them go wrong." Whether or not she agreed with the change, she certainly made it sound as if the idea had earned her full support.

And Raymond Sainz knew when to take an advantage and leave well enough alone. Down to the hard sell. "We know the signs when the Neo-Soviet empire is feeling bellicose. They haven't varied too much since the zero-nine invasion of China. They escalate, stockpile, and threaten. And then burn a good portion in one massive strike. We've held them off every time it's come our way. This time we hope to stop them during the escalation phase. Taking out Chernaya Gora will do that."

"And," Rebecca reminded them, "if we're caught before we finish the job, it might just drive them straight into their strike. So stay alert; on your toes and by the numbers. Here's where we prove the Seventy-first Assault Group is a cut above the rest."

A good end to the show, Sainz decided. He nodded, once and finally. "Dismissed," he said.

As the juniors headed off to their various posts, Sainz did not move from his spot alongside the Hades. "We'll talk under way," Howard promised, then she, too, left to make one last check of the columns.

Sainz had no doubt of that. If he was a bit more cautious, it was because he knew more of the report on the Angola incident and how some of the African phenomena compared with these local oddities. He also had a better idea of what was at stake on the mission, though first he had to prove that a large force could operate under stealth in the taiga lands of Siberia. And since that test directly impacted on the survival of his command, he ranked it fairly high. So far, at least, nothing seemed to stand in the way.

It was a thought Raymond Sainz hoped would not come back to haunt him.

3

As the airlock processors continued pushing Mars's thin atmosphere aside for a Terran-norm mixture, Brygan Vassilyevich Nystolov peeled himself out of his environment suit. "Brygan the Bear" never waited for full atmosphere or the heated changing rooms. Didn't have to.

He quickly broke the hard seal down the chest of his protective suit and shrugged it off his wide shoulders. Made from a dark material backed by an insulated liner of silver-gray fabric, the suit clung to him like a second skin. Where he pulled it away, the sub–zero Centigrade temperature stabbed through his undergarment.

Ignoring the air's freezing touch, he hiked the suit down to his thickset waist. This freed the wide neck skirting attached to his helmet, the thin material covering his shoulders and good portions of his chest and back. He'd designed the suit himself to be a system of overlapping folds in order to be free of the maddeningly rigid helmet collars most suffered when suited for Mars's hostile environment. The helmet and skirt came away easily, his beard rasping against the suit's inner insulation.

He cradled the headgear in the crook of one well-muscled arm and tucked the skirting up into the bowl of the helmet. Doing so, he caught a glimpse of his own face in the helmet's reflective bowl; dark eyes almost black, set in a red-tanned face framed by dark bushy hair and trimmed beard.

Drawing a deep breath of the cold, thin air, Brygan curled his lip at the trace odor of stale sweat so typical of Neo-Soviet bases on Mars. It spoke too easily of an overtaxed scrubber system and the press of bodies in close quarters so common in the Mars colonies. He would know, his duties as scout and surveyor having taken him to every outpost many times over. Some he liked better than others, the ones where he had room to get away by himself. But this one, the Baskurgan cliffside base on the lower slopes of Ascraeus Mons, was bad. The main control center for Mars operations, its narrow corridors connected deep warrens crowded with Neo-Soviet military.

The insulated gloves finally came off, and he clipped them to his belt after brushing a wispy cloud of red fines from the dark material. The airlock's inner door cycled open, and Brygan glided forward in a stride he had perfected for the two-fifths standard gravity of Mars. Though still half-undressed and carrying his helmet with him, he bypassed the changing rooms. Some officers frowned at his appearance on the lift up to command levels, but no one bothered him. No one ever did.

Down a long corridor, and then into the chaos of Mars control. Computer stations packed the room wall to wall, the colored wash from their screens providing better illumination than the dim overhead lights. The room felt electrically charged from all the equipment. Operators and military men worked their way along the narrow aisles between stations, looking distracted as they compared data and argued. Brygan frowned. When technicians *and* the military were distracted, that left no one in control.

Almost no one.

He spotted General Vladimir Leonov near the plex wall, hands clasped behind his back, staring through the thick, transparent material to the violent landscape beyond. The outside floodlights washed enough light back in to show the general's iron gray crew cut and uniform outline. The large man wore his officer's trench, a rigid-armor vest with ballistic cloth falling in straight lines from the waist.

Brygan maneuvered the cramped aisles with a casual grace belied by his stocky frame. Though only 165 centimeters in height, his thick body lent him the solid appearance that had earned him the nickname *Bear.* His rogue habits likely contributed to that as well. He had come to Mars for Mother Russia and the Neo-Soviet empire, yes, but also for the freedom of exploring a vast wilderness, alone. It was how he worked, trusting to his own skills and near-preternatural senses and his touch of *goryachee*—the *hot stuff.* The high-radiation environment so many Neo-Soviets were exposed to in their lives had developed many low-grade mutations. Brygan's gave him less need for insulation from the extreme cold temperature of Mars and the ability to survive on a thinner oxygen mix than most. Though he couldn't breathe the Martian atmosphere, he could stand fully exposed to the negative-ninety-degree Centigrade mean temperature for a fair length of time.

Joining Mars's commander at the window, Brygan stood at some semblance of attention. "*Strasvi*, Comrade General Leonov. Reporting as ordered."

Brygan did not salute. Though a ten-year veteran of Mars, he technically held no formal military rank. That would have placed him in the chain of command, and the Neo-Soviet military put little faith in rogue individuals such as Nystolov. The group would always be more important, and more desirable, than the individual. The empire did not mind exploiting talents such as his, but would never give him authority over others. And that suited him. So a semi-formal *greetings* would have to suffice.

The general nodded brusquely. "*Da*, Comrade Nystolov. *Strasvi*." His voice was muffled slightly by the armored vest's high collar. The thick guard up front was wired for sound augmentation to amplify the general's voice if need be, and also came with a concealed mouthpiece for five minutes of secure air even on a chemically polluted battlefield. On Mars, such a feature was not without uses. "Welcome back from oblivion."

A Mars-traditional greeting, held over from the early days of the red planet's exploration. Brygan stared out through the thick plex, taking in the landscape he had come to know and appreciate. Barren rock and dust, scarred and pocked from an ages-old shower of micrometeorites. Crimson streaked with darker rust reds. The lower slopes of Ascraeus Mons looked like a blood-drenched battlefield. "Oblivion and I remain on good terms, Comrade General. What was it our first cosmonaut to Mars said? 'Everything to be cautious of, but nothing to truly fear.' "

"Pavel Shtavyrik," the general said, with a nod. "Three

times he commanded missions here, bringing supplies to establish our first base. A hero of the people. Still, he died on Mars."

"The danger of familiarity," Brygan agreed, reluctantly tearing his gaze from the view and back to the general. The man was of solid build, topping Brygan's medium height by a dozen centimeters. Red-brown eyes—a cosmetic mutation. A scar ran from the general's left temple, curving toward the cheekbone, then back to the base of his left ear—a souvenir of last year's battle against Union forces trying again to win a foothold on Mars. Armored gloves covered each hand, fitted with a protective exoskeleton.

Many of the personnel assigned to Mars had some touch of *goryachee* in one form or other. An added advantage for dealing with a hostile world. The Neo-Soviets did not possess the refined terraforming technology of the Union. The empire made do on the sheer might of its people. The general was a case in point—his strength was legendary. With those gloves, Leonov could punch through the thick plex without so much as scarring his hands. He was the only other person Brygan knew besides himself who often worked out under full Terran gravity, though the scout could not match half of Leonov's weight press.

It did give him cause to wonder, though, about Leonov's position near the plex. A subtle warning against those who still thought the path to advancement lay in a carefully staged coup? Or simple intimidation? Brygan glanced back to the main floor where operators and junior officers continued to work, with the occasional nervous glance toward their general.

"We have a problem?" Brygan finally asked, obviously rhetorical.

"Only one? That would be a welcome relief." Leonov

glowered at the men gathered about a nearby console. "Our Mental has informed me that Union forces have landed a new expedition on-planet. We did not detect them, again, and skywatch offers only excuses. And *now* half of the alleged geniuses in this room cannot explain our communications trouble with Moskva." His glared even more mercilessly at one hapless technician who happened to look up at the wrong time.

"Well?" Leonov demanded of the man.

"Comrade General, we still are not sure," the tech stammered. "The disturbances behave similarly to interruptions from heavy solar radiation, but no large flares have been detected and radiation readings are nominal." He swallowed hard, looking to one of his fellows for support. "The satellite array *did* lose tracking on Terra for an instant earlier today, but no cause has been determined, and it does not appear to be related to current difficulties."

Leonov reached out one gloved hand to touch the plex wall. Brygan drew in a deep, silent breath of the stale air, just in case.

"You tell me what it isn't and what shouldn't be involved," the general said, his voice dangerously quiet. He brought his free hand up and slowly closed it into a tight fist. "I want communications restored with Terra, and I want it done now." Several men and women visibly paled under the general's gaze.

Mention of Ascraeus's Mental, one of the rare individuals who exhibited extraordinary powers of the mind, instantly caught Brygan's attention. Though pitifully weak of body and ostracized to an even greater extent than rogues like Brygan, it was the Mentals who'd helped save Neo-Soviet security when technology and manpower failed to detect threats. If a Mental said that the Union had landed on

Mars, then it must be so. And likely up to Brygan to track them.

"You want me to locate the Union expedition?" he asked the general.

Unspent, Leonov's anger continued to color his voice. "*Da,* Brygan. The Union controls Venus and Europa and who knows how many other outposts out here. Mars belongs to the Neo-Soviet empire. We fed it our blood and sweat while they built their precious atmosphere processors in the safety of Terra's gravity. We will not give it up now. It is ours by right."

Brygan ignored the speech. "Chaos or the Labyrinth?" he asked simply.

A grim smile touched the corner of Leonov's mouth. "Aureum Chaos," he said. "They always want to buy themselves time by putting down there or at Noctis Labyrinthus, thinking we will never find them in those twisted, broken lands. All they really do is pin themselves into an enclosed area with limited options, waiting for us to come destroy them." Only grudgingly did the general admit, "A mistake that many would make, though."

"I would not make that mistake against you, Comrade General." Brygan finger-combed red fines from his beard. There was no escaping the minute dust particles that covered so much of Mars. To live on the red planet was an agreement to ingest and breathe them. To feel the ultrafine grit against your skin and constantly shake the red dust from your clothing.

Leonov frowned, either at Brygan's challenge or the fall of dust in his command center. Brygan had made his peace with the red planet long ago. He knew where he could push, and where Mars would kill him if he paid too little respect. That relationship was what made him invaluable.

Amid the incompetence currently demonstrated by the rest of the command center, Brygan decided to remind Vladimir Leonov of that fact.

"I would take control of the orbital facilities," he began "and then land a base on the higher slopes of Olympus Mons—or perhaps the caldera of Pavonis Mons—against you. Make you expend energy coming up to meet me. Every time you launched missiles, it would give me a fix, and I could respond with gravity-assisted bombardment."

Leonov nodded slowly, his irritation forgotten as he envisioned such a plan. "Perhaps you could hold one of the magnificent mountains against me. You know Mars, how to fight alongside its strengths." He smiled fully. "And that is why you were born Neo-Soviet and not Union. *They* would remake Mars as they did Venus. So might we, one day, but not in our lifetime. The Union would accomplish it much quicker. And that would destroy you because the red planet would be no more."

He turned his gaze back to the plex wall and the red landscape beyond. "Find them, Brygan Vassilyevich. Find them, and I will destroy them. For Mother Russia, the empire, and Mars."

A light wind stirred the fines, casting a reddish haze into the air as Brygan Nystolov abandoned his rover to trail the last two kilometers on foot. There would be no easy retreat. But driving what was essentially a stripped-down Blizzard military crawler into what might be a well-defended Union encampment seemed the poorer idea. On foot, no one could match him in this terrain.

He moved past tall, standing columns of tannish and orange rock, and easily glided over one three-meter crevice that barred his way. Aureum Chaos was a fractured land the likes of which Terra could never hope to see. Mars's lower gravity allowed for higher rises and treacherously sheer drops that fell away without warning. But the light gravity worked in favor of the hiker. A ridge standing less than six meters high or a chasm less than four across was more annoyance than hindrance.

It was on the gentler slopes that Brygan was more cautious. Crossing open areas he was most vulnerable. In the confines of Chaos he had a better chance of spotting Union pickets before they noticed him. His gliding stride stirred the fines very little, and he knew to avoid the detritus piled below cliff edges. It was too easy to start a rock rolling along in two-fifths gravity. Hidden scouts or patrols would have no such experience.

Also, the easier slopes were usually signs of unstable areas that had shaken themselves down from a collection of steep cliffs and deep canyons. And, worse, might be ready to shake apart again. The underlying bedrock of such places tended to be layered with tiny faults, ready to shift and grind together in miniature imitation of continental plates back on Terra.

Brygan found the decoy site exactly where low-orbit spy satellites had placed the telltale shine of new metal. When Vladimir Leonov radioed him the information, Brygan almost took it at face value. Considering the century and a half of manned spaceflight, it still amazed him that the Union—and before them the Americans—never tired of making their spacecraft and satellites so easy to locate. Always a white or shiny metal finish.

An easy assignment—his first thought. Too easy—his second.

Chaos might not allow an army to concentrate its forces and move according to proper tactical doctrine, but it *did* make for an excellent hiding place. Nothing hiding in there would be seen, unless it *wanted* to be seen. He requested and won two hours' grace time to check the situation before the general assembled Baskurgan's army and flew out for deployment around the site. Not that Brygan believed he'd really get it. Leonov would assemble the army regardless, then wait only so long as he could control his desire to kill Union soldiers and keep Mars clean.

Brygan gave himself twenty more minutes. Maximum.

So, no time to waste. He watched the area carefully for a long and precious five minutes. A wide clearing. Cliffs on one side. Standing columns and a small ridgeline guarding two more. The fourth was danger territory, a fairly steep grade but not in keeping with the surrounding Chaos.

Finding no strange stirring of fines or flash of white Union space suit, however, he moved in slowly with his easy gliding step. Carefully approaching the lone vehicle, Brygan scanned the ground for evidence of further Union forces. The vehicle itself reminded him of the old exploration type, flatbed with eight caterpillar wheels, flywheel drive, and a simple steering cockpit. Something definitely was not right. The ground showed marks of a single large landing craft and some foot travel, but no large numbers.

If he'd been more of a true military mind, Brygan Nystolov might have recognized the trap sooner. His specialty was reading the land and recognizing immediate dangers to a single individual versus menace to large numbers. It cost him a few precious heartbeats and several loping paces closer to the flatbed lander before the alarm bells rang in his mind. He spun in the air, ready to come down and leap back for cover.

The vehicle exploded first.

The blast's shock wave caught him in the small of the

back, knocking him off his feet and hurling him back toward the standing columns. He felt sharp stabs of pain as a few metal shards lanced his suit and cut into his limbs and body. His breath squeezed from his lungs, as if a giant fist held him in its grip and then slammed him down against the surface of Mars, scraping him along and tearing away a portion of one sleeve already lacerated by shrapnel. When the blast's force finally released him, Brygan was immediately into a crouch on his hands and feet. Then he noticed the landslide flying toward him.

Flying was the correct term for it. The cascade of dirt and rock appeared to ride a cushion of air as it swept down the slope and toward the clearing. A few pieces might touch ground briefly, kicking off again to tumble airborne. Geysering fines and dirt and small rocks at the top of the slope promised that it had been set off by planted charges. A well-laid trap to catch anyone not killed by the exploding vehicle. Brygan's first instincts were to take cover over the ridge or in the forest of standing columns, and the columns were closer.

It surprised even him when his first jump bounded him toward the avalanche rather than at an angle to its path. He justified the directions he didn't move before touching ground again. If an enemy left a path of escape open, then that was a direction he did *not* want to travel. At the upper arc of his second glide, he realized something about the avalanche that might buy him a chance. It was falling slowly, not in the mad rush one might expect under Terran-standard gravity but powered by Mars's much weaker pull.

Partway up the slope he spotted a protruding boulder that looked likely to remain anchored, even after the slide hit it. He angled for the boulder, figuring he would lose the race by a long ten meters. He was twenty short when the first of the debris swept up to and around the boulder, throwing more red fines into the already-hazy air. At fifteen, the larger rocks were smashing into and sliding around the anchored boulder, and the first small rocks bounced off Brygan's legs. He allowed himself one last gliding step, then crouched and jumped for it.

Though well built for someone of his size used to Terran gravity, Brygan Nystolov weighed less than sixty-five kilograms after counting in his environment suit. His leap was poorly timed, but managed to net him eight airborne meters over the worst of the slide. He came down in the boulder's lee, a scant two meters short, and scrabbled for the top just as a new series of explosions rocked the landscape behind him.

Perched atop the boulder, panting with exertion, he surveyed the damage. The ridgeline had disintegrated under the last explosive chain, and a dozen of the tan-and-orange standing rock columns had crumbled to the ground. If he hadn't jumped free, Brygan estimated he would have been buried under several tons of Chaos rock. The bulk of the slide having swept by him now, he looked downhill and realized how close that still came to being true. He shook his head lightly. He had narrowly escaped a trap meant to catch and destroy an army. Or a good measure of one anyway. He swallowed hard.

He'd overestimated the Union's cleverness. They had not guarded against a single individual springing their trap early, thinking to catch the Neo-Soviet forces as they swept in on the decoy en masse. That had worked for him, too, since what did they care if one or two had been able to survive? But with that question came the realization that the Mental had been wrong and had steered the Neo-Soviet forces into a trap. Such a thing had never happened before.

The Union had also landed uncontested on Mars, and still remained hidden. That was a new concern as well.

Brygan sat down heavily—for all the two-fifths gravity—on one edge of the boulder. He felt the pain blossoming in his body from the rough treatment. Looking down at his left arm, he saw a large frozen patch of blood covering the area he'd scraped raw. He frowned, noticing now a few more ice-rimed bleeders on his legs. He was looking at a two-kilometer walk back to his rover. The Union force on-planet had still to be located. And if he had the larger picture in place, the best Mental on Mars was guessing wrong *and* communication was out with the empire on Terra.

General Leonov was right. Having just one problem would be a relief.

4

Arguing bursts of machine-gun fire echoed throughout the shallow valley—long, regularly paced statements from below answered by hard, chopped replies. The retorts echoed sharply from nearby cliff faces of pale tan stone, rolling into a thunderous peal as the violent debate mixed in the deeper folds of Gory Putorana.

Sergeant Tom Tousley hugged up to the back side of a large rock outcropping, he and his squad pinned against the slope halfway down to the valley floor. He felt the stone's freezing touch even through his thick fatigues, a few of the sharper edges jabbing uncomfortably. The terrain offered good cover behind large boulders or inside shallow trenches cut into the land by occasional heavy rains. Small, bushy alpine pines clustered on the valley floor and dotted the lower slopes, one patch stretching almost to the rim in a long but thin stand that likely followed some unseen water source. The lower edge of that wood had been fired. Red-and-orange fingers danced over the dry needles and snapped at pitch-covered branches. Wispy dark smoke trailed up into an overcast sky.

Tousley rose up in a half crouch, bracing his arms over the sandstone ledge. He watched for the telltale muzzle flash below. Found one. Squeezing off two bursts from his Pitbull assault rifle, the sergeant easily rode out the recoil and stayed on target until he saw the enemy crumple forward. Large, wearing heavy boots and military-issue pants but a heavily muscled chest bare to the day's chill. Even from seventy meters distance Tousley noted the abnormal bone structure of its upper body, the hairless head growing out of oversize shoulders like a thick knob, and saw the mask strapped over the lower face. Mutant. Rad Trooper, sure enough.

There was no end of the empire's own people who had fallen victim to high levels of radioactive contamination, and the Neo-Soviet military pressed them into service for their hardy nature and ability to withstand the chemical and radiological weapons so commonly employed. Rad Troops were fearless, taking pride in their final sacrifice for the empire. They branded themselves with the trifoil insignia commonly used to mark nuclear material. No great tacticians, they made up for it in determination. Armed with stripped-down Nagant 7.76s, a cheap-production rifle prone to breech jams, they fired steel-jacketed slugs tipped with hot uranium. Every bullet that shattered against hillside rock spread radioactive debris, and any nonlethal hit promised complications caused by internal contamination.

Even now return fire spanged bullets off the rock facing, showering the area around Tousley with stone chips and splinters. Many shots passed overhead with sharp cracks of hypersonic velocity. Tousley ducked and rolled into a nearby shallow dry wash, fetching up against the legs of PFC Brad Williams.

Williams carried one of the squad's two Bulldog support rifles, the over-and-under combination that relied on the same 5.56 millimeter as the Pitbull but included as well an M-81 20-mm grenade launcher. With the assault rifle the young PFC could punch a hole through a silver dollar at better than one hundred meters. The colonel had wanted to steal him away for sniper assignment, but Tousley refused to let him go and 'Becca had backed him on that one. Sainz could go poach from someone else's squad.

"How many you reckon?" Tousley asked, shuffle-crawling up beside the PFC. Williams never lost his cool in a firefight, and had a situational awareness Tousley admired. He noticed the new crease to the side of William's helmet. A very near miss.

"I saw yours go down. I accounted for two more, and Jerry picked off one. So no more than four is my guess." Williams shook his head. "And no sign of Hastings," he said, naming the scout Tousley's squad had been backing.

Tousley silently cursed Raymond Sainz for establishing a half-kilometer operations range for the Seventy-first's forward scouts. That the colonel had been the one to set a backup, and that the scouts had actually requested a wider range while searching for the Black Mountain facility, didn't matter. The fact remained that the sergeant had been too far back to render immediate aid. Corporal D.J. Hastings had radioed in nearly twenty minutes prior, frantically yelling through undiagnosed interference something about the sky "breaking open." Shortly afterward, his voice weak but the strange static fading as Tousley's squad zeroed in on his location, Deej had warned of contact with a patrol of Neo-Sov Rad Troopers. Then silence.

Williams seemed to read his mind. "He's been quiet too long. Think he bought it?"

"Some Rad Troops have been known to home in on radio frequencies. If he's still too close to them, he'd stay quiet." At least, Tousley hoped that to be the case. "He's not under orders to die this mission," he said. The Union army's traditional pledge was to keep searching so long as any doubt remained of a soldier's condition. "And we can't let this patrol report back in. We can only hope that whatever interfered with our comms has prevented them from getting through to Noril'sk."

Williams nodded, then checked his clip and swapped it out for a fresh one. "Call it," he said.

Tousley nodded. "Go!"

The young PFC rolled to his right, up to the edge of the wash, and snapped off a new burst of fire. As the Nagant 7.76s tracked in on his position, Tousley rose to one knee and sighted down the slope. The fire had spread among the small pines, and a gray haze hung over the valley floor. He held his ground for several long heartbeats, daring a Rad Trooper to spot him. Finally, he picked out a new muzzle flash. His time spent, he cut loose with a single, long burst of fire before dropping back down.

Williams quickly rolled back, chased by a hail of ricochets. "We missed. The smoke is getting thicker down there." His voice gave away his frustration.

"Not your standard Rad Trooper tactic," Tousley agreed. It showed a bit more creativity than most Union soldiers gave Neo-Soviet mutants credit for. Still, the smoke likely didn't bother them, and it did offer a decent camouflage. "It works both ways, though. They've got to come out of the smoke to spot us."

Putting it in words helped Tousley recognize what had eluded him before. "Deej set that fire!" he said. "He's making his way up that stand of pine, and started the blaze down low to cover his path."

William's answering grin and nod supported the idea, and Tousley quickly checked the positions of his squad. He picked out locations simply by sound. There was no mistaking the higher-pitched report of Union assault rifles against the heavy discharge of a Neo-Soviet-manufactured weapon. His people also relied on short, rapid bursts while the Neo-Sovs preferred steady but slower fire. He counted seven locations besides Williams and himself, fixing them in his mind.

Tousley reached up to his left ear, toggling the commlink built into his helmet. "Awright, list'nup," he said in good battlefield address, slurring those first words together. It didn't matter if the Rad Troopers gained a fix on his position by comms. They already knew where he was. "We think Deej is lying low in that stand of pine stretching toward the rim, but that fire is crawling up his backside fast. So by numbers, we're going to swing that direction and downslope, getting him the support he needs and putting down those *mutes* for good. Ready? Even numbers cover and odd numbers advance. Go, go, go!"

On his own command, the sergeant belly-crawled forward to the cover of a large rock while Williams popped up to spray the lower valley with a good burst from his Bulldog. The PFC also let fly with a grenade. Tousley then slipped off to one side. He glanced back up the wash at Williams, making sure he was unhurt, then set himself to provide the next burst of protective fire from between his cover and an adjacent boulder. The Rad Troopers were sniping in close on his position, so he wedged his Pitbull between the rocks, using the support to be able to fire one-handed his next few rounds. Leapfrogging, Tousley hoped to pick up Corporal Hastings and then make the valley floor to finish off the Rad Troopers. Preferably without losses, though he knew he would probably lose at least one of his squad.

He couldn't have known how prophetic that thought would be.

Tousley's next command, for even numbers to advance, was interrupted by a throaty snarl and then a loud scream. He whipped his head around, back toward Williams. A red-skinned canine stood over the soldier, left-side claws gouged into the PFC's back and fanged mouth buried in his shoulder. The dog was lean to the point of emaciation, its bones standing out in sharp relief and its muscles bunched and quivering beneath the tight-drawn skin. Open sores festered on its right shoulder, with pus running down its leg. A metal plate had been bolted down over the creature's head, capping the skull with some armor protection and shielding the eyes. A *mertvaya sobaka—death dog.*

Known as rad-hounds because they so often supported Rad Troopers, the mutant canines were lethal trackers. Steel-trap jaws could bite through protective gear and crush bones. They also sensed energy waves across a wide spectrum. No need for eyes, which was why the unreliable organs were capped beneath the metal shield. From background radiation alone rad-hounds bounded over the most broken terrain in perfect form. Mutant handlers often commanded them by radio signals. And they could be trained to hunt certain frequencies, such as the ones used by the Union squad.

Tousley cringed at the crunch of bone mixed with the muffled growls of the rad-hound. His Pitbull wedged forward, Tousley pulled his Pug ten millimeter from its chest holster and trained it on the hideous animal. All he could think of was freeing his man from the deformed jaws. As the Pug's laser sight spotted a tiny red dot just back of the metal cap, Tousley remembered at the last moment the collar device. All rad-hounds came equipped with some type of explosive device slung under their wide metal collars. It allowed their handlers to direct the hound into an enemy formation and then detonate the bomb. If Tousley killed the creature, it would detonate regardless.

Right then he knew there was no saving Williams.

The knowledge settled over him with a cold detachment. His teeth clenched tight enough to hurt his jaw, Tousley drifted his laser sight down from the rad-hound's head, across Williams's shoulder and to the man's just-visible chest. The red dot traced over one of the weaker points of the Kevlar flak vest, at the base of the neck and just off the shoulder. He caressed the trigger, twice, mercifully ending his man's terror and agony. The dog ignored the death of its victim, continuing to worry at its prey like some game it had run down in a hunt. The red dot swept again over the metal cap protecting its head, finding an unarmored spot just back of the skull.

His comms still open for the abandoned advance, Tousley gave his people one heartbeat's notice. "Everyone ground and freeze," he said in casual tones. He pulled the trigger and rolled to one side, taking cover around a bend in the wash as he abandoned his Pitbull and brought his arms up to protect the sides of his head.

The explosion bucked the ground, shaking loose several small slides and hurling a gout of dirt, small rock, and bloody gobbets into the air. The bloody stump of one *mertvya sobaka* leg landed in front of Tousley's face, two of the diamond-sharp claws still set into the large paw. The rain of light debris pattered against his back—small rock chips and burnt earth. The caustic scent of the explosives wafted around on a pale gray smoke.

Spitting out dust, breathing shallowly of the acrid air, Tousley inventoried all body parts present and accounted for. His Pug had been protected as well by the wall of the wash, but the Pitbull assault rifle had been mangled when the explosion's force had channeled between the boulders where he'd left it. He abandoned it there.

"Shake it off," he transmitted to his squad. As if to underscore the order, a bullet careened off a rock ledge above. The report of the shot and the ricochet itself was eerily soft after the deafening roar of the rad-hound's explosive device.

"The mutes down below haven't forgotten us, and we sure aren't forgetting them. Jerry and Maria, I want you to work your way back upslope and guard against another rad-hound sneaking down behind us. If you see its handler, I want him dead. Everyone else, we frog it straight to the valley floor. You burn down anything not wearing Union military issue." No Neo-Sov unit was going to cost him a man and live to tell about it.

"We'll locate Hastings and collect Williams on our way out. Keep heads low and off-numbers lay down a good suppressing fire. No slips.

"The price has already run high."

Major Rebecca Howard knelt next to her commanding officer at the head of one body bag. Colonel Sainz shrugged uncomfortably, as if feeling Tom Tousley's glare burning into his back, though she actually doubted he was even aware of the sergeant's anger. His attention was reserved for the lost soldiers. Three of the black containers lay on the ground in the shadow of a Trojan supply carrier—two showed that they held full forms, while the third was half-filled with pieces. The assault group's first casualties for the operation. Unlikely to be the last.

Howard pulled back the flap on the bag holding Corporal D.J. Hastings, though positive identification was only possible from his dog tags. The two officers stared at the blackened flesh, charred and cracked as if flash-burned. The burnt-pork smell turned Howard's stomach, though she weathered it. This wasn't the first burn case she'd seen in her Union army years.

The scout's uniform was little more than tatters, all of it singed black. Only the helmet had survived mostly intact, left on to avoid peeling away any more of the ruined skin. The wide, staring eyes showed a touch of madness.

"He's cold?" Sainz asked quietly, pitching his voice for a private conference, though several dozen men and women stood in a circle not ten meters around.

Howard nodded. "The CBR boys took their readings, and I watched. Whatever did this wasn't nuclear. And it wasn't a forest fire either."

"Why do you say that?"

"I was in the Two-oh-seventh Defense Force before joining the Seventy-first. We helped fight the Montana inferno, straight labor mostly, and then worked with cleanup crews. Fire victims are rarely burnt so uniformly across the body. And the alpine forests up here could never generate a blaze hot enough to do this kind of damage."

She lifted the flap back a bit more, pointing to three areas across the lower chest where charred flesh had been split and caked with the glossy red-black of dried blood.

"This is where the Rad Troopers drilled Corporal Hastings, *after* the burns were inflicted and before the small pine fire swept over his location."

The colonel's brown eyes sought out hers. They reflected a small measure of the pain his man must have experienced. "You're saying he lived through this?"

Her voice was rough but pitched soft. "It looks that way."

Sainz pulled the flap back up, covering the body. "Log this as an unexplained incident, then. And clear Sergeant Tousley of any negligence in the deaths."

That surprised her. Rebecca Howard had been the one to debrief the squad when they brought back Hastings and their own two dead. She'd placed Tom Tousley on notice right then that he faced possible charges for his reckless charge down the valley slope. Better she prepped him for it than for him to get it straight from Sainz. "He broke up his squad in the face of enemy opposition. It cost them a second casualty."

"He had to put Williams down himself," the colonel said softly, running fingers back through his dark curls. "It was a judgment call then, picking his priorities. Maybe he made a poor decision, but we weren't there, Major."

Rebecca Howard didn't buy into it. She read the tension in her commander's shoulders and knew the early losses were disturbing him. The unit was surveying the northeast quadrant of Gory Putorana, better than four hundred kilometers from Noril'sk. Here was the last place to expect a casual patrol, unless they were close to the Black Mountain facility. But no scouting party had yet to find good indication of it.

"There's something else, isn't there?" she said.

Sainz did not try to deny it. Still looking down at the black bag, he nodded. "The shoulder tattoos Tom reported on the Rad Troopers. The Fifty-sixth Striker. That's Colonel Katya Romilsky's command."

Rebecca didn't place the name. "And you know her?"

"I know *of* her. She's very competent. If she had a patrol out here, it's because she had an idea something was afoot. How she divined that I'm not certain. But when that patrol fails to report, it will be enough to draw out her command to come looking for us. I think we're in for a fight, and I don't need one of my sergeants with a possible court-martial hanging over his head to dull his edge." He glanced to the side, in Howard's direction. "You think I don't see his problems? Get his anger refocused at the enemy, Major. That's your job."

"Yes sir." Still, a nagging doubt convinced Rebecca Howard that Sainz had not divulged all of his reasons. There was more hanging over him than some Neo-Soviet colonel and the possibly early termination of the mission. More than a curious death of one of his men.

"You know what did this, don't you, Raymond?" she said, but it was a statement more than a question. Using his given name was a liberty she seldom took, and then only when he had first used hers. "What killed Corporal Hastings."

A flicker of wariness, as if careful of what might be showing on his face, showed in the colonel's eyes. There was something there. But when he spoke, Howard couldn't help but believe him at once.

"No, Rebecca. I don't know what killed Hastings." He shook his head in frustration. "The problem is, I'm beginning to wonder if anyone does."

5

Corporal Phillipe Savoign and PFC Amanda Baker stood their post at Tower 183, one of the small elevated buildings in Union territory that was responsible for observation of over fifty kilometers of Luna's fence line. Here on the back side of the moon the Earth would never grace the pale sky, but the tower was full into its fifth day of sunlight so cold-weather precautions weren't necessary. The two specialists stared out across the thin strip of no-man's-land, a barren gray landscape dotted with darker rocks. One hundred meters distant, on Neo-Soviet soil, their mirrors stared back from a similar building.

Luna's fence line stretched around the Neo-Soviet's semicircular territory, monitored by electronics and at infrequent points by manned stations. From the enemy's point of view, of course, Savoign figured the Neo-Sovs saw the fence line as surrounding the Union's position, but facts were facts. The Union controlled better than two-thirds of Luna, which included nearly all of the "live side" facing Earth. Only Point Gagarin speared over from the empire's "dead side," the one region left undisputed since it placed the Neo-Sov's main communication facility convenient to Union listening posts and satellite interceptors.

That might be a fact he wasn't *supposed* to know, but keeping secrets on Luna came hard. With the two nations sharing Earth's moon, tensions ran high, and too often survival depended on working closely with other rates.

"Tag, I'm in," Baker said, tapping him on the shoulder. Savoign switched out with the PFC and walked to the other side of the tower, leaving her to keep an eye on their counterparts.

He studied a landscape that had changed little in the century and a half since the original moon landing by Apollo astronauts Neil Armstrong and Buzz Aldrin. The moon's gravity remained one-sixth Earth standard except at Union bases and outposts with installed gravity-compensation fields. Hundreds of atmospheric processors strained to provide a breathable if low-ceilinged atmosphere, and a fixative agent had been added to bind moondust into something approximating the true weight of soil. Still, the local ground remained white-gray and would never be conducive to growing much in the way of vegetation. And then there was the problem of the moon's fifteen-day light-and-darkness cycle that still varied temperatures by as much as one hundred degrees Celsius and created a strong, eternal wind that constantly scoured the planetoid.

Gardens and light forests were maintained only where soil brought up from Earth supplanted the natural gray dirt, and large terrasim systems were installed to simulate a continuous Terran environment. Such areas were clustered about the Union's various crater colonies, and were a feat the Neo-Soviets could not hope to match. The empire was lucky simply to maintain the atmospheric processors they had captured twenty years before.

Savoign had seen those vids, the waves of rad soldiers, mutants, and armored vehicles that the Neo-Soviets had spent to claim their share of a Union-held moon. Having won their ground, they shipped up what few space specialists they possessed and worked to hold it. His gaze found Mount Remnant on the horizon, actually a massive refuse heap covered with a light coating of the moon's grayish soil. One of several mammoth piles of junked satellites and old solid-fuel boosters and even low-grade tailings from when the Union had pulled asteroids to Luna to mine them for precious metals. Though a Union dump, one of many dotting Luna, it still seemed more appropriate to the Neo-Soviets.

"Scavengers," he said softly.

"You say something?"

Savoign never had the chance to repeat himself. Suddenly the observation tower swayed and trembled as if under heavy assault.

"Movement!" Amanda Baker shouted, spinning for the secure commlink back to Tranquillity Crater. Being a comms specialist, her first thought was to call in the attack. As a weapons specialist, Savoign ranked that second. He placed his highest priority elsewhere.

He dived for his assault rifle.

It was an MD-11 Rottweiler, often called the *Mad Dog* for its military designation. Phillipe Savoign referred to it as *The Rott*. Modified for a low-gravity environment, like most other Union weapons on Luna, it had special outside ports to vent the gases in such a way as to cancel most of the recoil.

Savoign pulled it from the rack. Sure that the Neo-Sovs would be carrying unmodified Kalashnikovs, he crabbed low beneath the open window and popped up near the tower's corner support for what little cover it might offer.

As it turned out, he had more time than he'd first thought. The Neo-Soviet tower was still in a slow state of collapse as one-sixth standard gravity pulled it down. Both enemy sentries had jumped for distance, and were just now falling behind some boulders dragged into place for such an emergency. The boulders seemed to tremble as well, and Savoign realized that, as unlikely as it seemed, the moon was experiencing an earthquake. His first thought was to wonder what the Neo-Sovs had done to cause it. Caught without a procedure to follow, he burned several precious seconds in hesitation.

Then one of the Neo-Soviet sentries cut loose on full automatic, walking his line of fire up the tower and into the building's side. A few armor-piercing rounds picked small holes into the side of the tower building, and other shots whistled by as they found the open windows. *That* Savoign knew how to deal with.

Trusting his Kevlar-lined vest to stop all but the luckiest Neo-Soviet round, Savoign struck a classic infantry stance. Though the Rottweiler lacked the Kalashnikov's rate of fire, it loaded eleven-millimeter high-explosive rounds that hit with enough centimeter-gram force to throw a man back ten meters in lunar gravity. He didn't bother with the single-fire selector switch, sighting in on Neo-Sovs and boulders both and holding down the trigger. The tower filled with heavy staccato reports, and a hundred meters downrange a shower of stone chips and splinters burst skyward in an impressive geyser. Moonrock crumbled and split under the assault. No

Kevlar armor could stop such raw firepower, and both sentries flew back with chests and limbs shredded.

Savoign eased off the trigger and spat at the acrid taste left from breathing the Rott's discharge. The moon's trembling stopped a few seconds later.

"I'm through to Tranquillity," Baker said in the sudden silence. "They're reporting a planetoidwide quake." Covering the transmitter, she mumbled, "What are the Neos up to now?"

Guessing from the reaction he'd witnessed, Savoign figured the sentries had asked themselves the same thing about the Union. Their first mistake had been to shoot without thinking. Their second was to stack Kalashnikovs up against a Rott. The empire might have won its foothold on the moon through manpower, but with even numbers Union technology too often made the difference.

"You'd think they'd learn," he muttered.

Baker glanced at him sharply. "Say something?"

"I said I don't think this was a Neo-Sov event. They didn't seem to expect it either." He shrugged. It made little difference to him one way or the other.

Baker held the link away from her head. "What? You think the empire sentries are asking the same questions about us right now?"

Savoign retrieved a pair of field glasses and gazed over the open ground at the two dark-suited figures sprawled in the moon's grayish dirt. He shrugged again, and smiled grimly. "Not anymore they aren't."

Inside the Union's Tycho Crater Moonbase, Major Randall Williams continued to work among the science consoles as he avoided Captain Paul Drake. As a scientist, arguing with the M.I. mentality of a combat-rated officer placed high on his list of things to be avoided. Right behind a court-martial and just slightly in front of live combat duty.

Though the *M.I.* initials were known to stand for Military Issue, Williams often thought of them as representing *marginal intelligence*. It was an old slur even when he'd first begun to rise through the ranks of the military's Research and Development branch, but it rarely failed to amuse him—or annoy his younger brother, who had enlisted in the regular military just last year. An added bonus, he decided with a private grin.

The joke was slightly unfair to Drake, though. Williams knew that no one came into space without impressive skills and a certain amount of natural talent. Even now Drake held a corner of the room near the main door, standing at abbreviated parade rest and looking ready to repel boarders at any instant. He exuded that kind of military competence.

Williams knew what Drake wanted to talk about, but as far as he was concerned the discussion would be nonproductive and tiresome and so to be avoided for as long as possible. Avoided, but not ignored. He remained acutely aware of each restless shift and not-so-subtle throat-clearing. There was a limit to Drake's patience. Sooner or later the confrontation would be forced. Williams would rather it come later.

Fortunately or unfortunately—depending on one's view—there was plenty to occupy his attention besides Captain Drake's growing displeasure. Especially as a new tremor shook itself through Luna.

Major Williams spoke out quickly to keep his people calm. "Hold your places, everyone. Let it run out."

Along with others of the staff in Tycho Control and Direction, Williams hunkered down to wait out the quake balanced on hands and the balls of his feet. Those who sat clung tight to their chairs. Over most of Luna such a tremor would hardly rate as a problem, but the Union kept its military bases at Earth-standard gravity inside buildings and three-quarters standard outside. So they rode it out with care except for a few combat Marines simply too tough to take precautions. One of them lost his equilibrium and collapsed roughly onto the floor. Captain Drake remained rock-steady as any bulkhead or console, staring daggers back at Randall Williams.

Williams turned away and peered instead through the thin plex wall. The Earth hung full in the gray-blue sky, its form blurred slightly by Luna's atmosphere. Tycho Crater's terrasim environment currently simulated an Earth morning, dimming the Earth's reflection even more. Lost were the days of a crystal-clear image of mankind's birthworld. An easy trade, in Williams's opinion, when considering the moon's livable surface. Trees reached upward, growing taller and more slender than they would under full gravity. Around the base of the trees the life sciences department had cultivated a thornless wild rose of which Williams was particularly fond. Further testament to mind over environment.

The tremors subsided, and Williams rose smoothly back to his feet. Fastidious about his uniform, he straightened it with a quick tug at the jacket hem. Paul Drake stepped forward, obviously intent on using the interruption to open his case. Williams preempted him with a quick nod of recognition and stepped over to geology.

"Origin and cause?" he asked, doubting there would be any change. This tremor was merely the most recent in a series of planetoidwide quakes differing in severity. The fact that no one in the military sciences division had been able to formulate an explanation for them galled Williams's sense of order.

The lieutenant shook his head and gestured to the console screen as if that explained it all. "A nonlocalized phenomenon."

Which simply meant that the computers could not get a fix on a point or particular direction. "Nothing is shaking the entire moon at once, John. Keep on it." He turned toward the front of TC&D.

Captain Drake stepped forward to partially block Williams's path. Though a few centimeters shy of Williams's height, Drake outmassed him by several kilograms, mostly muscle. "Major Williams, I'd like a word with you please." His voice was a deep baritone, powerful yet controlled.

"I realize that, Captain Drake, but we're a little busy at the moment." Williams stared at the narrow gap left for him to squeeze by, and then back at the Marine. "Excuse me." Drake withdrew a step, and almost hid the exasperation he felt. Williams moved past him, then stopped short of completely brushing off the space specialist one more time.

"Tag along, why don't you, Captain," he said. Perhaps if Drake saw some of what Union forces on the moon were facing right now, he would appreciate the situation more fully.

"You're . . ." He paused, deciding to avoid using the word *upset*. "You're *concerned* about the postponement of your launch."

"Yes, sir. Brigadier General Hayes referred me to Colonel Allister here at Tycho, and the colonel pointed me in your direction. They both refused to overrule your decision to indefinitely delay the *Icarus's* launch."

"Awfully kind of them," Williams remarked dryly, deciding not to get sidetracked by Drake's efforts to have his decision countermanded. He paused at a weapons console, turning his attention away from the Marine.

"Did you finish the targeting solution for Battle Station Freedom, Erin?" he asked of the weapons specialist. Williams preferred first names, believing that his people responded better when he set aside military protocol.

She nodded, sitting up straighter under his recognition. "Beat Tranquillity Base by twenty seconds with a point-zero-nine percent improvement over their efficiency." Sergeant Erin Montgomery grimaced. "But we lost a full minute in transfer of the data and verification, so Tranquillity went with their own numbers. If I'd had Corporal Savoign here, we'd have come in well under the wire, but he's rotated out to the fence line today."

Williams smiled at the spirited competition. He also was disturbed that Phillipe Savoign had been pulled today of all days, but Union military protocol directed all enlisted combat-technician rates below the rank of sergeant to stand at least one watch in ten. A waste of good training to pull talented people off their station and put them at risk in the field, if anyone were to ask him. But then, no one had.

"So long as the job was done, Erin. General Hayes will know you aced his man."

Williams leaned in to study the screen, cupping his chin with his right hand and idly stroking the long, pointed sideburns that fell nearly to his jawline. Not quite regulation, but then the general allowed lunar bases some latitude. "Did you figure out what Neo-Soviet target they intend to strike at from Freedom?" Not that he really possessed a "need to know" such information, but no one had ordered it classified either, and the scientist in him could not resist any quest for information.

Beside him, Captain Drake stiffened perceptibly.

"Near as I can figure, Station Freedom will take down a Neo-Sov security satellite set to pass over central Siberia." She tapped a few commands on the touch-sensitive screen. "Since we rarely care if they see into their own backyard, I'm guessing they want the satellite downed before it passes over the European Commonwealth." She paused, then, "Any word on why we're handling the number crunching, Major?"

"Freedom is having even more trouble with planetside communications than we are, so all orders from Cheyenne Mountain are bouncing off Tranquillity. We're to handle all the critical data until they can run diagnostics on their computers."

Williams moved on, pulling Captain Drake in his wake. "Beginning to see the light, Captain?"

Drake folded thick arms across his chest. "That the moon is trembling and we have some comm troubles with Earth? Yes sir. But the *Icarus* is self-sufficient and under mission orders to maintain communications silence anyway for the first week."

"And after that week?" Williams shook his head. "If we don't know the cause of these events, we can't predict their duration or guarantee a solution. I refuse to send out an unsupported solar-system explorer."

"But instead you'll leave an unsupported mission on Mars?" Drake stopped, his tone urgent but respectful. "Major, no disrespect, but allow me to remind you that we've landed an advance force on an enemy-held world. They're expecting us."

Williams bridled at the insinuation that he would abandon men, but quickly controlled his anger. Drake saw only his compatriots sitting on a hostile world waiting for supplies his ship was supposed to drop. Of course, a few lunar quakes and communication problems were low priority in comparison.

"The Mars team is one of the largest forces we've ever dropped and has a year's worth of supplies, Captain. The barge you were to tow in with the *Icarus* is meant for expansion of a hidden base to accommodate additional forces sent *at a later date.*" He paused, thinking of faraway Mars. "I have friends out there, too. I helped train Captain David Hutchinson, the lead scientist. So yes, I'm concerned. But believe me when I say they can hold out just fine."

Drake visibly calmed himself. "I apologize for any implied insult, Major. I know they can hold out, but you have to understand what it's like to be on the ground and out of touch with your chain of command. It's hard on the nerves, even for experienced operators." He exhaled noisily. "I just find it difficult dancing to a tune called by the Neo-Sovs."

"And you think that's what I'm doing?" Randall Williams met the other man's gaze easily. "Comms," he called out. "Jason, have you broken the latest Neo-Soviet transmissions?"

From two consoles away, a communications-rated lieutenant pushed himself back from his screen. "Yes, Major. They're still worried about Sputnik-23's deteriorating orbit and whatever *we're* doing to shake Luna apart. Would you like the transcript?"

"Not yet, but make it available to Captain Drake if he wants it." Williams waited while the Marine digested that information. "If I, Colonel Allister, or General Hayes thought these problems were the effects of Neo-Soviet meddling, I can guarantee you we'd stop it and your launch would go forward. As is, I stand by my decision to postpone the *Icarus*'s departure."

Drake had the good grace to back down, nodding an

apology. Williams straightened his uniform and was about to turn to new concerns, then stopped. "It's a dangerous habit, Captain, blaming everything we don't understand on the Neo-Soviets. It awards them too much credit, and compounds our own ignorance.

"They may be the enemy, but right now they're as much in the dark as we are."

6

Brygan Nystolov felt General Leonov's menace as a palpable presence as they stepped from the lift and into *the cage*. Only Leonov's personal security code let them take the lift all the way to the uppermost level of the Ascraeus Mons base, and the general had stood in cold silence the entire ride, flexing his exoskeleton gloves as if preparing to choke the Mental. That he would never do, of course—Mentals were simply too valuable—but it must have helped the general work off some of his frustrations imagining it.

The doors they faced qualified for airlock-durability, and the general punched in another code with savage thrusts to a keypad. Any harder and Brygan was sure the control would shatter.

Vladimir Leonov exhaled a sharp breath, nearly a

growl, as the doors cracked open and began to roll back. He clasped his hands behind his back, removing his most obvious threat, but his tight face and narrowed red-brown eyes showed his fury. Then Brygan forgot about the general for a moment as the scents of fresh-baked bread and cinnamon spice wafted on the warm draft escaping the Mental's quarters.

He had never seen the Ascraeus Mental himself, or been to his quarters, which were called *the cage* for the heavy security it took to get in—or out. Brygan knew the empire pampered Mentals for their special touch of *gory-achee*, but had never known to what extent. Looking about the palatial room, Brygan knew a touch of envy for the luxury and understood a bit more the general's anger at the Mental's failure.

Perfection would be expected of anyone who enjoyed such privileges on Mars.

Pillows were strewn everywhere, from small, lap-sized headrests to large plush cushions that even the stocky Brygan might burrow into. The energy it took to heat the vast space to such a warm temperature must surely put a serious drain on base resources. The lighting was soft, accented by an enormous plex skylight that covered a full third of the ceiling and allowed a view of Mars's pale sky. A bowl of fresh fruit sat on a low table, along with a plate of vegetables and a loaf of brown bread torn in half. Incense burners occupied shelves and other tables. Colorful prints of Terra decorated the wall: arctic seascapes and forests and mountains. None of the empire's great cities, Brygan noticed. No portraits of party leaders, past or present. And no sign of the Mental.

"Close the doors, please, Vladimir Janosovich," came a muffled voice from among a mound of pillows. What a moment before had looked like a rumpled uniform tossed carelessly over a nearby cushion suddenly stirred. "The alcove is not well heated."

Brygan now picked out the form of a thin man sunk deep into the cushion. His dark-colored uniform was little more than a loose-fitting jumpsuit. Now that his head was visible, it did not look larger than the head of any non-Mental.

General Leonov flushed angrily, but he did close the security doors. "The Union force was not in Aureum Chaos," he growled as they shut behind him. "It was a trap."

"*Da.*" The Mental offered little more for a few seconds. "I felt the explosions. Your men should be more careful. I warned you that they might have already moved."

Brygan started at the criticism, which might have made him angry except that it was true that he had missed the trap until almost too late. Now it seemed that the Mental had warned Leonov, but the general had not told *him* that the Union force might already have moved on past Chaos.

"Well?" the general barked after a moment of silence among all parties.

The Mental shuddered. "I don't know where they are." His voice trembled with fatigue. "I haven't looked."

"Haven't looked?" Leonov nearly shouted.

If the Mental was trying to see how far he might push Leonov, Brygan doubted it would be much further. The general's anger rolled off him in waves—no extrasensory perception needed there—and his face showed the disgust so many Neo-Soviets felt for the physically weak Mentals. But staring down at the frail man, someone who surrounded himself with Terran pleasures but seemed unable to enjoy them, Brygan suddenly felt something else. Pity.

The Mental stared back, one eye blue and the other

green, as if surprised by the scout's presence. He was young, a sharp contrast to his voice, that of a frail old man. An uneven stubble darkened his jaw, and his hair was matted and unkempt, which made him look even more pitiful. Though Brygan did not feel physically threatened, he shifted uneasily under that stare until finally the Mental relaxed.

"*Tovarish* Nystolov," the Mental said in soft greeting.

Brygan nodded a careful salute, uncomfortable with the use of the familiar form of *comrade*. It was a liberty usually reserved for close friends. A pointed glance from Leonov prompted him finally to join the discussion. "If I am to find the Union force quickly, comrade, I will need to have a general area. Any help *is* appreciated."

The Mental frowned, winced, and looked in fear to Leonov. "Perhaps I should clarify. Something else eclipses the sight. I *can't* look."

Brygan noticed the general's hands clenched into trembling fists. "Can't or *won't*?" Leonov asked in deadly calm. "I don't believe you. You are playing a game against further privileges."

"It is a simple request for communication with a Mental in Moscow or Hong Kong. That is a privilege, Vladimir Janosovich?"

The general shook his head. "Communications with Terra are still sporadic." After a second's pause, he added, "At best. Mars currently stands alone." He was obviously losing the battle to subdue his anger. "Now what about the Union force?" he demanded.

"Then I shall need transport back to Terra," the Mental said as if he hadn't heard the question. "At once."

"To the wastes with your requests and demands and doomful prophecies," Leonov shouted, his temper finally winning out over the need to tread lightly around the overly sensitive Mental. His exoskeleton gloves slashed the air in front of the cowering man. "You and every Mental on Mars whimpering about wanting communications and transports. You are staying here, because *I* say so. Nothing you want could compare with what you owe the empire. And if I decide, you will take to the field with us." He took a threatening step forward. "That is how it will be."

The Mental simply retreated back into his cushions, while Brygan pondered the reasons for the general's rage. This was a man the great and strong Vladimir Leonov could not completely control and would never be allowed to harm. At least physically; the verbal tirade seemed to take as much out of the Mental as any beating might. And while the general obviously wrote off the Mentals' requests as pampered sniveling, it bothered Brygan to learn that the Mentals on Mars were suddenly interested in getting off the planet. Doomful prophecies? How big a force could the Union have landed?

"The Labyrinth," the Mental finally squeaked out. "Search the Noctis Labyrinthus."

"Good!" Leonov barked, still angry but calming down now that he had his answer. He turned for the doors. "Come, Scout Nystolov. You have your area."

Yes, he did. And it was a reasonable guess that even Brygan could have made. If you wanted to lose a large force on Mars, the choices were most often either Chaos or the Labyrinth. He stood there, looking down on the trembling Mental, who had buried his face in his hands. For an instant he sensed the other's pain, then the Mental lifted his face, his mismatched eyes seeking out Brygan's. It was an obvious plea for help, but what could Brygan do against the general's orders? He was responsible only to himself, for himself. It was the way he preferred to live. His reason for his being on Mars. Wasn't it?

He turned away and joined Leonov outside the security doors. The general shut and encoded them again. Brygan struggled with the idea that perhaps—just perhaps—he was on Mars to escape the same treatment he'd witnessed in the Mental's quarters. But even now Brygan knew he was just as expendable as the Mental, knew it with the same certainty he had about something else. Something he would not report to the general.

Brygan knew the Mental had lied.

With the map of north central Siberia stretched out over her desk, Colonel Katya Olia Romilsky circled around it, critically surveying the geographical chart from all sides. Gory Putorana figured prominently in the center of the map, colored in browns and oranges to show heights relative to sea level. She ran fingers back through her short, auburn hair, mimicking the silver stripe that curled up from her left temple and then slashed back down behind her left ear. Leaning forward suddenly, she pointed like a striking snake at the spot where her patrol had disappeared. Northeast quadrant, not too far south of the nuclear plant that supplied power up to Khatanga and other cities surrounding the Kordvik Inlet.

One of Noril'sk's stronger Mentals had warned of a possible Union incursion in the southwest folds of Gory Putorana, but all patrols had come back negative. Only Katya's natural suspicions had then placed patrols in other quadrants, and followed up the disappearance of one patrol with large troop movements. She stood prepared for battle, but the Mental's error still nagged at her. Mentals were either right or—unlikely but possible—wrong.

"It is not normal," she said aloud as her aide, Lieutenant Gregor Detchelov, entered the office carrying her lunch tray.

"Comrade Colonel?"

"Mentals," she said, waving a hand over the map. "I've never seen one off the mark by so much. Five hundred kilometers." She shook her head. A few failed nuclear plants and a number of hidden missile silos. Were the Union forces interested in those, or was this part of a larger search?

"Never trusted them anyway," Gregor said, referring to the Mentals. "But then you did mention that they've been acting very strange of late." He set down the tray on a side table. "Maybe the patrol simply fell victim to a slide or an unmapped area of lethal radiation. It happens."

"Rad Troopers?" she asked. "No. Not the entire patrol." She tapped the map with one long finger. "We have company." And the Mental had given her a name. *Sainz.*

The towns and cities bordering Laptev More reported no odd sightings or unusual disturbances in the last week that might account for a clandestine landing. That left Karskoye More, and the recent destruction of the coastal town of Dikson. Now it had become the bay of Dikson, the entire town seemingly ripped from Terra. Just like the rumors circulating through the upper command concerning Angola's recent catastrophe, which seemed to confirm that the Union was in possession of a devastating new weapon and did not hesitate to use it against civilian populations. That they had tested it against United Africa further proved the corruption of the West, a baseness they tried so desperately to hide behind a veneer of altruism and supposed-superior moral standards. Yes, Dikson's destruction pointed to Karskoye More as an insertion point.

Detchelov joined her at the desk. "What do you know of this Colonel Sainz?"

The question was more than just curiosity, Katya knew. It would be Gregor Antoly's duty to request all official files, and, when those ran out, to ferret out any additional information possible. Digging for knowledge she already possessed would be a waste of time and resources, and with a memory that was virtually photographic, her knowledge was likely to be extensive.

"Union special forces," she said, walking her mind back through reports so neatly pigeon-holed in her memory. "Part of a team that sabotaged our Leningrad Arms Facility and later led a Ranger unit that defeated security at Murmansk and stole our new armor alloy being tested there." She turned the page of a mental dossier. "Promoted to command the One-twenty-first Reconnaissance Force, and later accepted transfer to the Seventy-first Assault Group." She grimaced. "He has an unfortunate history of excelling against Mother Russia and the empire."

"You seem to know a great deal of him, Colonel Romilsky," Gregor said admiringly. "What more can I find for you?"

Her gaze turned wintry at the well-performed but false praise. She would make Detchelov pay for that. "You can find out more about the man who is Raymond Sainz. I know the general history, but nothing about how he accomplished his string of successes. What is his style of command? Where are his weaknesses? What was he like *before* joining the Union Army?"

"Before the Union Army?"

"We are taking the field in eight hours, Gregor Antoly, to link up with our own army. By then I want to know everything I can about what makes Raymond Sainz an effective officer. You can destroy an army, but you *defeat* its commander." She turned ice-blue eyes on her subordinate.

"Since you will also be on the front lines, I expect you to be properly motivated."

Gregor nodded vigorously, though his face was pale. "It shall be as you command, Comrade Colonel Romilsky. I will hand you the key to Sainz's defeat."

"That is good, Gregor. Because I have no intention of adding to the list of Sainz's victories. At Gory Putorana our forces will clash. And at Gory Putorana Raymond Sainz and the Seventy-first Assault Group will die."

She looked down at the map and smiled to herself as she began to plan her approach and deployment. "Nothing on Terra must be allowed to stand in my way."

7

A stream of bullets cut the air over Tom Tousley's right shoulder, the sharp *whistle-crack* of their near passage demanding attention even over the distant heavy chatter of a Kalashnikov assault rifle and his Pitbull's own higher-pitched reports. One slug clipped the shoulder plate displaying his rank and merit insignia, gouging into the Kevlar material and jostling his aim. His return fire scored into the rocky ground a hundred meters downrange, kicking up dirt and small splinters of rock a scant meter off the feet of two enemy infantrymen. The pair dropped down behind a slight rise in the land, and the other three members left in the pursuing Neo-Soviet squad followed suit. No poorly trained Rad Troopers these, but Neo-Soviet Vanguard well armed and outfitted and experienced in the conduct of warfare.

Tousley looked forward to taking them down.

In the dead zone between the opposing forces, a Union scout rolled from concealment and scrabbled toward the Union position. Tousley didn't wait for her, waving his team of four back another dozen paces before setting up a new line of defense, each man and the one woman grabbing their own supporting cover. A strange plant that looked carved from translucent stone sprouted nearby. Tousley kicked at it, smashing the offense to his sensibilities into small pieces. He was really tired of such strange terrain, and though it was nothing like what the Seventy-first had encountered earlier, he didn't need the distraction.

The scout made it another twenty meters before the Neo-Soviets rose up as a unit. Their opening fire drove her into the protection of a cluster of boulders. A few shots came close, but apparently none touched her. "Good," she said over the Seventy-first's common frequency. Not an appraisal of her current situation, which was precarious, but the standard call meaning she had finished her run and taken no injury worth mentioning.

"Far enough," Tousley said over the same channel as the Vanguard infantry began walking their fire uprange to his position. He squeezed off a quick answering burst. "Cover and freeze, Kelly. We'll take care of the rest."

"All yours, Tom. I got mine earlier."

Tousley grinned at her response, both brave and boasting at the same time. A fellow Texan and one of the Seventy-first's best forward scouts, Kelly Fitzpatrick rated as one of his favorite "loners." He'd be damned if he'd let her go the way of Corporal Hastings.

"So you sniped three from range. Hardly sporting. I think that's why they're so mad at you. Now stay down and pray they don't go prospecting," he said, referring to the grenade launchers built into the Kalashnikov which could reduce her cover to gravel in a matter of seconds. They were a very real threat, but to use them against a lone scout in retreat was overkill and the Neo-Sovs were not in optimal range to blast away at his small team. The sergeant was gambling on the Vanguard infantry holding off a few seconds more.

He flinched and dropped down as a steady stream of enemy fire blasted into the facing of the rocks that hid him. Dust and shards flew wildly, choking the air with an earthy scent. He felt the sting of a hit on his upper arm, checked it, and found he'd been nicked just above the elbow. No immediate concern. He also noticed that the hit he'd taken earlier against his shoulder plate had scored a funny groove over his rank and merit insignia, adding the rocker bar which Sainz had taken away with Tousley's demotion and removal as the Seventy-first's command master sergeant. All over a stupid remark. For an ex-Ranger, the colonel had thin skin.

But now Tousley owed him for dismissing 'Becca's promise of a review board. Life could have a twisted sense of humor, placing a red-blooded patriot under the command and in the debt of an officer like Raymond Sainz. And it wasn't bigotry. It was about fairness. In Tousley's eyes, the Union state of Mexico had done even less than Canada to deserve instant parity with the American contribution. It was no great secret that the average quality of life in the States dipped slightly after formation of the Union.

And no impressive prediction that he'd lose another soldier if he didn't stop grousing and mind his job.

Craning his neck upward, he used peripheral vision to quickly check the landmarks back along the way they had come. The five enemy soldiers were almost abreast of a boulder on which he'd placed a small rock as marker. Thick growths of brush, some of it petrified, dotted the ground.

Another few steps, he promised himself. Then a new bullet skipped off the stone near his face, stinging him with stone splinters. Close enough.

"Now! Able Team, cease fire. Baker Team, hit them!"

He shifted around to the other edge of the boulder he hid behind, catching the tail end of his carefully orchestrated ambush as three evergreen shrubs rose up and struck at the Neo-Soviet force with a withering cross fire. The enemy soldiers thrashed about as if shaken by invisible hands, their assault rifles falling to the ground and then gravity claiming the bodies as well. As quickly as that, the fight was ended. Ten minutes of terror put to rest by ten seconds of slaughter. Now the walking scrub moved about freely, toeing over corpses and shaking dirt from their fatigues. Tousley had worried about the camouflage job when ordering half his people into shallow holes as he tied scrub brush to arms and legs and kicked a bit of dirt and rock over them. From a distance, though, the land itself seemed to have come alive to devour the Vanguard infantry. With the strange terrain they were seeing, it would only half surprise him.

And as his adrenaline rush faded into the usual hollow weariness, he wondered if that might be the next surprise in store for the Union army.

Five kilometers back of where Sergeant Tousley worked to extract Kelly Fitzpatrick, the bulk of the Seventy-first Assault Group carefully worked its way over the Moyyero River. The antigravity transports and heavy armor skimmed the surface with ease, though no driver was immune to an uneasy downward glance. A deployed squad of Ares heavy-assault suits stomped over, ice chips flying out from beneath their diamond-tread feet.

The men and women of the command picked their way

across the Moyyero with greater care, each step treacherous. More than one cursed the cold touch as they slipped and had to pick themselves up off the river's surface. Nerves were strung taut and faces betrayed the fear many of them felt. Only a few of the more spirited souls in the command accepted the bizarre event with a casual shrug, whether feigned or real, and threw caution aside as they ran across the ground and jumped onto the Moyyero, quickly sliding and slipping across.

"Frozen solid." Raymond Sainz shook his head at Major Howard, the two of them walking the river's southeast bank. The cold radiated outward from the river, chilling the air and turning their breath to frost. "An entire river of ice. It's thirteen Celsius. How do you ice a river five meters deep when it's thirteen degrees above freezing?"

This latest affront to reality was the kind that could awaken the shadows dwelling in any person's mind. An anxiety that served as a reminder that the usual rules no longer applied. That nothing was safe. Sainz didn't let it show, however, except as a measure of concern to his exec, though privately the colonel admitted that he stood an easy step from the edge of fright. Not panic—no Union officer in command of an assault group would give in quite so easily to unthinking terror—but fear, yes that was definitely within reach and not to be pushed aside in denial. Fear kept you sharp and on the edge. Worry, that kept you alive. Sometimes it seemed that half an officer's job was to worry. About the equipment he was accountable for and the lives under his command.

A deep peal rumbled across the sky, like the roll of distant thunder or the passage of a hypersonic transport. Rebecca Howard glanced southeast, in the direction of the recently concluded firefight. "Artillery?" she asked, frowning at the unfamiliar noise.

Unfamiliar because of the clear, pale blue sky stretching overhead. Sainz knew the sounds of a battlefield, no matter how distorted. He knew this one. "Thunder."

He scanned above for any sign of clouds. The pale blue washed almost white at the horizons, as if the color was being bled from the sky. "No stranger than anything else—thunder in a clear sky."

Just one more indication that something was going on in the atmosphere, at any rate. None of the Seventy-first's comm specialists could raise Union command. Undiagnosed disturbances, they claimed. What it meant was no hope for reinforcements and no way to arrange withdrawal, should it become necessary.

The major held one hand to her ear, as if trapping in the small earplug she wore. More than anything a gesture for silence while an aide back in the Hades briefed her by remote. "The pickets have met Tom's squad. They brought out Fitzpatrick. She reconned a large Neo-Soviet force about thirty klicks southwest." A longer pause. "They're ready to fight—they know we're here all right. And you called it, it's the Fifty-sixth Striker. Lance Corporal Fitzpatrick has a rough estimate of force strength." She gauged the position of the sun. "If we angle harder west, we might avoid them for another half day. But the fight will be tomorrow for certain."

Sainz stepped up onto the ice. For a moment he thought it might simply run back to water and he would sink into its blue depths, but it held. He saw the first trails of water forming as the river began to melt. It would be a slow process at first, the water pooling on its surface, those pools being warmed by the sun and helping to melt the ice further. Toward the end the process would accelerate, until the ice finally lost its battle with temperature, broke apart, and floated down the resurrected river.

"The Seventy-first might be dissolved the same way," he said, not bothering to explain his observation. "The Neo-Soviets can shave us down bit by bit, always pooling more forces against us than we have. In the end, we'll shatter and be swept away."

"It's just the Fifty-sixth, for now," Rebecca Howard said. The two had worked together long enough to level with each other. And, when one needed it, to hit the other with a reality check. "If they came out to fight, maybe there's something here worth protecting."

"Chernaya Gora." Sainz nodded. "Black Mountain. I haven't forgotten." He stared up into Gory Putorana, to the southwest. "It's out there, somewhere on the southern slopes apparently. And it does us no good to withdraw without the ability to call in retrieval. Let's hope we find it while we're strong enough to take it out."

He stood there quietly for so long that Rebecca turned away to leave him a moment's peace. Sainz sensed her movement, knew she would keep the others away. So close to battle, everyone needed their private moment to ready themselves.

"Who is our best shot with a Bloodhound?" he asked, freezing her in place. The Weatherby Mk-VI *Bloodhound* was the Union's standard long-range marksman rifle. Read, sniper rifle. Sainz rarely authorized their use. Snipers tended to have short lives on the battlefield.

"I would have said PFC Williams," she said cautiously, thinking. "After him, I'd say either me or Sergeant Tyree." She paused. "You think this Katya Romilsky will give you the shot?"

"No. But then I also can't afford to overlook the possibility of a mistake, either. I want all bases covered. If nothing else, it might give us a hole card to play if he works into the right position." He nodded, as if to punctuate his decision. "I can't spare you on the field. Issue Tyree a weapon with precision scope.

"If we're going to drag the Seventy-first through the grinder, I want to be ready to chip out some teeth."

Randall Williams considered calling Paul Drake back to Tycho Control and Direction. He would set the Marine between him and the barrage of questions, requests, and demands being placed on him, defending a moment of peace and sanity that would let his scientist's mind work on one problem at a time. TC&D was juggling too many projects, each one critically important to someone's interests. The Canadian states were suffering massive communications blackout as several Union CanCom satellites shifted in their orbits. Battle Stations Independence and Liberty were under full manual control and requesting navigation assistance. Station Freedom, the third of the Union's three orbiting battle platforms and in a higher orbit, reported less in the way of disturbances but had been tasked with moving over Siberia though they had lost half their propulsion systems in what they called an *unclassified impact*.

Major Williams grew tired of such descriptions. There had been too many *unclassified, undiagnosed, and nonlocalized* phenomena of late.

Meanwhile, the lunar tremors had not subsided. They continued with increasing frequency, if not severity. No one paused to ride out the light quakes, though. They worked through the trembles, ignoring them as best they could as fingers flew over touch-sensitive screens and comm specialists manned links to Tranquillity Base, Earth, Freedom, Liberty, and Independence, and various military posts nearby on Luna.

"Phillipe, what do you have for me?" He paused behind the weapons specialist, who was busy manipulating numbers on a navigator's console. He rested a hand on the corporal's shoulder and gave it a reassuring squeeze.

"This isn't my seat, Major." He held up his hands in surrender. "I need at least another orbit to bring Freedom over this Gory Putorana whateveritis." He winced. "Maybe two."

"You know the basics of orbital mechanics, Phillipe. And you know the computer system well enough. My navigators are trying to keep Canada's satellites from spinning off into space or decaying into the atmosphere, and now the Pacific Ring system isn't looking too good either. We have forces on the ground in Siberia, and Freedom is their only chance of putting them back in contact with Union Command. Make it happen."

"I'll try, sir."

Williams's people were all giving one hundred ten percent, but sometimes that wasn't enough. "If you can't handle it, Phillipe, I'll turn it back over to General Hayes's people at Tranquillity."

That was, of course, an empty threat. With the Tycho workload, the major could only imagine the bedlam at Tranquillity Lunar Command. But, as always, the added push of competition focused his people. Savoign bent back to his console with renewed purpose.

Not that Williams thought it would do any good. Freedom couldn't maintain good comms with Union ground-based systems. How they would cut through the disturbance and link up with the Seventy-first Assault Group he couldn't see. But more than an order from the general, the Seventy-first was his brother's outfit. Major Williams had to try and get them support.

"New message coming in on priority override," Amanda Baker called out as a new quake shook Tycho.

"Another one?" One more problem might be the proverbial straw that broke the camel's back.

PFC Baker frowned. "This is coming in from the observatory. They say the stars are flickering."

That wasn't funny. Williams strode over to the console, picked up an auxiliary link. "Brigadier General Hayes has declared an emergency on Luna. Keep this line clear except for official traffic." Because he evidenced little use for military authority, most of the time, did not mean he didn't know how and when to use it.

"Sir!" a voice interrupted before Williams disconnected. "This *is* an emergency. We're losing star fixes. They're flickering out, and then back into view."

"Switch to red," Williams ordered a technician, who adjusted the lighting in TC&D from standard illumination to what had forever been known in the Union as *battle condition red*. The room darkened, but the red lights gave people enough to move around by, and console screens were actually better viewed this way.

The major looked through the plex wall, at the natural scene outside in the terrasim environment. "Kill the outside floods," he ordered. Tycho was still days away from its dawn. As lights came down, the stars were easily visible in the darkness of the sky. Even through the generated atmosphere they would be brighter and more numerous than the best night on Earth.

And some were indeed flickering. They would fade from view, as if occluded by some object, and then reappear. Those just off the base's line of sight with Earth appeared affected the most, though no section of sky was immune. The excited talk of a moment before, the entire room at work, faded as all eyes slowly turned to the plex wall and what they could see of the sky. No one spoke—not a whisper. Only a few consoles beeped for attention, and they were ignored.

Randall Williams continued to stare at the strange phenomenon. "Back to work," he said softly. In the room's abnormal silence, the whisper sounded exceptionally loud.

He swallowed, feeling his mouth suddenly parched and a knot in his throat, but managed to continue in his regular voice. "Everyone back to work, except consoles eight through twelve, clear your screens."

That was half his astrophysics consoles. He pointed at the disturbance. "Find out what that is."

8

The empire survey ship *Kolyma* hung against the star-strung backdrop of black space. The vessel pointed its after end along its direction of motion, the concave shield of its thruster port awash in a dull orange glow as the nuclear drive ejectors continued to fire a steady stream of fissioning material into the bowl. Though still traveling at several thousand kilometers per hour, the vessel appeared nearly motionless without any good relative point to judge velocity. Coming in at the back side of Terra made for a poor reference. The planet looked no more than a dark disk ringed by a thin solar halo, not to mention the immense difference in scale. And the *Kolyma* decelerated at only a slightly lower rate than the transport ship it pursued.

To an outside observer—had such been possible—the

pair of ships would have seemed to slowly drift toward each other. Though on slightly different approach vectors, they were quickly matching up on the same target. Terra.

Strapped into his acceleration couch on the *Kolyma*, sweating through the discomfort of four and a half gravities of deceleration, Brygan Nystolov focused on the nearby monitor and watched that gap narrow. He waited either for his missiles to come within range or for the *Leonid Sergetov* to answer his hails. He didn't want to destroy the ship, or its occupant, but unless the vessel answered and then slaved itself to his computers, he would have no choice.

His orders were very clear.

Brygan had never seen General Leonov so angry as he had been twenty-four hours earlier.

The general's teeth were clenched so tightly the muscles along his jawline bulged in solid knots. His red-brown eyes blazed with fury, and his face flushed red all the way up his head, lending a pinkish cast to his gray crew cut. Brygan felt fortunate that he only had to deal with Leonov via the small monitor screen set among the *Kolyma*'s controls.

"Scout Nystolov," Leonov growled, "have you located any sign of the Union forces in Noctis Labyrinthus?"

Brygan wondered what was really on the general's mind. If he'd checked his consoles at all, he already knew that Brygan had abandoned the Labyrinth and was currently gaining altitude over Arsia Mons.

"Plenty of signs, Comrade General Leonov. I believe they have separated into several forces, each laying false trails where we would expect to find them."

A curt nod. "So you plan to survey the nearby mountains?" The general obviously remembered Brygan's comments about how he would attempt to seize a foothold on Mars were he the Union commander.

"I wanted to look over Olympus Mons and the caldera of Pavonis Mons, yes. But to adequately quarter and search those areas will take a stronger force than just myself."

"I will assign such forces. You, Brygan Vassilyevich Nystolov, are to pursue a rogue vessel, manned by a possible traitor and defector, and destroy it." The venom Leonov gave to the words *traitor* and *defector* said that he had already rendered his judgment. "The military transport *Leonid Sergetov* is already past our outer satellite ring and setting a Terra-bound course, current acceleration of three standard gravities."

The *Sergetov*? "I couldn't possibly intercept her before Terra. Better to inform Neo-Soviet High Command." Even as he spoke, Brygan knew what the general would say.

"Communications are still unreliable." Leonov threw a sidelong glance of disgust at the communications crew no doubt laboring back in a corner of the Ascraeus Mons base. "We have no transmission capability and only intermittent reception from Terra, mostly requesting status reports or informing us of strange planetwide disturbances." The general shook his head. "Some of the reports make little sense, but it seems that our Union enemies have developed some new weapons. I believe High Command may be about to strike back with heavy assets."

"And the rogue?" Brygan asked, suddenly dreading who Leonov would name.

"The Ascraeus Mental." The general glowered. "Twice he sent you out chasing phantom trails. Now he steals a transport to make it back to Terra, at just the time when the Union successfully lands forces on Mars and war is imminent on Terra? That is too much the coincidence. He defeated security around the cage too easily, and has somehow managed to navigate an interplanetary craft."

"The *Kolyma* can make the trip, Comrade General. But it is a one-way mission. I will expend all my fuel to match the *Sergetov*'s acceleration." And every second of delay cost Brygan another 29.4 meters per second in speed. He cleared his current piloting program and took manual control of the ship, turning onto a fast-escape course from Mars's atmosphere. The small craft swung around in a tight arc, pressing Brygan back into the crash couch. Less than thirty hours' flight time to Terra. Better, if he hoped to catch the *Leonid Sergetov*. "I am altering course now."

"Good hunting, Brygan Vassilyevich. When you reach Terra, you will do what you must to facilitate a return of full communications with the empire, but that is secondary to your mission. If you cannot gain control of the *Leonid Sergetov*, you will destroy it. There can be no chance of the Mental defecting."

"I understand, Comrade General."

As Leonov ended the conversation with a disconnect from his end, Brygan could finally frown in confusion. No Mental had ever defected or been accused of treason before. The evidence was circumstantial, but still damning.

And Brygan noticed another item Leonov had not. That despite a physically weak constitution, the Mental would endure an acceleration three times Terran-standard gravity—six times that of Mars? Brygan had not mentioned that fact to the general, who, in his current state, would surely have twisted it into further evidence of treason. In Brygan's mind, it raised even more disturbing questions.

What could be so important as to drive the Mental to flee Mars, and in such haste? What was it he had seen, or sensed?

Questions that still plagued him as the computer cut back on the heavy G forces to a deceleration of only one standard gravity. A red icon flashed for attention on the main console screen. The *Sergetov* was now inside his extended range for missiles. He was fast approaching the troop transport as it continued a heavy-gravity decel. With only four missiles loaded on his ship, Brygan could afford no more than two risky launches. After that, if the missiles found no joy, he would have to match courses with the *Sergetov* for sure hits.

Terra was huge in the forward window, though still several hours away, as Brygan cut all deceleration. He swung the small scout craft 180 degrees and reached for fire control, intent on launching the first missile. He paused in midreach, noticing the sudden flare of white energy that streaked across Terra's shadowed side. A ballistic missile? Had the Union and Neo-Soviet empire entered into full-scale war again? Then the first tremor hit the *Kolyma*, shaking the vessel for ten long seconds.

A micrometeor strike? The odds were long that a spacecraft would strike a foreign particle large enough to do damage while traveling through the vacuum of space. The screens showed no damage, and he wasn't venting atmosphere. Brygan almost wrote it off to an engine malfunction, except that the diagnostics all read in the green.

Then another flare streaked across the dark face of Terra, quickly joined by three more, all at various angles to each other. Brygan Nystolov knew then that these were no missile strikes. In fact, at the relative scale, the flares were several kilometers in width and thousands in length. The scale boggled his mind for a brief instant of shock that ended when Terra suddenly pulsed a curtain of energy. No other way to describe it. The atmosphere glowed with illumination, allowing Brygan to pick out the Union continents sweeping by in what was their unsuspecting night, and then it strengthened to a solid white veil that rushed outward as a wave of energy that curled over the moon in a bright flare and swept over both incoming vessels.

No noise. No shaking of the *Kolyma* this time. Just an eerie wash of pure energy that pulsed outward and then contracted back in until it settled around Terra in a nebulous haze at about half the radius from Terra to Luna. The blurred streaks became titanic tendrils of energy that curled around Terra and reached lazily into space for hundreds—thousands—of kilometers in a silent storm of energies the likes of which Brygan had never witnessed or even dreamed possible.

The nebulous curtain dimmed and brightened to some alien rhythm, and slowly began to expand. Before its immense size occluded the moon, Brygan noticed how it bulged toward the planetoid as if drawn toward it. One tendril whipped past the survey ship, a solid white wall of pulsing force that hung there for several long seconds as he flew right toward it. Then it was past, and once more he faced a world snared in some cosmic storm.

And he flew right into it, with no hope for escape.

With one hand, Vladimir Leonov held the hapless major a meter off the floor by the front of his uniform and shook him roughly. "Do not mention again the advantages of being a guerrilla force or you will be ejected out the nearest airlock. I care nothing for losses to date. I want answers!" He slammed the officer down onto the floor and stood glaring about the control room of the Ascraeus Mons base. "The same applies to everyone in here. I want that Union force located, or we begin to make room for the next shipment of experts. I will toss you outside one by one until someone starts thinking."

It was amazing how much busier his people looked, though they continued to do the same jobs as a moment before. The power of positive thinking.

It infuriated the general no end that the Union continued to elude him. Neo-Soviet scouting squads had found traces of a large force, and several booby-trapped sites that had cost him fifty-two men so far, but no hard evidence of where the enemy had set up base. He regretted sending Brygan Nystolov after the renegade Mental, needing the scout's affinity for Mars more than ever. Actually it was the talents of a Mental he needed more than ever, but he hated admitting it. But Ascraeus Mons's Mental had gone rogue, the two at Elysium were beaten to death by Colonel Teklov for lack of cooperation, and now the rest were all reported as catatonic.

"Sir," a technician called out from a telemetry console. His face was dead white, looking almost bloodless. His voice faded to a hoarse whisper. "General Leonov, we've lost Terra."

Again, the general finished silently. Not that they had been able to maintain any kind of credible communications lock on Terra for several days now.

"Turn it over to communications," Leonov ordered curtly. He clasped his hands gloved in metal exoskeleton behind his back, forcing himself of think of anything other than smashing the nearest console into useless parts. It might make him feel better, but then the console would only require replacing.

"*Nyet.* I mean *Da,* Comrade General." The tech looked flustered and completely terrified, though not of Leonov. He turned back to his console screen with dawning horror. "I mean, we've lost Terra.

"Sir, she's gone."

9

An overcast sky the texture of gray cotton batting looked down on Gory Putorana and the conflict escalating within the southeastern foothills. The morning's light rain had passed, leaving the alpine meadows a touch slick. The pale blue buds of saxifrage and the yellow and pink of alpine primrose were quickly stomped into the earth by booted feet or chewed up along with the short bluegrass by the steel treads of Neo-Soviet armored vehicles. A few rifle shots routinely punctured the crisp air, at times drowned out by heavy guns or the *thump-whistle* of artillery fire that ended in roaring explosions of fire and shrapnel somewhere in the no-man's-land neither side yet attempted to cross in force.

But the building growl of Neo-Soviet Rad Troopers, their officers psyching them for the concerted rush at Union lines, promised that the full battle would not be long in coming.

To Sergeant Tom Tousley, the battle was shaping up into the classic confrontation between Neo-Soviet and Union armies. Both sides had drawn up into their line of attack, deploying and then shifting assets in response to the other commander's movements. The Fifty-sixth Striker fielded a larger force, especially with the high numbers of Rad Troopers and Vanguard infantry they would throw forward in a human shield. The Union held its edge in advanced technology.

Antigrav tanks, the hum of whose field generators were becoming high-pitched shrieks when stressed under tight maneuvers, currently faced off with their heavily armored Neo-Soviet counterparts up and down the line. Units would feint outward and then, more often than not, retreat in an effort to draw the other commander into a mistake. Occasionally, the unit might slip in and manage a solid strike against the enemy before pulling back.

If they could pull back. A Wendigo ag tank already lay burning in mid-field, caught and smashed by a lucky barrage of Neo-Soviet Thunder artillery. A few broken squads that had strayed too far came staggering back in singles and pairs, a few of them fleeing in panic from loosed radhounds. The *mertvaya sobaka* usually met a quick end amid Pitbull cross fire.

Across the dead zone, the Union claimed its due in one devastated Vanguard division and two smoking hulks that had been Avalanche troop carriers. A squad of Chem Grunts had strayed too far forward, trying to sneak around the Union flank with their toxin-wash chemsprayers. An Ares heavy assault suit on guard smashed them with a single discharge from his shoulder-mounted plasma cannon. Charred flesh and half-melted metal littered the ground where they had stood.

All the while both lines inched forward toward that point of no return. Like some chess match of titans, played out with living pieces by the opposing colonels Raymond Sainz and Katya Romilsky.

And out on the edge of that game, a very deadly pawn or perhaps a knight, Sergeant Tousley led his squad in repeated feints and strikes at the enemy line.

On the Union's curling left flank, where the fighting was beginning to turn brutal, Tousley led his men forward in the shadow of a Hydra transport. Tired of Sainz's cautious approach, he was trying to work his people in close enough to strike at the pair of large Class F *Cyclops* mutants that prowled the edge of the Neo-Sov line. These two-plus-meter monstrosities were partially armored by exoskeletons encasing their lower bodies, the better to support massive upper body musculature and implanted devices. Monomolecular-edged titanium blades replaced fingers that could easily slice a man in two or tear into vehicle-grade armor. The single laser-beam eye that glowed in the middle of the armored headgear was powered from a large system surgically embedded in the back and shoulders.

Take them out and the mutants lost two of their most-powerful members. Maybe that would finally persuade Colonel Sainz that it was time to press forward on the attack.

Tousley heard a low whistle building up into a higher-pitched scream. "Down!" he yelled, then obeyed his own order and tried to melt into the damp ground.

The Thunder barrage bracketed his men and the Hydra, rocking the ground and showering them all with bits of fire-blackened earth. Tousley had thought his squad outside their effective range. Stunned, his ears ringing from the explosion, he stumbled to his feet regardless.

"That was for sighting," he croaked out, then swallowed to clear his voice. "They'll fire for effect next time. Move it!"

The Hydra had already powered into a quick stop, spun around 180 degrees, and was heading back toward the relative safety of the Union line. It was a race the foot soldiers couldn't win. With his squad stranded and exposed, Tousley cupped his ears against the ringing-whine sound plaguing him and made the only call he could. "Forward at a sprint. Get under the arc of those guns." His people scrambled to their feet and forward, urged on by the distant thump of heavy artillery launches.

When the first shell slammed into the ground behind them, Tousley was certain they'd never make it. He dived forward, mentally railing at Colonel Sainz for having waited so long to commit to battle, leaving Tousley and his men exposed to the enemy this way. True, the Seventy-first could not hope to draw on reserves as could the Neo-Soviet colonel, but you didn't win a battle while on the defensive.

A wall of fire leapt toward the sky behind them, oddly mirrored as the gray clouds took on a strange red cast. The Thunders drew a line of destruction that fell directly across the retreating Hydra. A shell tipped in depleted uranium punctured the Hydra's armor, detonating inside. The vehicle's sides bulged outward, fire spilling out burst seams and shattered plex windows. It cartwheeled over, coming down on its roof. Metal shrapnel, razor-edged shards from the artillery shells and bits of the Hydra, cut through the air. They sliced into the back of Lance Corporal Danielle Johnson, who was a bit slow taking cover. She tumbled along the ground and fetched up against a dwarf pine, still alive but her lower back and legs covered in blood. No telling how seriously she was hurt, but the fact that she could still pull her legs up under her told him that at least she wasn't crippled. Not yet.

From the frying pan, Tom Tousley thought. He shook his head, still trying to clear the whining ring from the earlier close call. Already, sporadic fire from advanced Vanguard infantry was churning the turf just a dozen meters in front of his people. The larger mutants were shambling forward, scattering other Neo-Soviet soldiers, who scattered frantically to escape the path of their own monsters. The shouts of the Rad Troopers massed along the forward right flank of Romilsky's line rose to a deafening crescendo.

Tousley's squad staggered to their feet, a few bleeding from minor wounds as they returned fire. All were still hardy enough to fight, though facing certain death. Tousley ejected his Pitbull's spent clip and slammed in a fresh one, preparing to sell himself and his squad at a high price.

Then the first crimson-and-gold blur flashed by. And another. The whine that filled Tousley's ears peaked and then quickly faded as the Doppler effect muted the Aztec antigrav cycles' trademark scream.

Having moved forward under the shadow of low hills, two squads of the experimental Aztecs now burst onto the field, re-forming into a perfect double-column staggered formation. They swept by the besieged infantry squad, drawing fire that might have broken a ground unit but that the armored ag cycles could weather for a moment.

The Aztec cycles moved at incredible speed, crossing the contested ground and hammering the Thunder artillery sites with SPEAR missiles before many Neo-Soviet officers could react to their presence. The Separate Penetration Explosively Armed Radials each held five submunitions which, on contact, drove forward at obtuse angles to each other to detonate independently. Where standard Arrowhead or DART missiles might have merely hurt a target, the SPEAR almost guaranteed a devastating hit. The problem was their decreased range, which is why they were traditionally mounted on fast-intercept vehicles like the Aztec.

Earlier shouts of victory from the Neo-Soviets turned to dismay and outrage as the Aztecs completed their run with devastating effect. Only one of the expensive cycles was lost when a Cyclops mutant ranged in with its laser and burned through the chest and neck of one driver. Hardly a fair trade for half a dozen Thunders, which the Neo-Soviets relied upon to cover their massed forces.

Tousley felt the shift in mood along both lines, and knew that right now he held an advantageous position if he could make it work. With a final burst from his Pitbull, he crabbed over to where Private Alex Kipp had been sighting his Draco launcher on the forward Cyclops. Kipp now knelt on the ground, gazing up at the clouds roiling and shifting into a sky tiger-striped heavily in reddish hues.

"Whatsamatter? Never seen a red sunset before?" Tousley said, slapping Kipp hard on the shoulder. "Get that Draco up and hit them." He pointed not toward the Cyclops, which was angling after the returning Aztecs, its red eye blazing, but at the small command team that had been whipping the Rad Troopers into a frenzy.

Kipp's eyes flicked momentarily over to Tousley, but he still didn't raise the Draco. "Sarge, that ain't no sunset." He pointed to a glowing patch of clouds. "It's afternoon. That's the sun behind there."

Tousley felt the moment slipping away as fast as the blur of Aztecs racing for the Union line. It was now or not at all. And not at all meant certain death for his squad. He gripped Kipp's uniform, thinking to shake some sense back into him. "I don't care if the sun supernovas. You get that launcher up and fire! Everyone! Hit the Rad Troopers with everything you've got. Now!"

Weapons spat controlled bursts into the throng of Rad Troopers. At this range, killing one outright would be more luck than skill, but there was always that chance. Corporal Jerry Richardson, hammering away with his Rottweiler, dropped several wounded to the ground. Danielle Johnson managed to pump off two grenades from her Bulldog's M-81 launcher, one falling far short, but the other arcing into a cluster of Rad Troopers. Then Kipp finally responded, shouldering the Draco launch tube and instantly firing off the Arrowhead round. Spiraling out on a light contrail of smoke, the rocket flew unerringly into the knot of officers Tousley had pointed out, scattering them like cinders in a bonfire.

Whipped into a bloodlust, stung by the infantry squad's weaponry, and now bereft of leadership along a large stretch, the Rad Troopers hung in a critical balance. At first Tousley thought he'd acted too late. Then one soldier broke ranks to charge forward, his Nagant spitting its uranium-tipped death. Then two and then half a dozen.

Like a building avalanche, the charging warriors led packs forward until the Neo-Soviet wing crumbled in a mad rush for their Union enemy. Rad-hounds leapt into the forefront of the charge, their mutant handlers confused by the charge into thinking Colonel Romilsky had ordered the general attack. Two squads of Vanguard infantry moved forward, then paused when they realized that the main line had yet to advance with them. The Vanguard milled about in confusion, then retreated rather than support a poorly organized and doomed attack. Tousley laughed bravely, waving them a wide salute.

A last act of defiance, most likely. As the Neo-Sov right flank pressed forward in haphazard advance, he took stock of his situation and how slight was the chance of rescue. The Aztecs were too far behind and as yet unaware that the squad was in trouble. Two Hydras moved forward, but lacked the speed to rendezvous and extract Tousley's men before the rad hounds were on them and the first Rad Troopers could begin firing for effect.

"Scatter and grab cover where you can," Tousley ordered rather than risk a rout in the face of the enemy. Better a brave finish that wouldn't stall a Union advance.

Then twin shadows crossed over the ground, and two blackened-metal turrets fell from the sky just ahead of his squad and in the path of the advancing Neo-Soviet forces. Automated Defense Drones, courtesy of Major Howard no doubt—just another case of Texans looking out for each other when they could. The drones hovered on independent vectoring antigrav thrusters, the head supporting a quad-barreled machine gun that would fire 7.62-millimeter rounds. Suspended below each was a large drill mechanism, the sharp-ribbed bit spinning at a rapid rate. As the ADDs drew close to the Siberian taiga, the bits grabbed hold and quickly anchored the drones into the earth. They spat out their first bursts, taking down the forwardmost rad-hounds.

Tousley felt like cheering.

"Ribbed for your pleasure, boys and girls," he said, referring to the old but not obsolete drill anchors. "We've done our part. Recover our wounded and let's fade back."

Scrabbling to the side of Danielle Johnson, Tousley waved over PFC Brian Scott to help. Between them they shouldered her weight easily, one of her arms around each of their necks. Corporal Richardson brought up the rear, guarding against anything that might make it past or around the ADDs. Privates Nicholas and Kipp ran point, the latter unable to help frequent glances at the strange cloud formations.

All Tousley noticed at first was that the cloud cover was beginning to break up, the red-stained cumulus quickly burning away. A patch would thin, then break into small bloodred clots, and finally be drawn upward as if snatched away in pieces. No lightning flashed, but a distant thunderclap pealed. He didn't understand any of it—the strange terrain changes or frozen Khela River or now the bizarre weather, nor did he truly let it concern him. He was a sergeant of infantry in the Seventy-first Assault Group, and his job didn't change because of such abnormal events. But he bade the cloud cover good riddance if it would alleviate any distraction to his squad.

And then he saw the sky behind.

Commanding from the crest of a low hill just off center of the Union middle line, Colonel Raymond Sainz had also kept a watch on the strange atmospheric conditions while directing the opening feints of his battle plan. The whole time he and Colonel Romilsky traded goads and disinformation over open frequencies. It surprised him when Rebecca Howard brought him an unsecured link and informed him of the transmissions. What Neo-Soviet commander would bother to send the enemy a message when battle had already commenced? All doubts, though, were put to rest with Katya Romilsky's opening demand.

"The Seventy-first will stand down and surrender within two minutes," she ordered him in flawless English, "or I will be forced to destroy you."

"*Strasvicha*, Colonel Katya Olia Romilsky." His Russian was as flawless as her English. "A pleasant day for battle. *Da*?"

His grasp of the Russian tongue and easy disregard of her warning flustered her response for all of three long seconds.

"*Da*, very good, Raymond Sainz," she replied, switching to her own tongue. "But you know you cannot win. We have armies across your line of retreat to Karskoye *and* Laptev More." Her voice hardened. "The empire will not tolerate your obliteration of Dikson."

Dikson? Sainz recalled the name of the small city mentioned by Captain Fredriksson and the strange storm of that moonless night. "Dikson?" he asked. "Above Murmansk? We would never have beached near your military base there."

"If you know our language so well, I can only believe you know Neo-Soviet geography, too. You would not mistake Dikson for Polyarnyy. And we intend to prove you destroyed it as you did Novo Cocarada in Angola."

So *that* would be the empire's game, to make United Africa believe the Union had turned a new weapon against their soil. And they had apparently destroyed one of their own cities to give truth to the lie. A heavy price, to sacrifice a whole city for so little gain. Two could play such games, though. "We tracked the missile that destroyed Novo Cocarada to a site near here. We came for the proof, and we'll have it before we leave." He winced when a Union Wendigo fell beneath a Thunder barrage, weakening his strong claim.

"You're here searching for Chernaya Gora," Romilsky said. Was that a touch of humor in her voice? "You chased a phantom menace right into our hands, as the High Command knew someone would."

Sainz had been distracted maneuvering his Aztecs into

position on the left flank, and now her casual mention of the supposed supersecret facility threw him further off-balance.

"Chernaya Gora—" he began.

"Does not exist," she cut him off abruptly, her voice calm and cold at the same time. "Never did. And your time for surrender is up. I am sorry, Colonel Sainz, that you lose your command to a hoax. That is war."

Trying to shake the dread stealing over him that it *might* be true, Raymond Sainz simply said, "Well, so is *this.*" He nodded a signal to Major Howard, who ordered the Aztecs forward on the run.

"What?" Romilsky spoke rapid Russian to someone else, her words lost amid a sudden flurry of voices until a final, "No, that! Those vehicles there!" Then the link went dead as she remembered to disconnect.

Both commanders were certainly busy then, as the Aztec ag cycles destroyed the Thunders anchoring the Neo-Soviet right flank. And again when Tousley's squad managed to throw the entire enemy wing into chaos by goading the Rad Troopers to break formation.

The *human-wave strategy* with which Neo-Soviet commanders employed Rad Troopers was a hard one to break. Though Rad Troopers were among the weaker units fielded by the empire and easily put down, in sufficient numbers they were a serious threat not to be ignored. Direct too much attention toward them, and the heavy armor and Vanguard infantry following would tear the Union line apart. Direct too little, and the Rad Troopers would overwhelm many of his infantry assets. And despite the technological marvels possessed by the Union, infantry still remained the backbone of any army.

Finding a way to deal with the Rad Troopers piecemeal was always a preferable option. The chaotic charge against his left wing was doomed from the start. It was a windfall he had hoped to create himself, noticing much earlier that the battle shaping up on his left flank would be the decisive clash. But its early triggering meant he was not quite ready. He nodded permission to Major Howard, who suggested dropping in two Auto Defense Drones early. They would blunt the advance without turning it back, and also give Tousley's squad a chance to regain Union lines.

"Order the Aztecs back around. Have them strafe the outside edges of that formation, but stay far enough back to avoid a run-in with the real mutants." The armored antigrav cycles were safe enough from the Rad Troops' weapons, but then the Rads were little more than diseased civilians handed a weapon and promised a quick end to their suffering. Cannon fodder. The strong mutants such as Cyclops and Zyborgs were the real dangers, though Sainz had as yet spotted neither on the field. On his right flank Sainz sent forward a pair of Wendigos backed by drones and two infantry platoons, to hold Romilsky in place while he finished rolling up her own right wing.

It wasn't until he paused to draw breath between orders that Sainz took note of the peals of thunder growing louder and Major Howard's preoccupation with the sky. In all the excitement he'd forgotten the strange actions of the cloud cover, and now watched as it boiled and burned away to reveal a dead sky behind. The last of the clouds shattered and dispersed upward into a heaven bleached a uniform bone white. The ground shook with the thunderous clamor, as if the Earth itself was protesting the rape of its skies.

Sainz barely noticed when his deployed drones quickly ran out of ammunition and were overwhelmed by the press of Rad Troopers. By the time he looked back to the battle, the Aztecs had whittled the advance down to fragments, and what little remained were being mopped up by intense infantry fighting as the ground troops ran forward supported by their Hydra carriers. His right-flank offensive had stalled, no doubt stunned by the dead sky. Around him his aides and nearby forces were shocked to inactivity as well, and the same seemed true of the Neo-Soviet forces. The fighting on his left flank slowly wound down, the few remaining radhounds shot down and exploding, and the Rad Troopers in that area of the field broken and fleeing back to their own lines. No one pursued the rout, the Union soldiers in the grip of paralysis as each finally noticed the strange sky with no sun.

And then, the heavens opened. To the accompaniment of a ceaseless roaring thunder, long scars of crackling energy quartered the sky and then split farther apart to reveal a liquid darkness behind. It was as if Sainz stared through holes in the atmosphere and directly into deep space, though a space without stars. A space that had volume rather than vacuum, dark and thick as ink. He heard an aide off to his right begin to pray. "Our Father, who art in heaven, hallowed be thy name," he murmured.

Sainz disagreed. Whatever looked down on them from those great heights, it wasn't God. And it certainly was not benevolent.

And beyond that, the Union colonel was as lost a soul as any other.

10

Sergeant Tom Tousley stumbled forward as the ground shook again, long and hard. He helped Danielle Johnson onto a stretcher that two corpsmen had dropped as the quake knocked them off their feet. Another medic tried to assist PFC Maria Carr, who had taken a hot, uranium-tipped slug from a Nagant assault rifle in her left thigh during their retreat back to Union lines. Her wound required immediate cleaning—painful, but necessary before the spread of contamination into her flesh and blood caused more damage than the slug itself. She refused to be carried within the protection of a nearby Hydra, shrugging the corpsman away rudely as she stared up into the hostile sky.

Tousley was by her side immediately, helping her to sit and backing off the angry corpsman with the fierce scowl that came with sergeant's stripes. He knew he should be glad that the medics attended their jobs at all with the chaos unleashed overhead, but Tousley wasn't about to deny one of his squad the chance to confront the threat overhead.

"No one's taking you inside," he promised her, then crabbed back over to Danielle and helped to strap her down. Her wounds looked more superficial than serious, but she was obviously in pain and weak from loss of blood. The quake finally subsided with a last light tremor, and Lance Corporal Johnson was quickly carried into the waiting Hydra.

The rest of the squad had taken up a half-circle post around Tousley and their wounded. They divided their attention between the fleeing Rad Troopers and the final few radhounds bounding over the terrain, and long glances into the wounded heavens.

Tousley followed their eyes upward. More of the dark pools had erupted into the bone white sky over Gory Putorana. Some ran together like merging oil slicks, hanging large and heavy overhead. Others extended out into thin wounds, stretching over the horizon. No sign of the sun—no telltale glow the likes of which Private Kipp had pointed out earlier. Only a uniform glow to a bleached sky stained by pools of corruption.

The event lacked any semblance of reality, challenging the sanity of every person who looked upon it. Many soldiers wept openly. Some were caught up in prayer. Alex Kipp dropped his Draco launcher and began walking in a small, erratic circle, his mind unable to handle the stress. Tousley had seen such things before in heavy combat, often right before some man or woman stood up into enemy fire or began spraying bullets around at anything and anyone regardless of uniform. Tousley began walking toward the private, intent on relieving him of his sidearm. Angry yells and even more shouts of terror distracted him, and he looked up again at the skies.

The pools had spilled over, and darkness slowly crawled down through the atmosphere—a hundred titanic inkwells pouring their foul blackness upon the Earth. It almost looked as if the skies were melting, the muted light running before the onset of an everlasting night. Already the dark trails smeared down to the horizon, leaving thin cracks of white in between, which would soon be lost. Overhead the blackness poured closer, silently creeping down through the atmosphere and casting a shadow over Gory Putorana and the rest of the world. One black runner slammed silently into the ground two kilometers distant. A thinner line speared the no-man's-land between the two armies.

Bedlam erupted among Union and Neo-Soviet forces. A Wendigo charged forward, unsupported, rail gun hammering into the enemy and machine guns simply tearing into the earth and air for the sake of it. The Aztec antigrav cycles raced back through the Union lines and sped northwest in a final bid to outrun the falling sky, though anyone could see that horizon was already stained fully black.

A Hydra, in its haste to follow the fleeing cyclists, plowed through a formation of deployed infantry, adding to the growing terror and confusion. Many soldiers also turned and fled. A rare few simply suicided. Alex Kipp drew the pistol Tousley had missed collecting and used it on himself. Tousley barely registered the fact. Some others threw down weapons and raised their hands toward the Neo-Soviet force, surrendering.

It was these few who roused Tousley from his state of shock. In seventeen years of service he had never surrendered. Not one stretch of ground he'd taken or one advantage he'd won from the enemy. Watching the curtain of darkness falling over him, he felt neither fear nor defeat. He felt rage.

Another tendril came down over the Union center line, eclipsing Colonel Sainz and Major Howard. He looked straight up into the black arm reaching down at him. As if gazing through dark water, far above he thought he caught the reflection of a single white eye staring at them down through that column of darkness. He raised his Pitbull and squeezed into the trigger. Not panicked fire like so many others, but short, controlled bursts. One clip—eject, insert, chamber—and then another, directly into the face of the enemy.

And then the blackness rolled over him, and he too was lost.

Major Randall Williams remained too busy to be much frightened. He quickly isolated TC&D from the many panicked requests for information—mainly from departments with no immediate need for the answers he was unable to give anyway. When the cosmic storm raging around the Earth reached out suddenly to ensnare Luna, he turned his back on it and concentrated instead on the data coming in over the astrophysics consoles. Visual effects would be recorded for better study later. He had to focus his mind away from the hellish storm. Survival could hinge on seconds of processing time, or the ability of one person to make the right intuitive leap forward from the data as given. And as a self-respecting scientist, Randall Williams remained just egotistical enough to believe that the one person might indeed be him.

Armed forces officers didn't know what real pressure was.

The moon never stopped shaking now, as if the wash of energy surrounding them somehow caused a turbulence in space. Nothing they could detect, but that didn't mean it wasn't there. His own theory currently revolved around microchanges in the moon's orbit. As if Luna had cut loose from Earth's pull for a fraction of a second, and then snapped back into orbit. Unfortunately, there was no way to test that theory, at least not yet. Though it remained as likely an explanation as the event they'd witnessed earlier, when out the plex window the Earth faded to a gray shadow of its former blue-and-green majesty, then to a featureless black. On instrumentation, it showed the same as ever. Williams might have written that off to a trick of his own mind, except for the twoscore operators also in the control room swearing by the same thing.

Then the moon came under two standard Earth gravities, and no one did much of anything for a moment but remained pressed into their seats or found themselves relocated to the floor.

"Gravity generators all read normal," one operator reported as soon as the heavier gravity released them. "Reports coming in. High gravity experienced all over Luna. Even outside bases. One standard G."

So a fluctuation in actual gravity, coupled with interior generators, had caused a double-strength gravity field. Williams couldn't begin to imagine how that might be possible, and he possessed a remarkable imagination.

"Atmospheric processor numbers twelve, fourteen, and thirty-five all read off-line. Operators verify system failures and many injuries."

Without doubt. Being subjected to twice normal gravity was one thing. No one had complained of too much pain, so bruises and sprains were probably the worst they'd suffered.

But outside the bases, where one-sixth gravity had come under a full G, that kind of change broke bones and shattered skulls. Especially those weakened skeletons of lunar workers who failed to keep up on their gravity treatments.

"I want medical to make inquiries to all critical posts," he ordered. "Make sure we didn't lose anyone vital. Any word from Colonel Allister?" The Tycho commander had been returning from a meeting at Tranquillity.

"His transport is down, and he's stranded," a lieutenant reported. "But he's all right."

"It's clearing," someone yelled. All eyes went to the large plex window rather than the instrumentation, which was showing clear pictures regardless of what their eyes saw happening outside.

A dark wave of shimmering energies rolled over the landscape, leaving behind a trail of gray haze that glowed and swirled aimlessly for a moment. The shimmer passed on, leaving the moon behind and now completely occluding Earth. It also opened up to Williams and his staff their first glimpse of the spacescape.

Blackness. Only two stars remained where once there had been millions to count at a glance. High-magnitude stars at that. Even by the naked eye, Williams knew they were closer than anything seen normally from Earth. Peeking out from the edge of the collapsing sphere of dark matter, giving it some definition along the eastern hemisphere, an ice-blue nebula began to fill the sky. The cosmic gases competed with the nearer gray luminous haze, though even as he watched, the trailers of haze left behind were streaming away as if suddenly caught on an incredible solar wind. Trailing off away from the collapsing sphere, it reminded Williams of a glowing black comet with a gray tail streaming out behind it away from the sun.

Only no sun like he'd ever seen. As it broke around the cover of the Earth's shield, it banished the artificial night and returned the color of Luna's pale atmosphere. The shock of a sunrise four days early froze Williams for a full two seconds before his scientific mind took over again and began to evaluate the strange solar body. He estimated it easily three times the size of Sol in subjective appearance. Blazing white to the naked eye, roughly globular but nowhere near the perfect sphere their sun had been. Right then Randall Williams realized for the first time that he was already thinking of this as an alien sky. One that had somehow supplanted Sol and the entire Milky Way galaxy. And it surprised even him that the hardest thing for him to admit wasn't that it had happened.

No, the hardest thing was that he couldn't explain it.

What might be called normalcy returned to Earth slowly. Colonel Raymond Sainz was aware of the darkness and little else for some time. Next came the touch of a cold, vast space, and the sense of motion. Then from high above a pinpoint of light. It grew in size, the only interruption to the eternal night. Slender arms reached out from its globular body and then wrapped back in, tearing off chunks of the inky black. Sainz saw those arms as able to rip planets like the Earth to shreds, and quailed under their approach.

Something deep inside his mind promised that the Earth might be better off cloaked forever in the night.

A halo circled this source of light, and quickly washed outward to color the sky the pale blue-gray of predawn. It stretched over the landscape with liquid slowness, the dark shadows clinging for every last moment of existence.

The landscape around Sainz was not the same landscape they had left behind. Or not quite the same. Gory

Putorana still rose up in the northwest, though large streaks of coppery soil hinted at some changes. It was the most recognizable landmark around, those slopes gradually rising up to the Siberian plateau.

The battlefield was altered beyond salvage of the colonel's battle plan. The open land that had separated the two armies was a jumble of broken rock crusted with ice and permafrost. There would be no easy crossing for antigravity craft. To the west, about where he had deployed his right wing, an immense, rounded hill butted up where sharp cliff faces had before overlooked open ground. Steam vented from large cracks in the mountainside. The gentler foothills where he had placed the bulk of his forces were now sharp-edged dunes of dark rust red stone, their southern exposure capped by standing ice that flowed downhill like miniature glaciers.

Sainz stood on one crest, a position analogous to his earlier one, and he picked out Rebecca Howard and many of his immediate staff and guard, all of them either wandering about the strange landscape or looking about as if waking from a trance. He found little immediate evidence of his Seventy-first Assault Group. One Hydra and a Wendigo. A pair of Ares assault suits, one outfitted with a plasma cannon and the other a Harbinger rail gun. Some infantry.

Then the sky bled blue, its natural color, as the sunlike creation thrust itself into a late-morning position. Three times the size of the regular sun, it hung there, menacing in its blazing white fury but providing not quite as much natural light.

Sainz checked the late-afternoon position where the sun should have been, and found clear sky. No sun or even a remnant of the cloud cover they had seen earlier in the day. And as he turned a full circle, he suddenly wished to find blue sky, clear of everything but that ominous, misshapen sun. What he hadn't wanted to find were the grayish white contrails that arced from the northern and eastern horizons, trailing upward into the sky until finding the small white flares of ballistic missiles already flying.

Warheads already set on their mission, as the Neo-Soviet empire struck at the Union.

blue sky, clear of everything but that ominous, misshapen sun. What he hadn't wanted to find were the grayish white contrails that rose from the northern and eastern horizons, arching upward into the sky and finding the small white flecks of ballistic missiles already flying.

Warheads already set on their trajectories, as the Neo-Soviet empire struck at the Union...

UNDER AN ALIEN SKY

11

Eleven years in space could leave anyone jaded, and it was a rare occasion when an object under Randall Williams's study evoked in him a sense of true awe or beauty. The crystalline forest did both.

The formation spread over a small patch of the moon's surface, rising from the gray soil as if grown there, fifty meters across and just over one hundred in length. The crystals ranged from small, clear-diamond spikes only centimeters long to magnificent emerald heights thrusting four meters above, reaching a maximum diameter—as measured so far—of .9 meters. Their progress in development was apparent as the in-between stages varied their greenish hue according to size. The medium to larger crystals formed slender, delicate towers or sometimes melded together into angular archways and latticework walls. Small crystals grew along the edges of larger ones, especially in those places where Williams noticed that previous damage had cracked what he was calling the "parent structure."

A team of junior scientists trod carefully through the labyrinth, taking measurements and conducting some initial tests. They all glanced nervously at one another, while trying to deal with so foreign a substance, and here on Luna besides. Two squads of space-specialist Marines under Captain Paul Drake stood an uneasy perimeter around the strange formation, guarding against any run-in with Neo-Soviet forces now that the fence line had been smashed.

Williams left that remote chance to Drake, concentrating instead on the ultrahigh-frequency pulses being emitted by the formation. At first he'd believed the pulses to be a piezoelectric effect. Compress the crystals, or they compress under their own weight, and they generate a small current that might translate as a UHF signal. His assistant had outguessed him; Lieutenant Theresa Dupras went straight for a resonating effect. While Williams quickly disproved his own theory by physically stressing the crystals and reading no subsequent change in signal strength, Dupras graphed out the power of the UHF signal against radio communications between guards and the electrical field given off by an antigrav sled's generator.

"Efficient," Williams said, praising the crystalline formation and Dupras at the same time. "The formation reacts to frequencies in our standard comm ranges and above. Those variations are converted to a single, powerful pulse, part of which works in regenerative feedback to create the next pulse." He nodded to himself as thoughts clicked into place. "There must be energy degradation in there somewhere, or a method of stored power, but we're not seeing it yet."

"Photovoltaic?" Dupras asked. She was one of the few besides Williams who didn't seem unnerved by the appearance of the formation.

He nodded. "That's as good a guess as any." Just then Captain Drake walked by, checking horizons. He nodded cordially enough, though Williams didn't believe it for a second.

Dupras ran one hand over an emerald facet. "I'd like to get some samples of this back into the labs, but I'm leery about breaking off pieces. How much damage until it loses the properties we want to study?"

Kneeling down next to the base of one large specimen, Williams dug his fingers into the soft gray soil around its base. "There's no telling how deep they run. They're well anchored, but the lunar soil is not compacted at all like you would expect if they'd been planted or forced into the ground. Tranquillity reported some odd terrain changes as well, with a similar natural blend into existing topography." He shook his head. "I'd love to know how they got here."

Theresa Dupras smiled weakly. "I'd love to know how *we* got here." Her eyes flicked skyward, to the large blazing stain that had replaced the sun. On the opposite horizon the ghost of the nearby nebula darkened the color of the sky.

Randall Williams remained mute, and after an awkward pause Dupras went over to a pair of scientists to request an update for him. He wanted to keep his mind free of preconceptions until more facts were known. All Union resources on Luna that could be spared were focused on collecting data that might help to answer that question, as well as the question of where *here* even was. Until then, he would focus on such events as the crystalline forest—a phenomenon never before surveyed by Union forces, anywhere. And he knew that was part of the appeal. That they were so—

"Alien," Captain Paul Drake said, more of a loud whisper than a statement for public consumption. He stood a few paces off, having stopped in his rounds to study the crystalline formation up close.

"Captain?" Williams asked, surprised at how the Marine's thoughts and his own had traveled the same path. He stood up and brushed the grayish soil from one knee. The lunar-plain winds swept away the light dust.

"They're so alien. Major." Drake tacked Williams's rank on almost as an afterthought, as if reminding himself to be civil. "Not in your standard little-green-men sense of aliens, but different. Like they don't belong here."

So perhaps not *quite* the same path. Williams thought of it more that *they* didn't belong here, Drake and himself and the rest of Earth-descended man. Drake reached out tentatively to touch the crystal spear. He ran an ebony hand along one smooth emerald facet, then pulled back suddenly. "Are they dangerous?"

"The first question of a military man," Williams said, giving a tight smile to take some of the sting from his words. "Can it hurt me? The next being, of course, can it be used to hurt others?"

Paul Drake's bearing stiffened, though military protocol was too well ingrained in him to ignite an angry retort.

Williams waved away the protocol. "You may speak freely, Captain Drake. I know you resent my pulling you off a combat assignment."

Drake said nothing as he scanned the full horizon with optics. Finally, he said, "I don't resent you, Major Williams. But I would rather have fielded with Colonel Allister's men, yes. Or taken the *Icarus* after Sputnik-23. She was supposed to be my command, after all."

Williams shook his head. "I saw no reason to waste

your talents on the mission to retrieve Sputnik-23's log recorders. The Neo-Soviets cannot place men in space fast enough to save their imaging array from a rapidly decaying orbit. It's going to burn up, just as our Station Liberty did. We need that data, and when Twenty-three hits the atmosphere it will jettison the computer logs and our men will retrieve them. I believe you would call such an assignment *a milk run*?"

Williams shook his head. "And as for Colonel Allister, he did not request you or your men for active combat, which leads me to believe he would rather you remain attached to my command and out of this foolishness."

That struck a hard chord in Paul Drake. His eyes widened in disbelief. "Foolishness? We have reports coming in from all over Luna that the Neo-Soviets have smashed the fence line using their *human-wave* strategies. And Station Freedom monitored the missile launches against Union nations back on Earth right after . . ." He trailed off.

"Our arrival?" Williams prompted. He gestured to the pale sky and the large, misshapen body blazing down. Earth hung large overhead as well, a sight most lunar residents were indifferent to after their first year, but that was a fresh event now that the Earth was far bigger than ever before as seen from the moon. It was caused by a change in orbit, according to the best minds of three different bases. Fortunately not too drastic to cause much more than heavier tides on Earth when the moon strayed in closer.

"The *event*," Drake said, stressing his own preferred term.

"Stick your head in the sand if you want, Captain. I've seen others doing it, too. But we're missing the eight planets we normally orbit with, though we've identified six others out there we've never known. And I guarantee Sol is not one of those few stars you'll see when we hit our night cycle. Wherever we are now, we are not where we once were or anything close to it."

Drake stepped aside a moment, raised his glasses to check a horizon again. Williams followed his gaze, saw by naked eye the tiny speck darkening Luna's pale upper atmosphere. Spacecraft bound for Tranquillity, he guessed. Though it looked to be awfully low.

"Wherever we are," Drake said, dropping the glasses to his chest where they bounced easily in the light gravity, "the Neo-Sovs are the enemy."

"Well, they shouldn't be." Williams shook his head again. "They're in the same situation we are. We can steal the observation video from Sputnik-23, and it might show us something we haven't found ourselves, but how much more do the Neo-Soviets possess that we'll never see? How much of that is vital information, Captain? We should be working together."

"They launched nukes against us!" Drake protested.

"And smashed the fence line, so I've heard. So we should launch back and go parading about Luna to defend our territory? All right, but consider this. I lost half of my specialists when Colonel Allister fielded toward Point Gagarin. How many man-hours is that in lost observation and research?"

Drake considered that, checked the incoming ship again, and frowned. Williams couldn't say if the frown was directed at his logic or something about the descending vessel that Drake found peculiar. "I can't change who I am, Major. It's my sworn duty to engage and defeat the enemy whenever possible, with a minimum loss of life."

"I know the oath, Captain Drake. But did you ever stop

to think that the oath was specifically written not to say *a minimum loss of* Union *life*?"

For a moment, Williams thought he might have gotten through to Paul Drake. He read the doubts and frustrations playing over the larger man's face, as his training warred with common sense and the desperate necessities of their situation. Then his face cleared of everything but alarm.

"She's coming in hot!" he yelled, pulling Williams aside. In the one-sixth gravity, they leapt away in loping bounds. "Everyone scatter. Away from the crystals. Get away!"

In the top arc of his third jump, Williams looked back and saw that the craft picked out earlier against the low horizon was coming down sharply and on a line right for the crystalline forest. The blocky construction and forward-swept wings indicated it was a Neo-Soviet craft. A raid? Williams wrote that idea off during his next leap, identifying the vessel as a limited-range explorer. Not even a true military design.

Everyone was moving away at their best speed when the vessel belly-crashed into the soft soil a half kilometer distant, then skipped back into the air like some impossibly large stone skipping over a gray-white pond. Grounding at such a distance might have given the craft an adequate margin of safety on Earth, but in the moon's lighter gravity and without landing gear extended to dig into the ground, the vessel would not be so easily halted. It skipped and slid as computer programs or pilot reflexes fought the vessel into the crash landing. Its last low-arced bounce brought the spacecraft down on top of the scientists' antigrav sleds, smashing them into the soil or sending them tumbling over the landscape. Then the nose of the craft burrowed straight into the crystalline forest, shattering the emerald formations into millions of splinters and pulverizing those fragments as the bulk of the craft skidded over the patch and continued on another good quarter kilometer.

Dust hung in the air in a grayish haze that reminded Williams eerily of the cosmic storm residue he had watched trail off the Earth. Just proper moondust this time, however, choking the air and making it difficult to breathe.

Paul Drake helped him to his feet, checked him for damage, then chambered a round into his Pug autopistol. "Perhaps it *was* a good thing I remained behind," he said.

Then he was walking steadily for the craft, calling his men to him. This, the captain obviously knew how to deal with.

12

The petrified dunes rolled almost up to the wall of broken rock that now separated the two armies. The permafrost on the ground melted slowly, becoming a dark sludge that pooled in crevices and in the gulches between the dunes and the wall of rock. The ice that ran down the dune slopes had yet to melt and looked like miniature glaciers. In the sky, the misshapen solar body that had replaced Sol was three times larger and burned brighter, but gave off no more warmth than Siberia had known the day before.

From the top of one rock dune, Colonel Raymond Sainz could pick out a dozen small fights by the echoes of distant weapons fire, all of them within a few kilometers. Outlying remnants of the Seventy-first Assault Group were coming under attack by splintered forces from the Neo-Soviet

Striker as they struggled to link back up with the main body Sainz had pulled around his position.

Sainz had to steel himself against the desire to send further reinforcements into these fights. He'd already dispatched an extraction squad to each one to facilitate their retrieval. He couldn't squander any more of his strength, not if he hoped to pry his force out of the Neo-Soviet heartland. All told he had so far salvaged better than three-quarters of the Seventy-first, including the Aztec antigrav cycles that had come screaming back after the cataclysm passed.

He slid down the rock slope, wary of the ice. Two infantrymen waited below and another pair followed him, the minimum guard Major Howard had insisted accompany him to investigate what Corporal Fitzpatrick had reported. The forward two stood at the front of a petrified dune, staring with rapt attention at the its ice-covered face.

Sainz stepped over a narrow stream of sludge to reach them, then stared into the bluish depths of the ice they pointed out to him. Frozen into the small glacier was a captain, both hands reaching out, caught as if trying to swim up from within. Three fingers actually broke the surface of the ice, exposed to the air. A flaw in the ice occluded half of the face, but enough was visible to leave no doubt of his identity. Ryan Searcy, commander of second column. No one spoke, appalled by the captain's horrifying end. Sainz reached out and gripped the exposed fingers, the best farewell he could manage. The digits were warmer than he'd have thought.

"*Strasvicha,* Colonel Sainz. One of your men?"

Sainz spun at the familiar voice, even faster than his own guard, who were so mesmerized by the ice-encased body that they had relaxed their vigil. A Neo-Soviet officer stood fifteen meters distant, two Vanguard infantry flanking her with weapons drawing a line for his chest. The colonel had forgone the usual armored trench coat and carried no weapon. Still, the aura of command lay about her for anyone to see. It was in her easy stance and confident ice-blue eyes, the authority in her voice.

The pair of Kalashnikovs backing her.

The Union infantry were smart enough to leave their own weapons pointed downward, not about to aggravate the situation with their colonel in danger and the Neo-Soviets with the upper hand. The enemy colonel grinned humorlessly at their inaction, but the grin faltered briefly when she glanced at the body imprisoned in ice. Then a mutant handler led a Cyclops from a hidden ravine that led in from the broken terrain. The Union infantry guard tensed, obviously ready to act, but held off waiting for some sign from Sainz.

"Very smart," she complimented them offhandedly in English. "No one needs to get hurt."

Raymond Sainz did not believe that. "No one, Katya Romilsky?" he asked.

"I said *needs,* not *won't,* Colonel."

Sainz switched to Russian, one-upping Romilsky's attempt to intimidate his men by speaking English. "You would not live to enjoy my death," he said.

Her eyes narrowed with suspicion, glancing about for what she had missed. "How is that, Raymond Sainz?"

Slowly, cautiously, he bent to retrieve a large rock, then held it up for her to see. The Vanguard tracked him the entire time with their vented muzzles. He tossed the rock into the open, away from any people.

"Stand fast," he ordered his men in a calm voice. Then he raised his hands and pointed three fingers of his left hand into the palm of his right, closed that hand into a fist, and yanked down as if pulling a lever. The rock disintegrated into splinters with the sound of a ricocheting bullet. The sharp crack of a rifle shot echoed a split second later.

The shot was fired by Sergeant Tyree, who was Rebecca Howard's contribution to the small ground force of guards. He had retained his Bloodhound marksman rifle.

Romilsky laughed, short and hard. With her head thrown back slightly, Sainz noticed again the silver streak that ran through her short-cropped auburn hair.

"Again, very good," she said in English, then threw a quick, angry glance at her Vanguard. "What would you call this, Colonel Sainz? A Mexican standoff?"

"Insurance," Sainz said simply. "You wanted to talk?"

Slipping back into her native tongue, Romilsky turned deadly serious. "What I want is your unconditional surrender, Colonel Sainz."

"Nyet," he said simply.

"Nyet?" She gestured to the eastern horizon. "You saw the missiles, I'm sure. The Union's defense systems can't stop them all. I can send for reinforcements, but you, you are stranded in the middle of the Neo-Soviet empire with no way home."

Sainz knew that might or might not be exactly true. The Seventy-first had been able to contact no one in Union Command, but intermittent comms with Station Freedom offered some hope of contact and eventual extraction. "We have a mission to accomplish," he said.

Her face clouded with anger again. "A fool's mission, Sainz! I told you before that Chernaya Gora is a phantom. You throw your lives away for nothing. Nothing!"

She calmed herself, checked to see that the mutant handler had the Cyclops under control, then continued. "The false intelligence was acquired by the Coahuila Reconnaissance Contribution." She stumbled over the name of the

Mexican district. "A unit captured or destroyed on a resulting mission will discredit Mexico's Contribution Forces and drive a deeper wedge between them and the vocal Texans. The damage is done, Raymond Sainz. Now it is a matter of how many lives we—you and I—spend to finish the operation."

Sainz did not know where the information on Black Mountain originated, but if it did come from one of the purely Mexican Contribution Forces and it was false, then Romilsky's scenario might well come true. He didn't know whether or not to believe her. She might be trying to trick him, but even if it were all true, only one course of action lay before him.

"My duties are clear," he said. "Regardless of today's bizarre events, I'm sworn to defend my command so long as the means exist to resist you. If you want us, Katya Olia, you'll have to pay the price. We've already proved that your greater numbers are no guarantee of victory."

Romilsky's icy blue gaze got icier for a moment, then she spoke again in English for the sake of the Union guards. "Then it would appear our business here is concluded, Colonel. I will withdraw, and I suggest you worry about rescuing your comrade before he suffocates." She nodded to the man entrapped in ice behind Sainz.

He had no intention of taking his eyes off her, but one of his own men cried out, "He's alive! Captain Searcy!"

Sainz did glance back then, and saw the fingers sticking up through the ice flex stiffly. He hurried over and laced his fingers between those of the captain while peering deep into the ice. No sign of movement within. Searcy's eyes were closed, but there was no mistaking the subtle pressure as his fingers squeezed back. In a flash Sainz had his survival knife out and was savagely chipping away at the ice, scratching and gouging slowly through the clear wall.

"Get axes, saws! Someone call Howard and tell her we need combat engineers." He wasn't sure what the engineers might do to help, but they were the closest unit with any kind of experience dealing with structural integrity. Maybe they would know—or at least guess—how to split the ice flow. He briefly wondered how long Searcy had been trying to signal while everyone had turned toward Romilsky. Sainz didn't want to believe that Romilsky might have noticed but let the man suffer.

"Colonel!" The warning shout came as a large shadow fell over Raymond Sainz. The ice reflected back the image of a large Class F mutant moving up behind him commanded by its handler. With only his knife in hand, Sainz spun about and readied for an attack.

They stood there, the mutant towering over its handler, the power supply for its radiation-source weapon venting into the air above its thick, broad shoulders. It was so close Sainz could have counted the copper wire hairs covering the massive chest if he'd been of a mind to. Oversize hands tipped with titanium blades hung at its sides. The hose running from abdomen to back flexed and stirred in time to wheezing breaths. The creature's metal face mask stared impassively down at him, its red optics port glowing dully.

Romilsky moved to Sainz's side, laid a hand on his arm. "Colonel, if you please?"

She pulled him away, letting the Cyclops fire a low-intensity heat beam into the ice, which scattered as it turned bloody red. Water ran at once, the heat beam accomplishing in one swipe what Sainz could not have accomplished in ten minutes of hacking and chipping away.

When the beam splashed over Searcy's outstretched fingers, Sainz saw a flexing response, and noticed the skin reddening as if sunburned. No telling how much radiation the officer might absorb under that beam, but then radiation sickness was the least of the man's worries if he couldn't be freed. That the Cyclops didn't use a full-intensity beam at least boded well for Searcy surviving.

The beam carved deeper, exposing the captain's right hand, then the right arm and his left hand. Next came the whole right leg and the man's shoulders and head. Searcy fell forward, the last of the ice shattering under his weight. He hit the ground and drew his first deep, shuddering breath. His eyes flickered open briefly, staring but unseeing, then closed as shock sent him unconscious.

Sainz knelt at his side, checking for a pulse. He found one, weak and thready, but there. He pointed off two infantry. "Pick him up and get him back to the medics," he ordered. "Go!"

He stood up and turned to Romilsky while the mutant was led back toward the crevice. *"Pochemu?"* he asked simply. *Why*?

She answered in English, no doubt so the rest of his men would understand and pass along to the others. "By bullet or buried in ice, he is going to die. Better his end come as a soldier, *da*?" And with that she turned and followed her Cyclops back through the ravine. The Vanguard infantry brought up the rear.

Sainz stared after them for a long time after they disappeared from view. Wondering.

Rebecca Howard had heard the single, rolling echo from Sergeant Tyree's shot and demanded an immediate situation report. Tyree remained silent, and no one in the colonel's guard answered their comms either. She quickly classified the two alternatives. They were unable to respond. They were unwilling to respond.

Unable meant the death or capture of the colonel and his guard, and the sergeant as well. Not a likely scenario, since only Tyree had fired a shot and the Neo-Soviets rarely relied on silenced weapons. When they came for you, they wanted you to know it. The loss of Colonel Sainz would also bump her into the Seventy-first's number one slot, something she didn't like to think about. Though not always in agreement with Sainz, she managed to see past his Tamalipais birth to recognize his talents. Right now, few men might hope to pull off this mission and extract the Seventy-first alive. Even Tom Tousley would admit that, if he allowed himself a moment of complete honesty.

So that meant they were unwilling to respond, for which she could think of no likely scenarios. Maybe it had to do with the terrifying changes in the Earth. Whatever the reason, she would go and find them herself.

She had just told off a full squad to accompany her when Tyree broke the silence. "Stand down, Major. Colonel Sainz is all right, but we have a very tense situation, and you don't want to break in just now."

After Tyree's complete and full report, Howard handed out the initial orders to mobilize the Seventy-first and then paced a tight square, waiting for the colonel's return. Tyree kept her abreast of what he could see, and almost sent her racing off when the Cyclops looked about to attack the colonel. That they were able to retrieve Captain Searcy seemed little gain for the risk Sainz was taking.

Then came the two infantrymen carrying a live but unconscious Ryan Searcy to the medics, and Sainz followed soon after.

"But you don't trust her," Howard said, after the quick briefing. She read the hesitation on her CO's face. "You can't believe that she'd be so free with Neo-Soviet intelligence?"

Sainz frowned, rubbed a hand along one side of his jaw. "She paints a believable scenario, you have to admit. And she gave us back the life of Captain Searcy."

Rebecca Howard couldn't refute that. As for Romilsky's supposed scheme to create conflicts among various parts of the Union military, she couldn't deny that it would be a good one. Her own Texan birth biased her against the Mexican Contribution Forces, but she tried not to let it cloud her thinking. Tom Tousley, though, and others like him, would use such an event to push for American-preferred status in the Union.

"It's devious enough," she admitted. She glanced southeast with a strong measure of concern. "But I wasn't there. You're the best judge of her honor." She didn't mean for her latter remarks to sound like an accusation, though they rang doubtful in her own ears.

"We couldn't have predicted that Katya Romilsky would take such a chance, approaching with so small a force. I would rather you had been there, too, Rebecca," Sainz said, with neither apology nor rebuke. He always let her speak her mind. "As to her honor, I couldn't say. Yet."

His tone gave away the direction he was leaning, however. "Then what would you say if I told you a large Neo-Soviet force had been working its way around the southeast edge of that broken terrain?" she asked.

"You're sure of this?" There was a trace of wounded surprise in his voice.

"Sergeant Tyree has a good vantage point. He observed them working through the petrified dunes east of here once he could safely tear his eyes away from your confrontation. The whole time Romilsky kept you occupied, she was working a large strike force of Rad Troopers, Grunts, and some Vanguard onto our left flank."

"How many Vanguard?"

"At least one company."

"Vehicles?"

"None noted. Doesn't mean they aren't there, however."

Howard could almost hear the wheels spinning in the colonel's mind as he stood there thinking for some moments, and she wondered suddenly if she'd missed something.

"An impressive gamble," he said finally. "Katya Romilsky knew I'd refuse the order to surrender. She wanted to be ready to strike as soon afterward as possible. But if I'd known of the troop movements, I might have forced the issue and tried to put her down or capture her."

Howard stared at him in disbelief. "You don't see this as proof of duplicity?"

Sainz shook his head. "It's a fine line to walk, Major, but Romilsky did it admirably. She gave me no word to break, and there were no terms on the order to surrender. She even told me at the end that she was simply giving Captain Searcy the chance to die as a soldier. The clues were there."

He glanced around, apparently noting the preparations of the Seventy-first.

"I've already ordered preparations for a full mobilization," she said before he could ask. She knew Sainz well enough to predict that he would want to withdraw and decide on a battlefield of his own choosing, not that of Colonel

Romilsky. "Eastern-deployed units are regrouping with all haste. We recovered nineteen bodies and another two squads equivalent of infantry. I'm afraid Captain Foley was among the bodies recovered."

Vincent Foley was commander of the first column. His loss created a serious hole in the table of organization. "I recommend Lieutenant Dillahunty for field promotion to captain of first column."

"Seconded," Sainz said at once. "Give him two of our best sergeants, and make sure he knows to rely on them as he breaks into the position." He smiled grimly. "Officers lead men forward," he said.

"Sergeants keep men alive," Rebecca Howard completed their two-part motto. "I'll deliver the orders at once, and have the Seventy-first into staggered columns and fully mobile within the half hour."

"Battle alert," Sainz amended. "After a thirty-minute run, I want one column deployed on foot." He stared at her in easy silence, obviously waiting for her to disagree.

Howard obliged. "It will slow us down, Colonel."

"Over distance the Union infantry can outmarch any troops the Neo-Soviets field except for Vanguard. If they want to catch us, they'd have to leave behind the bulk of their forces."

There it was again, the feeling she had missed something Raymond Sainz had noticed at once. Then again, she'd already placed her confidence in him to pull the Seventy-first through in one piece.

"I'll order it so, Colonel. But if you still plan to continue the search for Black Mountain, that means we'll be fighting again. I'd rather give us a bigger head start, and the men more time to rest."

"Time is a luxury we don't have, Rebecca." Raymond

Sainz looked southwest, past the newly risen hill and toward what apparently only he could see. "Colonel Romilsky has proven she can walk the knife edge of honor and duty. Now it's my turn to gamble, but I'm willing to bet she knows how to cut with that edge as well."

13

Fighting constantly to retain the higher ground, Sergeant Tousley led the three men left to his squad in a rearguard action while herding a medic team and a Draco squad ahead. No one moved with much confidence over the great hill that had magically replaced what had been open territory in the shadow of Gory Putorana's steep cliffs before the cataclysm. How could they trust that the Earth wouldn't suddenly give way beneath their feet again? He saw his people glance nervously at the sky, fearfully wondering whether the nightmare heavens might return, and Tousley caught himself doing it, too.

Fortunately, the squad had some idea of its route. Somewhere farther up the hillside Kelly Fitzpatrick reconned their path over cracked and broken ground, past steam vents and the occasional deep fissure. Footing was treacherous enough, thanks to the occasional Thunder artillery round dropped in the area and the resulting sympathetic tremors shaking the hillside, but fortunately there wasn't much loose rock to threaten them with falls or set off an avalanche.

"Travel gets easier another sixty meters up," Fitzpatrick promised over Tousley's private channel. "I marked the best route."

"Great news, Kelly, except it's still the wrong direction. We need to double back to make rendezvous." Each step took them farther away from the main Union force and any hope of succor.

The mission had sounded simple enough. But then they usually did.

"Go in and find the stragglers," Sainz had ordered, outlining the area that surrounded the newly made mountainside. It lay west of the main Union position, on the other side of the ruined battlefield where the sergeant's squad had been posted before the nightmare. Major Howard had gone off to organize another relief force, one that would head into the debris-choked land that separated the two opposing armies, leaving Tousley under Colonel Sainz's control. "You're down another two soldiers, with Carr and Johnson under treatment. Do you need reinforcement?"

Did Sainz think Tousley couldn't accomplish the job on his own? "Throwing new men into my squad would create more problems than it solved at this point. We'll work better alone."

He did request Corporal Fitzpatrick as scout, though, and Sainz had recalled her from a recon of the strange red-rock dunes.

"In and out in ninety minutes," Sainz had ordered brusquely, then walked off, calling to his personal guard.

Ninety minutes. Sure, Tousley thought, if it weren't for

the Neo-Soviet splinter force that crossed their path of retreat. They'd run into a nasty combination of Chem Grunts backed up by Vanguard. If the Draco-equipped team hadn't found them and scattered the Neo-Sovs when they did, Tousley's squad would have gone down for good. Even so, Corporal Richardson was walking wounded and PFC Scott was coughing bloody phlegm, thanks to a dose from a chem-sprayer's toxic wash. Not to mention a nearby Thunder site the Neo-Soviets had contacted.

Only the occasional bullet rang past now, in between infrequent artillery barrages. As far as Tousley could tell, the pursuing force was down to a single Vanguard infantryman. The Chem Grunts, however, were the larger threat. Hunched over, laboring under large tanks strapped across their backs, the Chem Grunts were bandaged all over from the burns and blisters raised by contact with the chemicals they carried and sprayed with seeming impunity. If they gained higher or even equal ground, where gravity worked in their favor, they could shower the hillside with the vile substances stored in their tanks, and it would be all over.

"I'd be the last to complain about your pathfinding abilities," Tousley told Kilpatrick, "but our lines are back to the east."

"Not happening," she promised with false cheer. "And it gets better. We have a decision to make. Should we try for the cliffs, or make for the far side of the hill?"

Strand themselves with backs against a rock wall, or head downhill and leave the Chem Grunts free to pour lethal toxins over their heads? Not the kind of choice Tousley looked for. He stopped and fired downhill, putting a bullet just a handful of centimeters off the head of a Chem Grunt. It ricocheted instead off his tank of breathing air, but didn't penetrate and blow the tank. The Chem Grunt turned his sprayer uphill, washing a stream of greenish fluid in Tousley's direction. The stream fell short but its caustic smell overpowered the metallic scent riding up from nearby steam vents, and Tousley stumbled away, retching.

"You have any good news?" he asked, exasperated, taking cover behind a steam vent and hoping the white curtain would hide his ascent another few meters.

"Sure. A CBR tech with the medics reads high radiation from the steam vents."

Tousley climbed faster. A good thing as a jet of acrid waste washed over his previous hiding place, draining instead into the steam vent.

The ground shook again, violently this time, dropping him to his hands and knees on the rough ground. He heard a cracking noise, the grinding of pulverized rock. He looked back and saw that the steam vent had split wider, now ten meters long and two wide. He awarded the crevice two grenades from his dwindling supply, hoping to collapse the rock face into an avalanche that would take out a few of the Chem Grunts. The grenades detonated with muffled thumps, and the ground heaved and pitched more. For an instant Tousley thought he had outsmarted himself and brought down the entire eastern face with himself on it. Then the shock settled into a series of light tremors. The crevice had widened only marginally.

It did flush two Chem Grunts into the open, though. The heavily burdened soldiers moved as if they had limitless strength, clambering over rough terrain with their packs and chemsprayers. Tousley noticed Private Nicholas rise up from hiding at the same time he did, sighting downhill. The two of them caught the lead Chem Grunt in a cross fire, throwing out several short bursts each.

Red blossoms stitched their way over bandages and

what looked like a tattered and mold-covered uniform. Then one bullet struck a chemical tank, and the Grunt simply ceased to exist as the explosion of a high-pressure tank shredded him and rained foul waste over the lower slopes. The explosion triggered another quake from the unstable hillside. During the tumult PFC Brian Scott broke cover lower down the slope and made a scrabbling dash uphill without calling for cover.

"Dammit, Scott. No!" Tousley shifted his aim to fire a hail of bullets over his man's head, managing a burst of four before the Pitbull clicked empty. Jim Nicholas had missed Scott's break and dropped back down from sight. It took Tousley two seconds to eject his spent clip and snatch a new one from his vest, slap it home, and chamber a round.

One second too long, as it turned out. The final Neo-Soviet Vanguard rose up below, dripping greenish fluid and swaying as he sprayed the hillside on full automatic. One bullet clipped Brian Scott's right hip, throwing him to the ground. Two, then three yellow-green jets of toxic chemicals converged on his location, pinning him beneath a deadly wash.

When they eased off, Scott lay there twitching and vomiting in his death throes. The Grunts' mutagen mixture caused his flesh to erupt in fungus-like growths, rapidly mutating but without any controlled direction at all. The regular toxins blistered the flesh and attacked his internals as well. Tousley devoted one careful shot to end the man's suffering, then dropped back to cover as a violent new quake shook the hillside.

"Damn it all to hell," he swore aloud, then triggered his comm system on a general channel. "We've lost Brian."

Kelly jumped back in quickly, voice concerned. "POW?" she asked.

He knew the rest of his men would be hanging on his answer. Union infantry did not leave their people behind. In the Seventy-first, Raymond Sainz was fanatical about it, a marginally redeeming quality. Not even bodies were abandoned if it could be helped.

"No, not taken, thank God. But there will be no pickup." That was expected when facing Chem Grunts, but no one liked leaving a body behind. "The body's gunked. We have to leave it for the CBR boys."

He patted a number of empty pockets in his tactical load-bearing system. He switched back to a private frequency with Fitzpatrick. "I'm also down to three clips," he told her, warning her that time was short.

"What about your Pug?" The tension in Fitzpatrick's voice was audible even through transmission.

"I left two bullets."

"Save one for me," she said, voice again light and easy. Neither one of them would be taken alive, or wanted to end their final moments as Brian Scott had.

"Kelly, you've got the height up there. Try to tight-beam a message back to Sainz. Ask for instructions."

"Copy that!" Kelly Fitzpatrick said, sounding relieved.

Tousley hated to apply for Sainz's assistance, but after what happened to Brian Scott he had to do something before all his men fell to a similar fate. It bothered him that Fitzpatrick also seemed to think it the best move under the circumstances, making him wonder if he should have done so earlier. He cursed again, privately, then spent a long moment with Private Nicholas, riding the tremors and spraying lead down the hillside.

There was more grinding as rock pulverized under stress, then a huge portion of the eastern facing gave way. But instead of cascading down in an avalanche that might bury the Neo-Soviets, as he'd hoped earlier, it collapsed inward as if caving in over an immense space. Dust billowed up, carrying a heavy, acrid-metallic scent. Tousley clung to a nearby outcropping, several times almost pitching off to tumble down the hill.

The screech that tore through the air as the quake subsided reminded him of rusty hinges crossed with the crackling roar of a forest fire. It grated on his ears, and his survival instinct told him it was the call of something alive. And something dangerous. It sounded again as a new tremor finally shook him off his perch and fetched him right to the brink of the ledge on which he stood. It knocked the breath from his lungs and almost threw him over the edge before subsiding. Tousley held on for a second to catch his breath, hoping the worst was over.

It wasn't.

From the billowing dust, a gray-green tentacle rose and flailed about in the air. Most of it was covered in overlapping chitinous segments, but one side exposed creamy, black-speckled flesh with long, hairlike tendrils that waved and whipped about of their own accord. A dry, rustling-rattle sounded from their rubbing together.

Tousley stared at it dumbly, his head peering over the edge of the rock outcropping. When he shifted his gaze into the sloped tunnel from which the giant tentacle rose, he saw smaller creatures working their way up from dark depths beneath. They dripped a black fluid as some crawled and others leapt forward on slender but impossibly strong legs. One spread out membranes like wings and took to the air, circling around the tentacle like a strange moth fluttering about a moving light. Deep down one sinkhole, directly beneath Tousley's line of sight, something large—some *things* large—moved about in the darkness like the coils of a giant snake sliding around together.

Stark terror claimed him for a moment. This was no hill! There was something under it—within it—being disturbed by the fighting going on above.

He shook off the mind-numbing fright and collected his wits. Someone who had witnessed and survived the previous day's events could not be kept down long. He inched slowly back from his precarious perch, then froze when a half dozen Chem Grunts rose up from concealment below. They cut loose with chemsprayers and toxic grenades against the strange creatures and the violently moving tentacle.

Jets of toxins pinned two creatures against a rock ledge, sending them into convulsions. The grenades fell deeper into the tunnel, detonating and causing another of the hideous screeches. The tentacle smashed downward, crushing one Grunt into a smear of blood and chemicals. When the tanks blew, it shredded the creamy flesh and cracked the chitinous armor. Small, fleshy gobbets spilled out of the wound like some kind of semisolid blood. A cascade of the gobbets poured over one Grunt, which dropped its chemsprayer and began to melt. Clothing and flesh sloughed away, leaving behind metal and heat-blistered bone.

PFC Jim Nicholas had raised up to fire down on the creature, and now stood mesmerized by the horrific scene below. Tousley switched back to an open channel.

"Jim, fall back slowly and stay off the channel," he ordered, then returned to the scene down below. Tousley had known it would take some kind of intervention to make it out alive, but this wasn't exactly what he'd had in mind.

The telltale whistle of falling artillery forced his head down. It exploded downslope, and when he looked he saw the tentacle now mangled in a dozen places by shrapnel and withering like a dying vine. Its hairlike tendrils rustled and found one more Chem Grunt, wrapping about an arm and pulling it down after it as it retreated back into the hillside. A second later there was a new explosion and another of the nightmare screeches.

"Tom, I have Colonel Sainz on the squawk box." Fitzpatrick sounded way too cheerful. Or maybe only compared to the horrific scene below. "The main force is on the move and following along our own trail, moving southwest along the base of the hill. If we can hold, they'll pull us out. I've already warned them about the chemical spills." She paused a second. "I recommend the cliff-face approach. It will let us last longer."

Tousley watched as the last Vanguard infantryman broke cover below and retreated back along his route of ascent while waving the Chem Grunts forward. Sprayers held ready, the Grunts moved in pairs into the large tunnel, jets of chemicals clearing back the smaller creatures and opening up a path for them. Tousley hastily retreated.

"Negative," he ordered. "It's over the top and down the other side fast as we can go. You tell Colonel Sainz that he better button up the infantry and kick the vehicles into overdrive. And skirt this hill by a fair margin."

"Are you joking? What about the Grunts?"

"I've never been more serious, Kelly." A new tremor, and a long drawn-out screech from nightmares. "The Grunts are no longer our problem. There's something . . . *sleeping* under all this rock. And whatever it is, I'm afraid they're waking it up."

Fitzpatrick didn't sound amused. "The colonel will want more than that, Tom."

Catching up with Private Nicholas who was walking

unsteadily, shivering and with eyes wild, Tousley grabbed him beneath one arm and helped him along.

"If I had it, Kelly, I'd tell him," he barked back. "All I can say now is we'd all better pray that we *don't* find out more."

14

Four armies paired off in battle across the Solstice Plains below Luna's Point Gagarin. Neo-Soviet forces spread over two square kilometers, finding cover where able and laying down heavy fire against Union positions. The smaller Union regiment relied on Ares heavy-assault suits and automated defense drones to supplement what few space-specialist Marines they had deployed there. And in the reflective finish of the bizarre landscape, the grayish soil seemingly fused into a flow of perfect silvered glass, mirror images of both armies formed a second battlefield being fought by duplicates of the soldiers above.

Cocooned inside almost two tons of walking armor and weapons, the Ares assault suit made Corporal Phillipe Savoign one of the most powerful warriors ever to set foot upon a field. That only made it harder to admit that the Neo-Soviets were winning both battles.

Owning seventy percent of Luna's surface gave the Union a large area to defend, better than thirty-five million square kilometers. When the fence line had been in place to warn of Neo-Soviet incursions, they'd accomplished that defense via fast response and technological superiority. But what little of the fence line remained after the strange event—what Major Williams called the *Induction*—the Neo-Soviets had smashed and poured through large numbers of troops and equipment.

More troops, in fact, than anyone had thought the empire possessed on Luna. Mostly Vanguard infantry and mutants, they had already captured two atmosphere processors and the base at Montlake Crater. Union intelligence had obviously underestimated the full extent of the Neo-Soviet lunar warrens and the ambition of the empire's local commander. With the Union's first line of defense crippled by the Induction, General Tamas Yorikev had made several vicious and successful stabs into Union territory.

The Neo-Soviets also fielded equipment never before encountered. Battle platforms the size of a small desk were driven around on small treads by a kneeling man. These platforms allowed a single soldier to move missile batteries or heavy machine guns into place in much the same way that the Union relied on ADDs. Though slower than antigrav drones, the platforms allowed the Neo-Sovs to hold a strong rear line while Vanguard and the larger mutants pushed forward.

Still, it shouldn't have been enough. And wouldn't have been, except for the treacherous terrain the Neo-Soviets had discovered and now exploited. Twenty thousand square kilometers, as smooth and shiny as glass. Boulders and the occasional crater still rose up in familiar grayish white, but everywhere else the soil of the Solstice Plains had been replaced by the mirrored terrain. The reflections played all hell with visual-imaging software, forcing the Ares suits and drones to rely on the less accurate thermal imaging.

And that was only one of the problems presented by the alien landscape.

Savoign tried not to think about it, finding it an affront to his sanity. Combat, fortunately, had a way of diverting a person from just about anything else. Now a red bar flashed over a small area of the virtual landscape projected onto Savoign's visored helm. The VR lens clusters mounted outside the Ares' cockpit focused in on the threat and the suit's computers magnified the image to show a new spearhead of Vanguard infantry moving forward under cover of missile fire. Reddish contrails streaked overhead to fall on Savoign's location, one impacting the Ares' upper left leg and blasting away armor but little else.

The large gyrostabilization module bulking out from the assault suit's back kept Savoign on his mechanized feet. His shoulder-mount option held a fifteen-centimeter Harbinger rail gun, but Savoign knew that was not quite the weapon of choice for smashing infantry. He drew a bead on the lead Vanguard elements with targeting software that responded to his eye motions, then raised his right arm, which brought into play the more precise antipersonnel "enforcer" weapon mounted on it. The APE mauled the advancing soldiers. Eleven-millimeter steel-jacketed slugs hammered one man into an unrecognizable mess of ruined flesh and cracked and splintered body armor. The others fell back to the protective wall of a crater.

Savoign had stalled the advance, but the missile site remained a problem. He moved his jaw forward, enabling his transmitting ability. "This is Twelve. I'm angling forward-right for a missile platform."

An answering call came back at once from Lieutenant Chilsun. "Copy, Ares Twelve. Five, forward-left and assist."

Savoign frowned behind his visor, considering the backup unnecessary. One assault suit could handle the job alone. For a few seconds he said nothing, knowing he lacked formal tactical schooling.

Then again, he recalled, so did Chilsun. "Twelve can handle this. No sense putting two suits at risk."

"Thank you for the *advice,* Corporal. But if you get in trouble out there, I want Five ready to cover you." Chilsun sounded more flustered than angry.

Savoign bit back any reply, then risked several dozen powerful strides forward and to his right, wary of the slick surface and the semiliquid pools that had already trapped two Ares and pulled them down beneath the reflective surface. Without any way to spot the quickglass areas before putting weight on them, every step put the man and machine at risk. One of the faster-acting pools had caught Captain de Rico's Hades while trying to set down below the lip of a crater wall, which was why Chilsun was now trying to salvage something out of this fiasco.

The Vanguard infantry that had taken cover not two hundred meters downrange fired away at him with their Kalashnikovs, but the slugs ricocheted harmlessly. The chances of an assault rifle bullet, high-explosive or armor-piercing, damaging an Ares were slim. Even a Rottweiler needed a lucky hit in just the right spot to cause trouble, but to the Ares it would still be only an inconvenience, not a disability.

Of more concern were the Kalashnikovs' grenade launchers. Though the moon's lighter gravity allowed them to fire over these ranges, accuracy was another thing. Savoign's Ares shrugged off one blast that slammed into the shoulder shield plate and another that clipped his left shoulder and destroyed the searchlight not in use anyway. Then Five moved up and behind him, drawing their fire away while Savoign searched out the missile platform.

He flicked his eyes around the four corners of the virtual-reality screen, while the Ares' computer cycled through the various imaging systems. Thermal was less than ideal for range. Upper right, magnetic. Lower right, back to straight visual.

"Magnify, times ten," he ordered, verbally overriding the automatic threat-analysis package built into the left-shoulder pod's extensive electronic gear. The lens clusters refocused, and imaging software firmed up the lines. He found the mobile missile platform crouched between two boulders a half klick away. In Luna's light gravity, an easy shot.

Savoign focused on the upper line of the small crawler, and with the squeeze of one hand sent out an ingot from the shoulder-mounted Harbinger rail gun. The imaging software failed to paint the projectiles onto the VR landscape, but the small platform suddenly burst apart in a fury of shredded metal and sympathetic detonation of the remaining missiles. The boulders channeled much of it upward until they disintegrated under the force of the explosion.

Savoign thrust his jaw forward again to activate the comm. "Scratch one missile site."

His victory was to be short-lived, however. "Magnification off," he ordered, noting that Ares Five held a position just forward and off his left, having swung completely around behind him. A pair of Vanguard had rushed forward from the cover of the crater to work at the Ares with heavy fire, slipping beneath the assault suit's large weapons. Now they retreated before Five could readjust for close-in support. Five took another dozen steps forward, intent on following them back into the crater and clearing it like a nest of vermin.

"Five, no!" Savoign yelled, his own voice deafening in his helmet. Ten meters short of where the Vanguard had begun their retreat, Ares Five took one final step and froze in position. Then he began to sink rapidly.

It was no accident. The Vanguard had snared Ares Five into a quickglass pool. They seemed to know where all the pools were. Savoign had a vision of the Neo-Soviets marching their Rad Troopers over the area, using expendable warriors to map out each pool's location. Likely he wasn't far off the truth.

"Ares Five is trapped and evacuating," the other suit broadcast, sounding angry at himself.

Chilsun was angry, too. Three Ares suits lost and the captain gone, and nothing to show for it but Vanguard and a few missile platforms. "Get out of there, Davies. Twelve, make pickup."

Savoign shook his head. "He's not going to make it," he whispered to himself, not about to transmit and make those the last words Corporal Miles Davies would hear. It was a fact, though. It required ten seconds to extract oneself from the cockpit of an Ares, and that usually with help. Five seconds later, Davies' heavy assault suit was gone, vanished into his reflection without a ripple, just that rapid melt into the alien matter. Savoign shivered, his brain trying to grasp the event and unable to truly accept what his own eyes were relaying to it. At least, with the quickglass making radio contact impossible, they wouldn't have to listen to the screams of a man buried alive.

"Five is gone," he said simply.

"That's it," Chilsun ordered. "Fall back, Twelve. All units retreat. I want every Ares to lay out a smoke screen."

Gritting his teeth at the order, Savoign cycled his control from the Harbinger to the grenade launchers that rose up on either side of the cockpit hatch. His left hand selected four, wide dispersal; he pressed forward with one palm and they spat upward in high but narrow arcs. As he stepped back deeper into the curtain of smoke laid out by the grenades, Savoign wanted to shake his head in disgust.

Pitfalls, he said to himself. They beat multimillion-dollar equipment, and they effectively did it with pitfalls. Just what was going on? When would the strangeness end? Never, his own mind whispered up from the darker recesses. And he doubted this would be the last oddity, or the Union's last defeat.

These were not thoughts that sat well with the weapons specialist, and ones he knew would continue to plague him. It was a long walk back to Tycho Crater.

The room was only big enough to hold a long table with three chairs to a side. It had been painted an antiseptic white to increase the edginess of subjects brought there. A large mirror was set into one wall, no doubt one-way glass with a video camera and who knew how many people on the other side.

Brygan Vassilyevich Nystolov relaxed back into the uncomfortable molded-plastic chair. He knew that most other Neo-Soviet military personnel in his position, being held by the enemy, would be sitting ramrod straight and answering any question with stony silence. Acting the part of regular military would be a fast way to the detention cells, at best, a firing squad, at worst. So he leaned back and scratched idly at his unkempt beard, grown long during his week in space, or ran blunt fingers back through his shock of thick black hair. He slurped at the American coffee provided for him, finding it weak and bitter, and smiled gregariously at the two men facing him in this game.

Move and countermove, as each side worked its own strategies. His captors trying to ferret out the truth and he working desperately to hand them a carefully crafted story. Not a lie. Lies were too easy to break through. No, it was a variation so close to the truth as to be indiscernible. Brygan Nystolov, not represented as a military auxiliary but simply an exploration specialist. His background of exploring Mars would help him pass himself off as a minor scientist. He knew enough of the basics—no matter that the empire would never have trusted him with truly critical data.

Already Brygan had identified the dangerous one of the pair, a thickly muscled man with black skin and an air of competence. The space-specialist rating on his Marine uniform gave his rate away and warned Brygan to be all the more cautious.

The other one had so far demonstrated a tolerance not consistent with military bearing. Of medium height and build with dark sideburns that grew to sharp points, the Union major tended to be magnanimous, especially in front of the captain. At first Brygan had thought the affected behaviors a variation on the classic good-politburo, bad-politburo interrogation. Now, he wasn't so sure. If these men were acting, they were very good.

Better than he was, in fact.

Captain Drake, the dangerous one, consulted a small electronic notepad. "Review of your ship's intact logs bears out at least part of your story. That you left Mars over six days ago, according to *the ship's* clock. A clock that is five days out of sequence with the correct time as we measured it here." A disconcerting pause. "We found no evidence that you reset the internal clock, and Major Williams has pressed for acceptance of the fact that following Earth through the *event* cost you five days outside of"—pause again—"reality." His tone suggested his own belief in that idea. "Where I have trouble accepting this is that the *Kolyma* does not have life-support capability for that long a span."

"You made some modifications to life support," Major Williams said, his tone softer but dark eyes no less sharp. "With the extra scrubber you created, you might have extended it a few extra days, but five?"

Brygan sighed heavily, because it would be expected of him. He had expected to give up this personal information, but there was no sense in seeming eager to do so.

"Mistakes the empire has made," he said carefully, as if worried his words might reach back to Moskva, "leave me with ability to breathe thinner air than most." He spoke English, in deference to his captors, knowing that it wouldn't be held against him. He knew that most Union personnel in space, military or civilian, also learned basic Russian. He preferred to believe his accent was not nearly so atrocious as theirs were likely to be. Besides, it would help him appear less the foreigner. Less the enemy.

"This is why I choose space exploration for my specialty," he added. The pair looked at each other. Neither one of them had completely bought his story—not yet—though the major seemed on the verge of doing so. Drake would be a harder sell.

It was Williams's turn to open a new gambit. "I've cleared you of most of the charges against you, including sabotage of a sensitive Union project under investigation. The pulses emitted from the crystalline formation interfered with the *Kolyma*'s improperly shielded electronics. It drew you in like a landing beacon and brought you down right on top of it. A regrettable loss, but if it hadn't you might have flown off into the Maelstrom with no hope of recovery."

The Maelstrom, Williams called it, referring to the vast debris-choked system in which Terra was now one of many planets. Half a hundred detected so far, Williams had said, as well as a few very tiny suns, small but thick nebulae, and that strange sunlike body wounding the sky. An incredible count of asteroids and planetoid-size fragments told of worlds already lost through violent cataclysm. They had allowed Brygan to study the sky. It was dark and forbidding, a frightening and curious place. He hadn't needed to feign a scientist's interest.

"Thank you for your assistance," he said politely, nodding to Williams. "I would never wreck such a site as you describe."

The major deferred to his companion with a glance. "Actually, that was another of Captain Drake's investigations."

The dark-skinned man smiled sarcastically. "I don't believe in charging a man for crimes he did not commit."

Implying that the empire certainly would. Well, there Brygan could not disagree, especially after experiencing General Leonov's iron rule over Red Mars. He remembered the general's treatment of the Mental, the reason he'd been out in space to begin with, and winced at the memory. Had the Mental made it to Earth? Brygan suddenly found himself hoping so, though neither of his interrogators mentioned the *Leonid Sergetov*. Perhaps they were testing him. If so, it was a gambit he could turn to his advantage.

"There was another vessel," he said slowly, noticing the reactions of both Drake and Williams. They knew nothing about it. The bulk of his mission files were still safe on the *Kolyma*, then. It was time to play out toward his endgame. "An infantry vessel carrying men back to Terra. I was chasing it down when . . ." He paused, frowned as he hoped a true scientist would at being unable to put the proper name to any event or phenomenon, ". . . when storm struck."

Major Williams leaned forward with sudden interest. "I would be interested in knowing more about this storm you witnessed building around Earth."

"I would be interested in knowing more about this military transport," Drake interrupted. "You said in your statement that you were sent to reestablish contact with Earth."

"We lose complete contact with Terra shortly around time the *Leonid Sergetov* left Mars. I was dispatched by General Leonov to carry several messages back to Terra, including news of your recent landing on Mars."

Neither Union man could hold back a satisfied grin. The intelligence Brygan had just handed them might once have been considered priceless, the news that Union forces were finally in the position to bid for a strong foothold on Mars. Brygan considered it inconsequential now, unless Terra could escape whatever held it. "I had hoped to meet with the larger vessel—safer for all concerned. Especially when storm struck." He looked to Drake, the military man. "Did the *Leonid* make it through?"

Drake held back a moment, then shook his head. "Not that we know of, though if you spent five unaccounted-for days coming through this Veil the major talks about, no telling where your other vessel ended up. And we experienced some gaps in our surveillance net when your empire launched missiles." He features clouded, his dark eyes narrowing slightly in accusation. Not at Brygan specifically, but for his allegiance.

The scout bowed his head in what he hoped was a manner properly subdued. "The empire makes mistakes," he said again, softly. He looked back up at his interrogators. "Is the Union perfect?"

Williams shook his head ruefully. "Not all the time. In fact, rarely. But we continue to try. Though certainly our advances in technology and *space exploration* prove that the sciences prosper."

There it was, the typical Union effort to encourage defection. Brygan thought it might have come off better if Captain Drake had handled the vague hint, but a tightening about the eyes argued for Drake's distaste for encouraging defection.

"I have duties . . ." Brygan said, hesitant to go too far along that road and playing to Drake.

The Union captain read into the hesitation. "Understandable. Still, all diplomatic channels are closed right now." A way of saying that the fighting continued. "You will continue to be . . . a *guest* here. Perhaps you would consent to opening your computer files to Major Williams and me, since you would be carrying no military secrets? Call it a gesture of goodwill."

And if Brygan had done a good job of doctoring the

files, they would back up his story and exonerate him. He nodded slowly. "The encryption key is the date of Yuri Gagarin's first flight into space—military time, day, month, and year." There, they had their prize. Or so they thought. Drake and Williams looked surprised that he had caved in so easily on that point. "But I would make a request."

Williams nodded. "Yes?"

Brygan stared hard at Williams, ready to test the scientist's good word and seeming to dismiss Drake. "Any work my observations figure into, any conclusions they help you draw, they are to be shared with me for delivery to the Neo-Soviet empire."

They had the key. Here was where he moved his final piece into place, playing his role to the limit, and tested how well they bought in to his story.

Drake started at first, obviously about to refuse on general principles, then seemed to think the better of it, as though he would bow to Williams's judgment. A good sign, though Brygan thought it might have more to do with Drake's proving a point to Williams than his actual leanings.

Williams hesitated, his own ethics called into question on the idea, then nodded. "Very well, Brygan Nystolov. You have my word on that."

The familiar use of the scout's name twinged deep inside Brygan, though he quickly wrote it off as Williams's knowing no better. He leaned forward and offered his hand to the major and then to Captain Drake. Both accepted the handshake.

"That is good," he exclaimed, again the gregarious Neo-Soviet. "Then you had better reverse the reading of date I gave you. Enter it backward, or you will wipe the computer memory clean."

Williams started, shocked for the moment that Brygan would have risked the loss of data. Drake nodded once, a grudging respect. Not between equals, though, one military man to another. It was a military mind acknowledging a game well played by an inferior. By a scientist.

Check and mate.

15

Katya Romilsky had fumbled her field glasses when the creature's monstrous head first reared up from the dark hollow of the hill. Seventeen years of service had dulled her unease when dealing with mutants or those disfigured through the more mundane violence of warfare. Her older brother had succumbed to a ruined genetic heritage, and she still remembered the forced pride in her parents' voices when they told her of the honor he had reclaimed fighting and dying in a Neo-Soviet Rad Troop. Katya's own touch of *goryachee* had manifested in more useful forms, though a physical reminder stared back from any reflective surface as the silverish stripe that marred her auburn hair. But this creature, this *alien* thing her Chem Grunts had awakened, it assaulted her sensibilities.

It frightened her.

Black chitin, ridged from the endoskeleton poking through from beneath, flared out at both sides. It lent the creature's shovel-shaped head the hooded appearance of a cobra, though there any major resemblance to a Terran creature ended. Gray-green fluid runneled down from its head and neck, washing free of long stripes of fleshy, yellow muscle that ran along the outside of the chitinous protection and added to its more horrible aspects. A vertically slit mouth began under the hood and trailed down the neck, creating a fanged maw that looked capable of swallowing an Avalanche crawler whole. Several black tentacles reached out of the mouth, thrashing in the air as if looking for prey on which to lay hold. A tangle of bloated pustules and fat tentacles crowned its head. It rose up toward the sky, as if straining to reach that uneasy excuse for a new sun, and with its neck fully extended it released a shriek that set every soldier clapping hands to ears to shut it out. A broken scream of sharp nails scraping across slate, supported by a hideous crackling that reminded the colonel of dry, breaking bones.

Scores—hundreds—of smaller creatures also poured forth, dripping the grayish green fluid as they jumped, crawled, flew, and even floated. Most of the winged creatures took to the air at once and raced away along eight cardinal points, perfectly coordinated. Katya watched a dozen wasp-shaped bodies on impossibly strong legs jump up toward the monster's long neck, fastening into the ridges there and apparently feeding off one of the fleshy, ropelike muscles. Their translucent white bodies flushed a deep ocher. Others fluttered on diaphanous wings around its head like moths to a flame. Bloated creatures looking like nothing better than large balls of gas-filled intestine drifted out to ring the alien—the *Sleeper,* as Gregor called it.

"Magnificent," Gregor Detchelov said, moving up beside her.

The two surveyed the Sleeper and the Union forces from a sharp ridge to the southwest, where the colonel had ordered the bulk of the army moved even before she'd gone to meet Sainz. It had taken the creature an hour to completely free itself of the confining shell. Clusters of chitin-covered legs sprouted out from beneath an armored carapace that protected its large body. The spiked limbs dug at rock and earth, pushing it forward. The long neck would reach out and settle its base onto the ground, dragging a great deal of weight forward in the manner of a serpent. Thick ridges occasionally tore themselves away from the back, exposing themselves as armored tentacles with a corpseflesh underside. They flailed the air a moment, then resettled over the back and resealed themselves into hardened armor.

"Magnificent," Romilsky repeated, her voice lacking his enthusiasm. "What do you see that is admirable in this thing?"

"What is not to admire, Comrade Colonel?" Detchelov gestured toward the beast as it towered over the Union forces retreating before it. Heading westward, right past their vantage point. "Its sheer size. Its defenses. The way it works in concert with the smaller creatures for its own good." He shook his head. "We have yet to perfect a symbiot program."

Romilsky had not even been aware that was a field the empire pursued, though it did not surprise her now. She compared Gregor's current enthrallment to the man who had gone pale back in Noril'sk when she commanded him to accompany her on the front lines. But then Gregor Antoly Detchelov had come up through the ranks as a mutant trainer and later, with his commission, as a program evaluator. She had taken Gregor as her aide for his uncanny ability with mutants and Rad Troopers, and for his utter lack of ability to command disparate units. He was an asset in deploying the more exotic troops but would never be a threat to her command of the Fifty-sixth Striker. Naturally, he saw more to this Sleeper alien than she did. She wondered, however, if he was looking with open eyes.

"Do you find it magnificent in the way it destroyed our auxiliary force?" she asked him, a touch of steel to her voice.

The feint she had set on the Union's eastern flank had tracked them right into the creature's shadow. The on-site officer had ordered an attack without orders. Through field glasses they had both watched the monstrous alien shred several packs of Rad Troopers. A brave squad of Vanguard had scaled the Sleeper's back while it fed on the Troopers and mutants, only to be struck down by electrical discharges that leapt from the back of the Sleeper's head and danced over its armored carapace. Smaller drones had swept in, then, finishing off the balance of the force.

Gregor had the good grace to wince at the bite of her words. Still, he quickly spun the unfortunate defeat into a positive light, in good Neo-Soviet form. "The Vanguard were an unfortunate loss. Rad Troopers and Cyclops we can easily request replacements for. And they taught us more of the Sleeper's strengths. The creature is effective in smashing numbers, but not so well equipped to defend itself against individuals. For that it must rely on its symbiotic partners. And it has the electrical defense for those who work in too close, a mistake we will not repeat. And once we gain control of the Sleeper, learn its secrets, the empire will be stronger."

A goal she applauded. Except, "One thing, Gregor Antoly. You laud the Sleeper's strong defenses and alien nature. How do you intend to control such a thing?"

That visibly bothered the junior officer. He made several attempts to speak, then broke off each time. Finally, flustered, he said, "To control a thing, you must discover and control its needs."

A sound theory, when dealing with the mutants created by the Neo-Soviet empire. "And those needs are?"

His shoulders slumped in defeat. "I do not know." But to end on a strong note, he hitched up his chin, and said, "Yet. Perhaps that Mental can assist."

"Hmm." Katya Romilsky nodded curtly and returned her attention to the view through her field glasses. The silence stretched out uncomfortably, until Gregor apparently could not bear it.

"May I ask what it is that you see, then, Colonel Romilsky?"

In the creature's path, a rear guard of the Seventy-first Assault Group continued to fire at it but with little effect. It stretched its long neck out again, shrieking its soul-grating scream. If the Seventy-first were to turn its entire firepower against it, then perhaps they could injure the great monster. A few men buying time for the main force would do little but annoy such an alien.

She swept her view forward to where the Union force loaded up their Hydra ag transports, pulling in all but the rear guard as they prepared for a fast run out from under the Sleeper's immediate path. Where her auxiliary force had been intended to drive the Union forces into her ambush, now the alien monster did the same.

"I see an opportunity," she finally answered.

* * *

When Captain Drake escorted Brygan into Tycho's Control and Direction area rather than back to the interrogation room, Brygan accepted it as a positive sign. Not that he had any doubt about his remaining under tight surveillance. Or that most classified material would be blanked from the console screens or, better yet, altered to provide false information. So he studiously ignored a tactical station and another running comms, and instead swung away to study a screen that ran a simulation. Near as he could tell, the simulation showed what it had looked like when the strange storm cleared away, leaving Luna staring up into a hostile sky. Terra remained lost behind the gray-glowing fog, and from around one edge of the glimmering shield that white-fury eye cast a hostile glare at the moon.

No one interrupted him. Brygan watched the simulation start over and run again, only part of him ready to continue on while the rest hung mesmerized by the unveiling of that alien sky. This time he caught something new.

"There," he said, stabbing a thick finger at the console screen. He glanced over at Major Williams, who stood next to a man of higher rank and more decorations on his pristine uniform. Brygan glanced back to the console, preferring to avoid the colonel's scrutiny. "I caught a halo of cold blue along rim of the eastern hemisphere. What was that?"

"Nebula," Randall Williams said.

The scout traced the ridge where the dark blue had shown before vanquished by Luna's lightening atmosphere. "Nebula?" Nebulae were immense areas of glowing gas, any one larger than a regular solar system. Stars were born in a nebula. "How close?" he asked.

"Three hundred million kilometers," Williams answered. "About the greatest distance possible between Earth and Mars."

"Not anymore," Brygan said quietly, for the first time feeling a sharp stab at the loss of Mars and his relationship with the red planet.

Williams covered the awkward silence with a cough, then quickly brought the conversation back on track. "We've dubbed it the Styx Nebula, and it is apparently a lot smaller and more condensed than any known nebula. You can pick it out on our horizon, but it won't be adequately visible to Tycho until we swing around the Earth and find it in the night sky. Stations Freedom and Independence have made extensive observations of it already."

"Not Liberty?" Brygan asked, with a frown, uncertain whether he had been meant to catch the omission.

"Station Liberty did not survive the Induction." A new voice, rather high-pitched. The colonel's. "The disruption knocked it into a rapidly decaying orbit, much like Sputnik-23."

"Twenty-three is gone? *Proklenath,*" Brygan swore. He turned, reacted to the colonel's presence for the first time. "Apologies, Colonel . . . ?"

From over Brygan's shoulder, Captain Drake made the introduction. "Brygan Nystolov, this is Colonel Travis Allister of Tycho Base and currently second-in-command of Luna."

Brygan ignored the full import of the man who stood in front of him. "Apologies, Colonel Allister. Sputnik-23 was one of our best achievements in space observation."

The colonel smiled thinly. A big man, larger than Drake and Brygan both, the tenor of his voice seemed at odds with his bulk. "Not a total loss. We recovered its logs."

Military man or Neo-Soviet scientist or scout, Brygan

Nystolov reacted as any citizen of the empire would, with thinly veiled anger. "I suppose it would be too much to ask for their return?"

Allister smiled, obviously enjoying his control over the Neo-Soviet. "Well, that depends. Major Williams here has filled me in on your agreement to share information that results from the *Kolyma*'s data. If you were to help us explore some leads developed from Sputnik's log recorders, I could see allowing a similar agreement. You would be free to deliver this information back to the empire, as soon as hostilities cease."

Warning bells rang in Brygan's mind. The colonel was a bit too free with such intelligence, though by right it did belong to the Neo-Soviet empire. There was more being proposed here than a simple sharing of information. "What is it you mean, to explore leads?"

Colonel Allister turned more officious. "By order of General Hayes, we are going to try and search out a way back to our own universe. We need to send out exploration teams to detect any final traces of the event that brought us here, and a path by which to return. Your late arrival in the *Kolyma* lends hope to the idea that such a path exists. The missions will also be responsible for exploring any nearby phenomena, to ascertain their threat or benefits." He nodded toward Williams. "Major Williams will head the science team aboard the *Icarus*."

"And I would be allowed to accompany? To observe?"

"To work," the colonel said. "The major has asked for your participation, and has suitably impressed on me the need to be a bit more open-minded considering our mutual . . . position."

Brygan faced Randall Williams, amazed. "You would trust me as crew?"

"No," Williams said evenly. "As staff. Captain Drake will actually command the vessel, for that you would have to deal with him. But it's only fair to warn you that he was against your inclusion on this mission. At any time he or I can put an end to your involvement, though that runs both ways. You may simply confine yourself to your quarters at any time and end your participation."

Bluntly spoken. Still, Brygan warmed over the offer—that implied trust given to him by Williams. And it was the kind of challenge that had endeared the *Bear* to Mars. Holding up under Drake's suspicions could hardly be worse than the oppressive presence of men like Vladimir Leonov. He looked forward to the exploration with more enthusiasm than he would have thought.

"When do we depart?" he asked simply.

That seemed to settle matters for the three officers. For Brygan, it was merely the beginning. He would have to be careful to maintain his credibility, always on guard against a slip. But the opportunity, both for the empire and himself! The slightest twinge deep down worried him that it had all been too easy. Too perfect. But then it was known that the Union could be overly trusting when it came to the single individual.

Brygan could even cite a few cases from history where similar deals had been struck. The scout smiled. It felt good to know that he was valued, even if under *slightly* false pretenses. That he could be valued for himself and his own contribution, not looked down upon for an inability to conform. Something he had never realized could be so important. And more than any note in a history book, this was the ultimate answer behind his enthusiasm.

He wanted to believe.

16

Colonel Raymond Sainz had ordered the rear guard loaded into the last Hydra antigrav transport, and then the Seventy-first Assault Group was fully mobilized and with a half hour's lead against the alien creature. Lieutenant Landvoy's Aztecs served as flanking guard as the Seventy-first worked its way out of the deeper folds of Gory Putorana, the cycles' generators whining a protest as they raced over hills and swept around steep cliff faces. Always angling southwest. Twice, the columns were forced to double back when canyon walls ran too steep for antigravity drives.

Then the assault group hit the Kotuy River, and by following it upstream managed to avoid such blind turns. Where the Kotuy swung northwest the Seventy-first quit its banks. Raymond Sainz hated abandoning the guiding waters, but by maps he knew that to follow it any farther would mean climbing up toward the remote Irynutsk Nuclear Power Facility and then on to the river's headwaters. Also more of the creature's symbiots flew overhead to the north, their dark bodies easily spotted against a cloudless pale blue sky, as if reconnoitering the landscape for the monster.

No other word for it, either, that thing that had clawed its way out from a den in the earth. A monster. At first Sainz had considered the idea that it was some new creation of the Neo-Soviet empire. A colossus mutant—could that be the Chernaya Gora aim? Then he recalled how the hill had materialized after the sky changed. This abomination was no Neo-Soviet creation. It was a new scourge, alien, released in the Russian heartland and welcome to it. The colonel's responsibility now was to his command, keeping them alive. Chernaya Gora, if it existed at all, would have to wait until the Seventy-first could rest and regain the initiative. And if he had to ride an ADD straight down that creature's throat, Sainz vowed to buy them that time.

So instead of turning with the river, the assault group cut across country straight west. It ran them toward easier terrain, where the antigravity vehicles would be able to easily outdistance the monstrous creature or any Neo-Soviet patrol that happened to run a crawler across their path. Buttoned up in the Hades command transport, along with Major Howard and their immediate aides, Colonel Sainz followed the course plot being figured by a transportation specialist corporal. By his calculations, the Fifty-sixth Striker had to be several kilometers to their rear. Now they had only to clear the broken-ridge territory of the southeast Gory Putorana. Fifteen minutes to clear into open terrain and then a few hours until nightfall cloaked them. That was all Sainz asked for.

Then the Neo-Soviet Fifty-sixth Striker attacked.

Little warning preceded the assault. There was no hearing the whistling descent of Thunders through the Hades' armor or over the stressed field generators of two nearby Wendigo tanks. The driver up front yelled a quick, "Incoming!" and then the Hades rocked over as if shoved rudely from the left. In the back, the colonel managed to get a death grip on his command chair. Rebecca Howard was thrown against the opposite wall and then fell to the floor.

"You called it," she said weakly, trying to rise even while the driver threw the command vehicle into a series of tight turns.

Sainz shook his head. "Can't be. Crawlers can't move this fast."

When Sergeant Tyree had reported a large force of Rad Troopers and Chem Grunts moving against them, but few Vanguard, the colonel had guessed it a feint to drive them west and that his Neo-Soviet counterpart had moved the bulk of her force into position for an ambush. Against Rad Troops alone he might have turned and smashed them first, foiling the trap, but Chem Grunts brought with them a horrible death, and Sainz had not wanted to see any of his people ending that way. He had backed Major Howard's order for a forced movement west, but with half the assault group deployed and ready to meet the ambush.

Only it hadn't come, and instead the Seventy-first passed right under the shadow of the monstrous creature Sergeant Tousley had discovered. Rearguard casualties had run high. It cost two squads just to rescue the two and a half Tousley brought in with him—three bodies irrecoverable when the creature lunged forward to bury the fallen beneath its massive bulk. A pair of Wendigo heavy armor completely shorted out when they slipped in too close to the creature, some kind of electromagnetic field, and then were picked up by the strange tentacles that separated from the monster's back, crushed, and tossed aside. Several of the symbiotic creatures had fallen on the ruined vehicles, driven back by the infantry just long enough to recover bodies. Sainz had been about to commit power armor and a squad of Ares heavy-assault suits when Neo-Soviet forces had hit the alien creature from behind and diverted its attention long enough to escape.

This wasn't Union soil, and the colonel had seen no reason his men should die for it.

"Message coming in from the Aztecs," a private on the communications board called out. "Lieutenant Landvoy reports under attack by Vanguard. Two Crawlers." She paused, listening intensely. "Elements of the Fifty-sixth Striker, confirmed." Then she tore away the headset, a look of pain flashing across her face. She stabbed several switches on the board, then tried the headphones again. "Jammed. I'll try to cut through."

Gunnery Sergeant Daily monitored a different channel. "Everyone is running sawtooth patterns, but we need to commit to a direction fast."

Sainz slammed an open palm down against his armrest. "She can't be here," he said hotly, rising from his chair and locking his large hands around the overhead runners. The Hades swerved hard right, its antigravity generators shrieking protest as the colonel's arm muscles strained against the effort of hanging on. He studied the numerous monitors, which offered real-time video in eight different directions.

The major clawed her way back into a chair, began typing rapid input onto a touch-sensitive tabletop screen. A topographical map flashed over the horizontal monitor. She placed Vanguard on their far southern flank. The two-dimensional screen was no substitute for being outside, able to observe and better read the lay of the terrain, but it was better than commanding blind. She traced a quick line from their previous battlefield to this one, seeing Sainz's point. "At their best speed, Crawlers should've fallen into our rear quarter five klicks back." She looked to Sainz. "Transports?"

"Neo-Soviet command is not in the habit of giving their field officers long-term control over a transport. They prefer that their senior officers be reliant on the upper echelon for retrieval." Sainz worked his way forward toward the Hades' cockpit. "We can't extend radio comms better than ten kilometers. I refuse to believe they've contacted Noril'sk."

At the door that separated the command functions of the Hades from the small two-man cockpit up front, Sainz leaned through to study the terrain with a critical eye. On one of the dashboard monitors, the view aft, he saw the ruined and smoking remains of a Hydra and two Trojans. Even as he guessed their positions, the tech riding shotgun confirmed, "We lost Hotel Seven and Tangos Four and Nine."

Sainz gritted his teeth. Tango-Trojan-Nine was powered armor support. "Major, circle two Trojans back to make pickup on any survivors," he yelled into the back. "Detail a Wendigo for protection. Any idea where those Thunders fell from?"

"Dead ahead," Gunnery Sergeant Daily answered from his weapons station.

Sainz assumed the man meant dead ahead on their original track. That placed them beyond a small rise that could be hiding anything. One they were fast approaching. "So close," he whispered. The Seventy-first had been within minutes of their goal.

"Hard targets," Daily yelled, and Sainz ducked back

into the Hades. The sergeant manned the targeting system for the command transport's light rail cannon. "Typhoon missile crawlers, backed by Vanguard and Grunts, all across our left flank."

Sitting in between the Aztec patrol and the relative safety of the Union assault group, Sainz noted. And no way of warning Lieutenant Landvoy.

The sergeant squeezed off a shot, then shook his head when another hard turn fouled his aim. The explosive ingot passed its target wide, raising a cloud of fire and smoke against an impotent knoll. Daily cursed in time with the muted thunderclap of the explosion. "Give me a steady run, damn you!" On the screen a cloud of smoke rose over the four missile crawlers as they launched a coordinated barrage.

"Hard left," Sainz ordered. "Howard, turn the columns into that barrage."

This was not the kind of fight any commander wanted to be forced into. A battlefield not of your choosing, where the enemy revealed itself only when convenient and usually to devastating effect. If the Union relied on wheeled or tracked vehicles as the empire did, the battle would be all over. Fortunately the ag transports and armor could skip over the terrain's rough spots without severe trouble.

Sainz's mouth ran to a metallic dryness as he watched the monitors to see the first missiles begin falling around the forward edge of the Seventy-first. Two clipped another Trojan, this one carrying the Ares assault suits, but did little more than shred some armor off the back and side. The main barrage passed overhead, unable to compensate their arc for the Union's maneuver. However, it also left the Seventy-first charging the enemy line, and who knew how many reinforcements.

"Reverse the second column. Tell Dillahunty to run sawtooth patterns north." Raymond Sainz gripped Sergeant Daily's shoulder. "Get me one of those Typhoons," he ordered.

The second barrage was late in coming. As the Union line split, half the vehicles reversing course and zigzagging away from the Neo-Soviet position and the other half barreling down, someone took a few seconds too long to choose targets. The over-canopy missile launcher on the third Typhoon from the left suddenly erupted in an incredible blossom of fire and thunder as Daily put an explosive rail round right into the full launch tubes. The force picked up the Neo-Soviet Typhoon and sent it spinning into the air to the right, slamming into a second Typhoon and caving in its side. The surviving Union Wendigos slammed several more shots into the immediate area, but none with Daily's accuracy or success.

Colonel Sainz gauged the remaining distance by eye, then backed up his estimate with a quick glance to the computerized range finder. "Split off first column's Hydras and Trojans, Major. Same orders as Dillahunty." That would leave only combat vehicles sweeping forward. And the Hades, of course. "Corporal, get through to Landvoy and let him know he's riding into hell out there. Gunny, you get one more shot. Make it count."

Daily selected a Shredder shrapnel round, one of the rail-gun ingots that would detonate in a storm of tiny drill bits spinning outward so fast that no body armor could hope to deflect them. He centered crosshairs on a group of Chem Grunts. "Give me three seconds on a steady line," he called out to the driver, "now!"

The turreted rail gun up top spat its load dead on into the Grunt formation. Daily had chosen his target with the eye of a man who understood ground forces. As the Grunts' chemsprayer tanks exploded, pierced by the flying metal screws, the harsh chemicals sprayed out over other Grunts and even washed over a squad of the Vanguard. A few infantrymen dropped at once, while others stumbled a few meters before succumbing. Three other squads broke formation and scattered rather than face their own chemical weapons. Enough to throw the southern line into a few seconds of confusion. Sainz reached over to slap Daily on the back for a job well-done.

Then Landvoy led his remaining Aztecs right into the budding disaster.

Down another antigrav cycle to a total of five, the Aztecs tried to shoot the gap opened in the Neo-Soviet line without realizing what had caused the disruption. Jets of dark green and others of brackish yellow still washed over the area from the Chem Grunts' ruptured tanks and hoses. The Aztecs wove through the nightmare, and almost made it until one final tank blew outward and enveloped two of the rare machines in a greenish cloud. They flew through and on, even as Sainz gave the order to reverse all of first column and get them the hell out of there.

"Landvoy back on line," the comms corporal yelled out, unaware of the Aztecs' return to the field.

Sainz gaze never wavered from the monitors, following the Aztecs from one screen to the next as the Hades swung about hard and began running sawtooth evasion patterns to the north. One of the contaminated cycles wavered from their runs for a few seconds, then straightened out and continued to close with the retreating Union command. The third wove about more erratically, getting worse every second. The high-speed antigrav cycles caught up and fell into a formation with the Hades, except for their stricken companion, who rocketed past and slammed into a rock outcropping. The corrupted body flew on another thirty meters before tumbling to a final rest. The Aztecs and Hades passed within ten meters, but none slowed. It would take a CBR team to recover that body, and there was no time. A new wave of Thunders fell into the area. Though off by a wide margin from any Union vehicle, they argued against any further attempts to delay.

Daily slammed his fist into his outside thigh repeatedly, not trusting himself to vent fury against the delicate electronics in the Hades. Sainz grabbed the sergeant's wrist, held it tight. "Not your fault, Sergeant. Bad fortune."

Daily tensed against his colonel's grip for a moment, then eased off. "Yes sir."

"I've got an arroyo marked out half a kilometer north that can head us back on a westward track," Major Howard called out from her station, focusing on the Union retreat. "Dillahunty would need to make his move now."

The colonel shook his head, stepped to Rebecca Howard's side, and braced himself over the horizontal monitor. "Romilsky is to the west, damn her. I don't know how she managed it, but she's there." He dropped the volume of his voice. "I knew she was setting up an ambush, but I didn't give her enough credit."

Howard covered one of Sainz's hands with one of hers. It looked frail and delicate alongside his, though that was more a function of size than any real measure of strength. "Bad fortune," she said, using the same consolation the colonel had offered Daily. "Sure you don't want to take a stab in her direction?"

"One of the first rules of engagement—never let the enemy choose the battlefield." Sainz shook his head again.

"She knows what she's doing. I won't underestimate her like this again."

Howard gave his hand a light squeeze and returned to the screen. She moved the topographical data to show their path heading north, and Sainz studied the terrain with as much interest and concern as she. They would hit the Kotuy River again when the rise of Tommat Plateau forced them on a sharp jog back to the east. The Tommat was a small break away from the main range of Gory Putorana, and the hard country the two steep rises framed would slow the Union force down considerably.

"What makes you think it's clear?" she asked.

"Major?"

"The northern route. Romilsky might have us boxed on three sides."

Sainz nodded, not in affirmation but acknowledgment of her concerns. "There was a reason she hit us where she did," he admitted, "giving us an area large enough to maneuver. To think, and decide we didn't want to butt heads. We know south and west are covered. East means backtracking. She's herding us north, because that's the one direction she does not have to guard." He reached above to one of the vertical monitor screens, tapping the skyline where several of the symbiots flew their missions back and forth into Gory Putorana. "She's turning us right into that thing's path."

Rebecca Howard paled visibly at running up against the alien creature again. "If that's what she wants us to do, then why oblige?"

"Because it's the one direction where there is a certain amount of uncertainty. We'll have to drop a rear guard back to monitor the creature and slow it down as necessary, but we *might* slip free around the upper side of Tommat and make the Oritskanly Tunguska, the Upper Tunguska River." His voice grabbed a hard edge. "If we move west, we *will* lose people. The Seventy-first has donated enough lives for today."

"That's bad territory," she said, tapping a finger over the terrain west of the Irynutsk Nuclear Facility. "More suited for crawlers. And it's nearly night. We get stuck in there, we'll be walking home."

They get stuck in there, the Seventy-first would never make it out. "It's our best chance. With any luck we can follow the Oritskanly Tunguska out on its westward run."

"And without luck?"

As always, the Seventy-first's two senior officers could level with each other. No punches pulled. Sainz spitted her with an even stare, matching her hard expression.

"Without luck," he said, "we're dead."

17

The gray armored skin of the *Icarus* almost blended with Luna's natural soil. The large vessel rose from the moon's surface by dint of raw power, its twin fusion drives blasting back at the barren slopes of Mount Symphonia. Though a delta-wing design built with an eye toward aeronautical lines, the *Icarus* was not truly intended to fly in atmosphere. The moon made for a good base only because of its light gravity and large areas of barren land where the spacecraft could be landed and properly guarded. It represented a significant investment by the Union—only Tranquillity's *Argus* and the *Prometheus* docked at Station Independence were larger, more advanced vessels.

Independent vectoring ports beneath the ship helped it achieve lift, and could even manage completely vertical takeoffs and landings though VTOL ops were hard on the vessel. When it cleared the moon's low atmospheric roof, those ports were closed off in favor of standard attitude thrusters. The *Icarus* was free in space, swinging wide around the Earth to begin one of many data collection runs.

Standing at a plex portal, watching the sky bleed away its pale color and then fade to a pitch-black studded with the few colored lights of planets and fewer stars, Major Williams still felt as if he was returning home. It had been a long time since he'd been in real space. Even if Paul Drake technically commanded the vessel now, the captain was still subject to Williams's orders with regard to mission parameters. And of course, the scientific labs and various stations in the *Icarus* were totally within the major's domain. Twelve people at this station alone, all keying off his direction. All twelve, but one.

"How long we orbit Terra?" Brygan Nystolov asked from a nearby image-rendering table. He studied and contrasted shots of the Styx Nebula taken from both Sputnik-23 and Station Freedom, ignoring one of the live consoles he could be using for up-to-date information.

Williams moved to one such console, this one feeding the direct video from the *Icarus*'s most powerful imaging array. Currently it focused on a blurred Earth and the Siberian heartland of the Neo-Soviet empire. Through atmosphere he would never get the resolution needed to search out the Seventy-first, if they still lived, but he wished for it. And for Brad's safety. "At least Freedom is finally on station," he murmured.

"Until Freedom is on station?" Nystolov asked, looking up from his comparison.

"Sorry," Williams said, pulling himself away from the image of Siberia and returning the screen to a wider view of Earth as a whole. "I guess I was talking to myself. Station

Freedom has finally come on station over Gory Putorana." He stumbled a bit over the Russian words, but close enough. "There's an engagement—at least there *was* an engagement—happening down there between Union and the empire. They hope to cut through the interference still cloaking much of Earth. My younger brother is part of one of the units."

Nystolov's faced showed more interest at the mention of Brad, maybe even a touch of concern. "I am sorry," he said, and even sounded as if he meant it. "I hope he makes it through."

"I'm sure he's fine. He has a good commander." Williams shifted uneasily. "Do you . . ." he began, but trailed off.

"No," Nystolov answered easily. "I no family on Terra. Mars is my home." His dark eyes narrowed. "*Was* my home," he amended gruffly.

Randall Williams had taken to Brygan Vassilyevich rather easily, though much of that was thanks to the other man's efforts. Brygan wasn't as moody as other Neo-Soviets Williams had met, though it was hard to compare because most of those had been prisoners. Nor did he seem to suffer from the chip on the shoulder many foreign scientists acquired because Union technology was so advanced.

The Neo-Soviet was bigger than Williams, but didn't use it as a way to throw his weight around. He did have a kind of bearlike gruffness, but it seemed more a sign of his seriousness. Williams respected that edge; it was the natural toughness a person needed if he or she was to survive any length of time in space.

He checked his work crew, found them about their jobs easily enough. "What are you so fascinated by in the Styx Nebula?" the major asked, looking for more insight into his *guest's* nature. "I thought you were more interested in planetary exploration."

"*Da*, I prefer to put my feet on what I study. This Maelstrom space is cluttered, compared to *before*, but it is still vacuum."

Williams waved a hand over the enhanced photos. "I don't see you finding anything in there to study then." He frowned, not in displeasure but the pique of having discovered another phenomenon he couldn't begin to explain. "Whatever makes up the Styx, it acts like a volatile substance. Like nothing we ever considered a nebula would be like. We've monitored a small planetoid and any number of asteroids hitting it. That ice-blue cosmic gas lights up brilliantly and explodes."

He saw the mischief glinting in Brygan's eyes.

"I can't see how a larger mass could exist in there."

More amused silence.

"What did you find?" he asked, suddenly unsure of himself in the face of Brygan's complete self-confidence.

Brygan scaled one of the photos around. "You would find it sometime," he said. Whether that was meant as a gesture of consolation for Williams's missing it or the reason Brygan had decided to share his find, Williams could not be sure. "There was planetoid in there. Not on scale of Luna, but big. Say, size of Buryat, or your New Jersey."

In his enthusiasm, Randall Williams missed the past tense for a moment. He studied the exposure, found the dark shadow of actual mass within Styx's volatile gasses. "How did I miss that?" he asked, berating himself and impressed that the Neo-Soviet had spotted the landmass. There was no denying the man was observant. Then the Union scientist finally caught up on the other man's assertion. "*Was*? It's gone?" He frowned again. "Destroyed by Styx, eh?" Well, it was like he had said; no matter could exist in there.

"*Nyet.* Not destroyed." Brygan tapped a large thumb on a sheet of photographic negatives. "Sputnik-23 filmed it more than twenty-four hours before your Freedom. Two hours into Freedom's tape, it disappeared. Not destroyed though. It faded away."

Williams began snatching up slides and photos as Brygan indicated them. "How does something just fade away?"

The Neo-Soviet shrugged. "How did Terra end up here in Maelstrom? Myself, am glad it faded out."

The proof was there on the film. Williams sighed in exasperation—scooped by an amateur. "Glad? If it phased away, it might have led to a door back to our own universe."

"If it had not, we might never have looked at it twice. At least now is *maybe* proof that not everything here is permanent."

The major conceded Brygan's point. "Still, too bad we're too late to see the phase up close, with the *Icarus*'s instruments."

"Try to get in there, *Icarus* would be cosmic dust," the Neo-Soviet reminded him. "Not everything should be known. You should not want everything to be known. That is why we learn, sometimes slowly." Then Brygan glanced away, unsuccessfully hiding a look of concern as if he'd said too much.

That brought the scientist in Williams up short. He cupped his chin in his right hand, stroking the pointed ends of his sideburns. Was the Neo-Soviet scout trying to warn him, or hitting close to something more relevant to himself? "I would like to learn how to return Earth home," he said, then sighed, "but I would never want to know for certain that it wasn't possible, you're right." But what more was

Brygan trying to say? "So we file this as yet another mystery of the Maelstrom. A list that is growing fairly long in relation to our list of answers."

"Eh? How many answers have you found so far?"

"Well, none yet. But if they're out there, we'll find them." He hoped he sounded more optimistic to the hearing of others.

"Then where do we go after our passes 'round Terra?" the Neo-Soviet asked. "How many planets inside our range?"

"Of the *Icarus*? All of them," Williams said proudly. "This ship could make it as far as . . ." He trailed off in exasperation. "Damn, that's one I gave you for free. We should stick to mission parameters, not Union technology."

"If it makes you feel better, we know ranges on all your primary vessels. *Icarus* could technically have made it between stars on a small crew that wouldn't tax life support."

"Yes, that makes me feel better," Williams said, then realized what that meant, "I think." Well, the Union knew as much about Neo-Soviet spaceships. "A more politic answer would be to say there are five planets in *convenient* range. No worse than the jaunt from Earth to Jupiter—maybe Saturn. And that's currently. With the variation in orbits, those can change rapidly."

Williams nodded toward a console displaying a cross section of the Maelstrom that Tycho and Tranquillity had collaborated on, and the two of them moved to it. It showed a supercolossal solar system in orbit around that misshapen, alien sun. From Luna or Earth, this sunlike phenomenon appeared to be roughly globular, like a splash of white paint hanging brilliantly in the sky. As the Union scientists had managed to image it, the Maelstrom's Eye—Williams's name for it—was at least six times larger than Sol and twice as distant, and created of some exotic matter rather than the fusing of hydrogen. It reached out into space with thick tendrils, some of which had elongated to reach deep into the Inner Ring. The Central Ring was a mess of planets in close proximity and thick belts of asteroids, still under evaluation for distances and total numbers. Williams gestured to the small portion of the Outer Ring that was confidently mapped out, and with a few deft instructions input, he expanded that region. Earth and Luna. The Styx Nebula. Five other planets and a variety of large asteroids and small planetoids.

"We'll orbit and do the initial survey on this world here." He pointed to an orange dot on the screen. "I don't expect much as it is a gas giant with no detectable moons. Then it's on to a rogue asteroid that is passing at an angle to our ecliptic. On our way back, we might survey one of these two worlds that lie close enough along our path."

Brygan did not ask the obvious question, about any of the other nearby worlds. Instead he asked, "What is so special about asteroid?" As if he trusted Williams to be ready with a good answer. The major punched up a request on the console which called a computer-enhanced satellite-imaging photograph. "That's from Sputnik-23," Brygan said at once, noticing the format marking along the bottom. "That was not included in the material you presented me earlier."

Williams shrugged an apology. "We have not made a hard copy of this, because we suspect it contains some very important findings."

"Such as?"

"Sputnik-23 tagged it as high in metal alloys. Also, there is this." He pulled up another image of the same asteroid, specially enhanced to find patterns in the supermagnified blurs. It showed the cold blue of rock, veined with lighter colors that ran in a network of patterns that suggested—

"Right angles!" Brygan reached out and traced the boxes. "Nature does not build straight lines and squared angles itself. This is man-made."

"It might be a piece from Venus or Mars," Williams admitted. "Or any number of outposts our nations have seeded over our old solar system."

Brygan narrowed his eyes in suspicion. "But you do not think so?"

"Most of these right angles are complete, as if framing buildings that are still standing. That is a giant rock in space. If it was torn from a Neo-Soviet facility, could the buildings have all survived intact?" He didn't need an answer. "Those were built on the asteroid to begin with, and that rock does not conform to any known shape of an asteroid cataloged in our old system."

The implication hung heavy in the air for several long minutes. "This seems very important. Why not go straight there? Why the stop by this gas giant?" He flicked a nail over the dot as if removing it from existence.

"The gas giant is on our way. Also, it allows us to approach with more caution. In the Union everything is done efficiently and in order." He regretted his choice of words at once. It was as if he'd thrown water on the moment of camaraderie the two had enjoyed.

Brygan nodded slowly, dark eyes clouded as he buried any show of feeling. Suddenly he seemed very Neo-Soviet. "In the empire, we have no resources to waste. We would go and take the objective quickly."

It was the first time Brygan Nystolov had separated himself from Williams by nationality. Before, they had both been men of science. Now, because he had forgotten twice in as many minutes that there were still a few military distinctions between the two men, he had wounded a man whose skill he might have need of. To say nothing of a chance that Brygan could still consider a change of allegiance. But they were words that could not be taken back.

If he had the chance, if Brygan Vassilyevich gave him the chance, he would try to make up for them later.

18

The smaller creatures rushed the Irynutsk Nuclear Facility just before a late dawn broke over the southeast horizon. All was dark except for the one light over the main gate on the chain-link fence. Thin wisps of steam escaped the tower, replacing the usual funnel of thick white effluent and indicating that the Neo-Soviet personnel had at least enough sense to shut down the reactor before abandoning the power plant. Several of the winged symbiots flew overhead and straight down into the large tower, disregarding the thin steam which still vented from the turbines within. Others dropped to the ground near walls posted with yellow-and-magenta trifoil warning signs—areas the CBR rep had already verified as highly contaminated. They sank tentacles into the ground, anchoring themselves firmly to the earth. From hiding, Union troops fired on them, and two of the airborne things erupted in the cross fire. Their sagging, flesh-sack bodies split open, spilling gobbets of translucent flesh over the ground.

Sergeant Tousley hunkered down among some hardy thistle growing near the pump house's concrete wall, squeezing off quick bursts from the Bulldog assault rifle he'd traded for his Pitbull. Inside, the pumps continued to hum loudly as they pulled water from the nearby Kotuy River. The area was relatively uncontaminated and gave him the commanding view of the eastern approaches that he would need. This would be his squad's last stand.

They might have stumbled another kilometer and hoped for pickup, but the odds weren't good. At least here they had some cover. He had already shot the lock out of the nearby pump-house door, creating a place to which he could fall back. Corporal Richardson and Private Nicholas held the roof over the main administrative building, and Lance Corporal Johnson and PFC Nash had the reinforced overhang that surrounded the tower. Kelly Fitzpatrick was on the ground, escorting the CBR rep Sainz had seen fit to attach to the squad. That brought them back to seventy-five percent strength. It was a strength that could crack under too much strain. Danielle Johnson was still little better than walking wounded from the shrapnel picked up in the first battle. Nash was new, an outsider, brought in from the Draco squad Tousley had pulled off the hill. And Loveday, the CBR guy, was all but useless in a firefight.

Not the strongest squad for a rearguard action. Tousley knew it, and Sainz did, too. But with the alien creature moving up behind them too quickly, it came down to the simple fact that the Union forces had little choice anymore. It was make do, or do without.

"At least he gave me the choice," Tousley muttered,

switching his line of fire to the gate as the first aliens smashed aside the meager protection it had offered. Some scuttled on crablike armored pincers. Others on thin but strong legs, their wasplike bodies hued a deep ocher.

"Say again?" Jerry Richardson asked.

Tousley had left his comms open. "Disregard," he ordered. "Concentrate on those fliers. I see two perched on the side of the tower. Maybe they act like scouts."

It made sense. Major Howard had explained something about symbiotic organisms. If they did work together, why not in a tactical sense? That would make the first creatures on the scene scouts or pathfinders, though why they probed the ground with those tubular tentacles he didn't understand. The armored things rushing in now he classified as common infantry. A shriek tore through the crisp morning air, that unbearable sound that shook Tousley to his core.

And that creature out there, an army unto itself, waiting for his squad if they didn't manage to turn its course. The creature was a kilometer distant, across the Kotuy and advancing along the southern cliffs of Gory Putorana. Its shovel-like head rose high into the air, about the same level as those bloated sacks of flesh that simply floated in a half-kilometer radius. They must be a picket, Tousley had decided. Expendable, early-warning sentries.

"Tom, we're evacuating the tower," Kelly Fitzpatrick called. "It's filling up with fliers. They've broken through several walls and are loose in the plant."

"Anything that keeps them away from here," Richardson said. "We're busy enough."

Tousley nodded his agreement, sighting in on a large specimen that slithered along, leaving a shiny, grayish trail behind. No chitin or carapace protected it. One burst tore it clean in two.

"Well, it looks like we're getting busier," Fitzpatrick said. "I swear some of them are growing."

Tousley thumbed a recessed button on his Bulldog's trigger guard, chambering an M-81 proximity grenade into the launcher. His next target, a walking black dome supported on tentacles and millipede legs, also had a thick carapace. He sighted in on it carefully, depressing a special button on the trigger stock and waiting for the red telltale light to flash a range lock. The strobe registered in the corner of his eye, and he squeezed off the shot. The grenade fired off on an echoing blast. The proximity feature would detonate the grenade as the range locked in, trying for incidental damage on any missed shot. He didn't need the feature this time. His aim put it right on the forward-right quarter of the dome, blowing a large hole through it and spattering yellow-gray gunk over a ten-meter radius.

Showing a measure of intelligence, the creatures began to fall back from the well-defended power plant. Tousley noticed at the last second that a few different types did not retreat. The ones he had thought of as alien scouts, still with tentacles probing the ground were, as Kelly Fitzpatrick had warned, getting larger. The ocher, wasp-bodied jumpers held their ground. Long, hairlike strands began to rise up on their bodies and whipped the air over them. One turned in his direction with a quick jerk and leapt.

The thing was coming for him. Tousley saw that in the purpose with which it moved. He fired two bursts while airborne, missing the first time and tearing one leg away with the second, but that didn't stop it. The thing landed, spitting a reddish brown globule of liquid and thick slime at him. The mess splattered off to his left, sizzling against the ground. He nearly retched at the caustic scent left behind—ruined meat mixed with the biting smells of volatile fuels. It hit him with the shock of tear gas, just as the globule began to hiss and spit even more loudly.

Instinct took over, and Tousley pitched himself backward and rolled to the right. The substance detonated a second later, some of the fiery debris setting the thistle patch on fire. Tumbling across the ground, Tousley held on to the Bulldog with strength born of desperation. He rolled to a stop. Flat on his back, barely able to breathe through the stench, he watched as the jumper again took to the air, looking as if it would land right on top of him.

One-handed, he brought up his assault rifle, firing it in one long burst and praying that this wouldn't cause one of the ammunition jams for which the Bulldog was infamous. The assault rifle waved around at the bare edge of control, cutting a line of armor-piercing bullets through the air and right across the creature's head. It fluttered in the air, fighting the hail of bullets, even as the sergeant rolled to his side and gained full control over the rifle with both hands. He drilled the creature hard and steady, stopping its powerful leap and driving it back.

"Watch the jumpers," he called out in warning over the squad's common channel. "They can spit some kind of—"

The warning came too late. Screaming cut him off in mid-sentence. Tousley crabbed about, keeping to the ground while trying to find his men in trouble. Fliers were now rising slowly from the tower-funnel and heading back toward the advancing alien. A few were also stirring about on the ground; having grown too bloated to fly, they walked on stunted legs.

He cut the feet out from under one with a quick burst of fire, then left it thrashing about helpless when he finally spotted where the trouble was. Richardson and Nicholas were on top of the administration building, and two of the wasp-bodied jumpers were clinging to the corner of the roof, bodies hanging halfway over the side. Some new fliers were also dropping in, but not the sagging-flesh ones of before. These were hard-bodied, looking like chitinous spears flying on membrane wings. They dipped and dodged over the roof. Higher up one of the floaters hung motionless, as if overseeing the entire attack.

"Nash, what are you waiting for?" Tousley screamed, his voice loud enough to carry to the reinforced overhang where the Draco-packing infantrymen hid. No need for radio. "You see those jumpers? Take them out! Everyone else give them some covering fire. Keep those fliers off them."

The fire from three assault rifles streaked across the rooftop at the spear-shaped attackers. One blazed briefly as it slammed into the corner of the building and threw an ocher-hued Spitter over the other side. Confusion reigned among the creatures for a moment, and a figure in green fatigues took a chance and ran for the side of the building. He stooped long enough to pick up another body, then threw himself and his buddy off the roof. It was a long fall, nearly six meters. The bodies hung in the air a long second, and then bounced off the ground once, hard, and were still.

"Still . . . here . . ." A voice strained in pain and faint from lack of breath. Tousley placed it as Jim Nicholas rather than Jerry Richardson's bass voice. "Broken ribs . . . and hand burned . . . badly. Corporal's dead."

Anger made Tousley clench his jaw so tight it hurt. "Kelly and Loveday, get them out of there. Danielle, give them supporting fire. Nash, keep hitting the jumpers where you see them." The battle was slipping from his grasp, and he knew it. Too many creatures, not enough Union. He would retreat, if they had anywhere to retreat to. And if they made a run for it, the jumpers would have them in less than two hundred meters. He searched the area for a solution, and saw only the thrashing flier he'd wounded earlier. Its bloated body gushed more of the small gobbets, just like the stuff he'd seen when the Neo-Soviets wounded the alien's tentacle. He could still picture those gobbets pouring over the Chem Grunt, which had—

Melted. Blistered, burned, and melted.

He looked around frantically, finding the largest concentration of fliers near a large tank suspended above the ground. "Loveday! What's that area on the side of the tower? The tank—it looks like it's set up to drop something into a waiting truck below."

"Ion resin exchanger. You flush old resin into it, and then from there it's loaded into special carriers."

"Radioactive?" It had to be, Tousley knew.

The answering voice was a mixture of curiosity and exasperation. "Of course. Highly radioactive. Next to the fuel, it's about the worst stuff you can pull out of the reactor compartment."

That was exactly what Tousley wanted to hear. He brought up the Bulldog, sighting in on the tank as he chambered a new grenade. The first one fell low, blowing a flier into shredded flesh and those translucent gobbets that he thought of as blood. His second shot hit the tank on the lower taper, rupturing the thick metal at a welded seam. Resin beads trickled out in a small but steady flow, small and clear and looking much like the capsulelike flesh globules the creatures bled. Looking very much like them. The fliers did not evade the deadly substance as his people would have. They flocked to it, driving the tentacles deep into the growing pile of resin.

"We're getting out of here," Tousley said at once.

"Head for the rear fence line and don't fire unless attacked. We'll blow a stretch and make our way northwest."

Kelly Fitzpatrick and her group were hobbling in that direction, she bearing up a wounded Nicholas and Loveday struggling under the weight of Corporal Richardson's body. Danielle and Nash, from their vantage point, could not have seen the resin exchanger.

"What gives, Sarge?" Danielle asked. "I thought you said we couldn't hope to make rendezvous. Better to go down fighting here than in retreat."

Tousley followed his retreating squad, swinging wide around the deadly jumpers. "Those fliers, they aren't scouts, Danielle. They're feeders. Those things thrive on radiation—look where they're landing. They soak it up—ingest it somehow—and take it back to that . . . that thing bearing down on us. We're not gonna turn it away from here. We're sitting *on its food source*! If there's a worse place to be than between an animal and its food, I don't know it. We're gonna take the chance and try and slip away. Now move it!"

As his people fell back in good order, Tousley still felt a twinge at the order to retreat. At any other time, he might have agreed with Danielle and stayed to fight it out. He was certainly tired of running away, and it seemed like that's all the Union had been doing of late. Running from the Fifty-sixth Striker, and now from this alien thing. He ejected his clip and slapped in a fresh one. At some point someone had to draw a line and say "no farther." Everyone had that point buried somewhere within, and he knew himself enough to feel his wasn't far off. Perhaps not now, or even today.

But sometime soon.

"I believe we were speaking of how to control that *Sleeper*," Colonel Katya Romilsky said, turning a withering eye on her aide. Gregor Antoly should have seen this—guessed this. "Do we have doubts any longer as to what it needs?"

The two of them stood among the ruins of the Irynutsk Facility. The ground was torn up from the Sleeper's passage, and several buildings had caved in from being sideswiped by its massive bulk. The tower had been ripped open when the creature smashed aside the thick walls and burrowed down into the underground reactor. The administrative building stood with only a single hole blasted into the wall near the roofline. It could be remanned, but the operators and officers would be overseeing a dead plant.

Gregor held a detector capable of registering gamma and beta radiation. Not one single chirp bounced the needle, except when too near one of the Fifty-sixth's own mutants.

"Clean," Gregor said, obviously in awe. "Not one bit of contamination left. And every piece of nuclear fuel is missing as well. Could you imagine what we might accomplish with the ability to clean up all our radiological problem areas? What that creature could do if we could release it against the Union?"

"Can you understand what it is doing to *our* empire?" Romilsky snapped at him in frustration. "I want to know how to kill it."

"You can't kill it," Gregor said. "It needs to be captured. Studied. The advances the empire might make are inestimable."

She shook her head angrily. "It became too late for that once the Sleeper destroyed Irynutsk. It is a danger to the empire. I am not about to allow it to wander around ripping open our power plants or *missile silos.*" Or anything more critical. "We are out of time, Gregor Detchelov."

He flapped his arms in frustration. "What do you mean,

no time? It's heading into the deeper folds of Gory Putorana, chasing the Union force up the Kotuy."

"*I* know exactly where it's heading. Colonel Sainz did not fall back along the Kotuy on purpose. He wanted the Upper Tunguska. With the *Leonid* we would have been there to meet him, but he missed the only pass his antigrav craft might have taken. He is now trapped in between Gory Putorana and the Sleeper, and so presses deeper to the north. Right where I placed him." She sounded concerned, even to herself.

"But that is a good thing," Detchelov said. "Let the Sleeper destroy him for us."

Komilsky didn't respond, not trusting her voice. Gregor was becoming an unknown factor in the battle, and the last thing she wanted was to give him cause to doubt her commitment to destroying the Seventy-first.

"I will find a way to bring the Sleeper to heel, Comrade Colonel. I promise you."

"You are not listening, Gregor. By this afternoon I will have to make some difficult decisions, but one of them will not be how best to capture this creature. The next time I spend troops against it, I expect to kill it." She let an edge of steel touch her voice. "And you will help me do that because that is how I order it. Is that understood?"

It was clear that he wanted to argue, but the hard look she gave him obviously changed his mind. Katya Romilsky saw the anger give way to wariness in Gregor's black eyes. She nodded to dismiss him even as she gestured forward the slight man waiting off to one side under guard.

Gregor Detchelov frowned slightly, then bowed his leave to Romilsky. She watched him as he passed near a group of Rad Troopers, suddenly imagining him grabbing a weapon or acting out some other form of rebellion, but then she eased as he continued on without incident. Gregor could be wily and devious when it came to ferreting out information she needed, and in battle he was an asset to draw upon. Katya Romilsky knew now she had almost made a mistake.

Because she had never once, until now, believed Gregor Detchelov capable of being a threat. But she had read the murder in his dark eyes. He would bear watching.

"Yes."

Romilsky started visibly. She rounded on the Mental who had landed the *Leonid Sergetov*—nearly crashed it, actually—near her position during the cataclysm that had robbed Terra of its familiar sky. He had been unable to speak coherently for half a day, mumbling to himself but not recognizing anyone else around him. Slowly he'd come back to some semblance of awareness, though he still trembled in silence when asked about the crossover.

The man was stoop-shouldered and frail, as if he'd spent too many years under some tremendous weight. Only his eyes were truly alive, one blue one green, with a piercing quality that bothered her. She decided not to ask, though, if he saw danger. If he did, he would say. Anyway, the next Mental to give a straight answer to a direct question about their abilities would be the first in her experience.

"Comrade," she said, using it as more an official title than a friendly custom, "I regret that you may not yet be returned to Noril'sk. We have"—she gestured around at the devastation—"several problems to attend to, and the *Leonid* is desperately needed here."

"Not the least of which is your tale to Colonel Sainz about Chernaya Gora, *Tovarish* Romilsky."

She worked hard not to show that she was disturbed by the Mental's familiar address, and his foreknowledge of the story she'd told Colonel Sainz. "The *Leonid* can serve to block any attempt by Union Command to reach Sainz, yes. Though it is a matter of time before a battle station is brought overhead, and then they will be in communication with their superiors before we are."

The man frowned. "I'm certain the Mentals in Moskva are coherent again. By now they have certainly informed the empire of this monster you face, and what it will take to defeat it."

"Then you see reinforcements on their way, *da*?"

"*Nyet.* There will be none sent."

"If you know what's at stake, you know that they must send them."

The Mental sighed wearily. He swayed on his feet, looking like he might fall over at any moment. "There are no reinforcements to be had. The empire is engaged heavily against the Union, and everything must be weighted accordingly. Reinforcements will go where they are most needed."

Romilsky swore silently. She had so little time left to decide. "Are you saying that I will not require reinforcement to stop the Sleeper?" A simple yes or no question, though the chances of receiving so simple an answer were slim.

A slight pause, and then the Mental gave her more than she had wanted. "None you do not already have access to."

And that was the answer Katya Romilsky had most feared.

19

There could be no concentrated line of battle in the rough country below Gory Putorana. Deep canyons and slopes too steep for antigrav craft broke the Seventy-first Assault Group into four separate and uneven forces as soldiers and vehicles fought against the creature and its symbiot army. The creature's tortured-soul shriek reverberated off cliff faces, echoed in part by Union antigravity generators screaming their labor. Wendigos, especially, fought for sheer volume while the four remaining Aztecs worked for an earsplitting pitch. The constant chattering reports of assault rifles and the occasional hard clap of grenades blended and rolled over the mountainsides as artificial thunder for a cloudless day. It reminded Rebecca Howard too much of the nightmare they had all lived through—was it only yesterday? It seemed as if the

Seventy-first had been fighting for days. She certainly felt the strain.

So many creatures. They swarmed over the rise to the south or soared in the air overhead, worrying her flanks and waiting for that opportune moment to attack. The Seventy-first never had any idea of the alien's full resources. Many of these must have trailed the parent creature, kept back as a reserve. That spoke of intelligence or a highly evolved sense of tactical instinct. Worse was the idea that this thing was learning with each engagement, though certainly they were showing a great deal more caution than when they had met against Tom Tousley's squad. The sergeant had thought so as well, calling back earlier from her forward line.

The Aztecs had been left under her command while the colonel led most of the heavy armor in complicated maneuvers meant to harass and hopefully wound the alien. So far Sainz was reporting back little success. Now the ag cycles picked up a flanking maneuver by the creatures on the right without her orders, Lieutenant Landvoy charging forward confidently at the head of the pack. It was her strongest position, anchored by the antigrav cycles and one squad of Ares assault suits. As opposed to her middle line tormented by spear-shaped fliers with their stinger-tipped pseudopods and the wasp-bodied Spitters. The front line sagged back as the fliers swung down again, stingers raking one man across the face and shoulders.

"Damn!" she yelled, feeling cheated and helpless at the rear while her soldier up front fell into a violent fit and then lay still. She carried a Pitbull assault rifle and a holstered Pug but had yet to fire either, more intent until now in directing her troops and trying to force some kind of advantage. She hated admitting that this was the kind of battle the

Neo-Soviets were better suited for, where mobility was curtailed and personnel could be expended with more impunity.

"Order a general move back on our position. We need to concentrate forces as much as possible." It would further limit their mobility, an asset the Union constantly relied upon, but she saw little choice. She cursed herself now for placing the bulk of the Hydras under Captain Dillahunty's command. They would have given her a stronger fallback position. But then Dillahunty was holding the Seventy-first's rear against a possible Neo-Soviet threat, scouts having placed at least some elements of the Fifty-sixth Striker behind them now, coming down out of Gory Putorana. "Tell Colonel Sainz he's about to lose his left guard and that we may need to order a fighting retreat."

Not before she claimed her own ounce of blood, though. Rebecca Howard all but threw her Pitbull at a nearby corporal and grabbed the Weatherby Mk-VI Bloodhound he held out for her. "Tell Sergeant Tousley to swing right and help swat those fliers," she ordered. It left Tom vulnerable to the press coming in, but the major trusted Landvoy's Aztecs and the Ares to handle that. And Tousley was also the most experienced in leading a rear guard, though that kind of experience no one liked acquiring.

She wrapped the rifle's carrying strap two hard turns about her left wrist for steady control, chambered the first round, and brought the rifle up to her shoulder. She paused for a practiced flick of her gaze over the battlefield, then raised the marksman rifle to her shoulder and sighted in where she expected the Spitter to land. The high-powered scope left little room for error, two meters in either direction and it would fall outside her sights. However, she knew better than to close her left eye, a mistake common among those not trained as marksmen, and so tracked in even when the Spitter made another last-second correction to its arc. It fell dead center and she squeezed off a round, then bracketed it with two more off center.

The first 5.56 round took a fraction of a second to make the four hundred meters, tearing into the Spitter's wide neck. The take-down power of the Weatherby knocked it sideways and ruined its tensing for a new leap. One of her follow-up shots passed overhead, but the second took it square in the thorax. The wound that opened up spat small pieces of flame at the air, then erupted in a gout of fire and flesh. She swung around, ready to send precision death at any creatures still pressing in on the right.

Just in time to watch the Aztec's SPEAR missiles fly outward on thin contrails of gray smoke and slam into the formation. The explosive radial submunitions tore through chitin and flesh, spilling that strange mixture of radioactive material most of these creatures called flesh and blood. Now one of the hovering Feeders moved down from above, coming in behind to avoid direct fire and hopefully scavenge any usable "food."

Major Howard had silently cheered the complete destruction of the probe, though already the effects of their solid victory were apparent. More fliers moved in, and on the ground, anywhere that the creatures gathered in tight knots they now spread apart to make such destructive power less effective. She did note it was not an instantaneous change, but that it swept over the alien line like a wave starting with the creatures nearest the Aztecs and spreading over and onto other battlefields no doubt.

"Message from the colonel," Lance Corporal Bo Huffer called out. "It's faint—I think he's dropping too deep in the canyons. He's lost three—that is three—Wendigos and is already falling back on this position. He asks you to hold."

The comms specialist swallowed hard. "Says to remind you we got nowhere left to go."

And they didn't, except to implement the escape plan Raymond Sainz was so dead set against. Break the Seventy-first into small squads and each flee at best speeds. The creatures could not hope to stop but a small percentage. The danger came from Colonel Romilsky and her Fifty-sixth Striker. If she was ready, she could conceivably wipe out the Seventy-first. But it gave some of their people a fighting chance to survive. A tough call to make. But as the exec her responsibility was to lives, a natural check against the commander's oath to engage the enemy. She would have to argue her case again.

"Say again?" Barnes asked into her headset, one hand cupping the earpiece as if it could help improve transmission. "Who is this? How did you get this freq?" His face screwed up in half shock, half anger. "Major Howard, I have someone coming in on one of our secure frequencies, but unscrambled, and trying to reach the colonel. It's faint, and he's in a communications shadow right now. It's got to be some kind of joke."

"Who is it, Corporal?"

"She is identifying herself as Colonel Katya Olia Romilsky," he said, slurring the Russian names slightly.

Howard nearly leapt for the comms specialist, grabbing his spare link. There was not time to hunt for it in her own headset. She wasn't sure exactly what she expected. A new threat, most likely. "This is Major Howard, executive officer, Seventy-first Assault Group. How do we know you are who you say?" she asked by way of opening.

"I can bring a Class F mutant and Vanguard escort again, but that would take more time than you have. And one mutant cannot help you here."

"And you can?" The major harbored no doubts that this was Romilsky, though she lacked any idea of what the Neo-Soviet colonel might be up to.

"That is my intention, *da*. I have a transport and will rescue you. But I will not risk the vessel without a guarantee that no weapons will be fired on the *Leonid*. Not without the word of Raymond Sainz."

So Romilsky *did* have a transport. Rebecca Howard stared at her comms specialist, then reached out and took the man's headset. These kinds of conversations were sometimes best kept in the upper echelon. She walked several paces away, keeping a wary eye on her force's fallback maneuver. "You are asking us to surrender again. He won't agree." But would *she*? Her primary responsibility was to the lives of the Seventy-first after all. Tom Tousley and many others would rather die fighting, she knew. Truth be told so would she. But what she wanted did not always mesh with what was required of her.

"*Nyet,* not surrender. A truce. What you would call *a deal.*" Slight pause. "I rescue you, and you agree to help me destroy this Sleeper."

The Sleeper being the monstrous creature which had twice forced the Union into a near rout. "How do we know your word is good?"

"My word is good as that of Raymond Sainz. Also, you have little choice as I see it. If you do not want to accept my assurances, I will leave you to be finished off by the Sleeper. Maybe you will wound the Sleeper enough that I can kill it, but I don't think it is so."

Howard could see where the monstrous alien posed a threat large enough to force Romilsky into such a position, that she might deal with Union forces. That meant, though, that they had no way of requesting reinforcements from

Neo-Soviet High Command, or that reinforcements were not available. Howard found herself wanting to believe the offer, though she knew that under any other circumstances she would turn it down flat. Trusting the Neo-Soviets was just not an idea she would ever be comfortable with. But the commander, he would take the deal. The major knew it. And her commander's opinion carried a lot of weight with Rebecca Howard. "All right," she said, voice catching on every word, "I'll agree."

"I desire the personal word of Colonel Raymond Jaquin Sainz."

"There's no way to put you two in direct communication yet, and minutes might count. I'll give it for him."

Romilsky sounded more than a little surprised. "You can do that? He is trusting you very much."

"No." Major Howard shook her head. "I am trusting him."

Raymond Sainz did not truly believe the deal his exec had struck until the *Leonid Sergetov* actually landed and Union forces began to move up its two loading ramps. The transport was an interplanetary vessel, and looked as if it had been through some major scrapes of late, but would serve well enough. Vanguard infantry spilled down from the immense vehicle bays, taking up flanking positions to keep the alien creatures off the loading Seventy-first. The colonel sent Howard back at once to gather in Tom Tousley, anticipating that the sergeant might not react too favorably to the Vanguard presence and wanting to avoid any difficulties. Tousley was the most reactionary of all the juniors. He wanted the man under control.

The large bays were marked off for crawlers, though the Union antigravity vehicles fit in well enough. Infantry quickly posted themselves at every possible ingress point, forming a living wall to protect their unit. Trojan supply carriers were placed in the middle, surrounded by Hydra transports. The assault group's four remaining Wendigos boxed the corners, each turned to cover a possible danger spot. The miscellaneous vehicles spread out in between. The transport had barely risen from the ground, coming up in vertical takeoff on huge thrusters, when the Neo-Soviet commander made her appearance.

Romilsky was first through the door, unconcerned with Union efforts to secure the bays. She left her Vanguard escort by the door and proceeded through the bay. The Union infantry stepped aside for her, a little too eager to place themselves in between the enemy colonel and her escort. The Vanguard shifted uncomfortably, but held their positions.

"*Strasvicha*, Katya Olia Romilsky," Sainz said as she approached. Both he and the major gave very formal nods of greeting. Romilsky returned the salute. Major Howard stumbled her way over the awkward Russian pronunciation, then Sainz continued in the same language. "Your timing was exemplary. One might almost say prescient." Why that would cause a temporary tightening around Romilsky's eyes, Sainz didn't see. Until then he had been willing to believe the timing simple chance since he did not believe the Neo-Soviets had cracked their communication system. He filed the new doubt away for future review.

"You have questions, *da*?"

"Nyet," Sainz said, surprising her. At least, he hoped he had surprised her. Romilsky was too sharp to allow her to control the conversation. "The arrangements were explained to me. For the rescue, we help you destroy this creature—this Sleeper as you call it. But I'll make it clear up front that

the Seventy-first will not be used as part of your *human wave* attacks."

Where his disagreement earlier had not fazed her, now she reacted as if insulted. Her voice held a sharp edge to it. "If you thought I would suggest that, you would never have come aboard the *Leonid* and bound yourself to the agreement."

As may be. But Sainz had not forgotten Romilsky's applied dedication to destroying the Seventy-first Assault Group, and how tightly she watched what she said. The comment was not meant as an insult, but the opening move in how they would coordinate an assault against the Sleeper. The *Leonid* rocked off center, and the Union colonel frowned. "Your pilot needs practice."

"The ship was recently salvaged from a crash site. Appreciate that we had it at all to rescue you." She glanced around the bay at the heavy force the Union assault group still commanded. "The Sleeper is threatening empire soil," she said. "Our homeland. I will devise the plans. You may review them, and propose changes. No battle is set until we both agree. Is that acceptable?"

"Very," Sainz said at once. Too easy. "You speak as if this was arranged, Katya Olia." He shortened her first name, implying that he would talk more openly if she would. "Has Moscow authorized your deal with my forces?"

She shook her head. "I anticipate a great deal of . . . you would say *controversy* . . . regarding this action." The ship pitched again, and she frowned forward in the general direction of the cockpit. "But let me only say that Moskva will not find this unexpected and leave it at that."

"What about our forces?" He nodded at the hostile attitude between her Vanguard at the door and his infantry blocking them from the two officers. He also saw Sergeant

Tousley, Bulldog held easily in his hands, waiting off to one side and not bothering to hide his mixed expression of anger and revulsion. "Will they accept it so easily?"

Romilsky shrugged. "That depends on you and me, Colonel Sainz. Doesn't it?" She offered him her hand.

Slowly, the Seventy-first's commander took it. "I guess it does, Colonel Romilsky." He couldn't shake the feeling that he was bargaining with the devil herself. It was a creeping sensation that worked its way from the base of his neck up over his scalp. But proof enough of her sincerity existed to balance out those remaining doubts. He would watch her, as no doubt she would him, for that first misstep.

"Here's hoping," he said in English, "that we each live up to the other's expectations."

20

The crystalline formations hung against the black backdrop of space. Three of them, moving in a rough triangular pattern at a constant speed that the *Icarus* slowed to match. The smallest was of a size similar to the crystal forest Brygan Nystolov had inadvertently smashed on Luna; a hundred meters wide by two hundred long, but fifty meters thick, which suggested that the forest had been buried deep in the lunar soil. The second was double the size of the first. The third was two times bigger than the second, an impressive kilometer in length and a half klick wide. Laser sampling from a distance confirmed a similar emerald coloring that the *Icarus* staff could not pick out by naked eye. With the *Icarus* coming in on the back side of the formations, only their outlines were visible as light creased the edges. Light from that hideous scar in the heavens—what Randall Williams had named *the Maelstrom's Eye,* and now everyone was calling *the Maw.*

Williams was one of the three people still paying attention to the imaging array that continued to feed the scientists information on the Maw. He and Brygan Nystolov, and Paul Drake, who had just come down to the main science station to discuss procedures. On the console screen, the blazing wound altered its shape. One thick arm appeared to shorten—actually it moved so that it pointed more toward the *Icarus* and beyond it, toward Earth—while two others stretched out even farther into the void of the Maelstrom's Inner Ring.

The Maw's heightened activity was what had led them to the crystalline formations, which had drawn their attentions toward the system's source of light. Light, but not heat. Or at least, not heat that behaved as anyone understood it. That had been Brygan's discovery, one among many the scientists made on approach to the gas giant they had—briefly—surveyed earlier. Even though he was reeling from the unexpected travel time between Earth and the next planet, Williams was the first one to catch the physical changes to the Maw.

He had been arguing with a lieutenant manning an astrophysics console. "Did you check your numbers?" he asked.

"Three times," Lieutenant Boucher informed him, sounding hurt by the question. "I can run a new check if you'll let me swing an auxiliary array back toward Earth for an accurate observation."

"Do it." Williams had no time for fragile sensibilities or bruised egos. Two gravities of constant acceleration for twelve hours and then a like decel period should have dropped them neatly into orbit around the planet. So Darcie's announcement only four hours into deceleration that the gas giant was not near as large as they'd thought, but in fact was approaching fast, made for a large discrepancy. Three million kilometers, even by the incredible distances covered by spaceflight, was *not* a rounding error.

"Confirmed," she finally said. "Distance to Earth, based on direct observation, eighteen million four hundred sixty-two thousand kilometers. And change."

Drake called Williams on the link. "Our flight profile is just as clear, Major. Taking into account velocity and time, we've covered only fifteen million klicks."

Nystolov frowned. "Numbers do not lie. Someone is wrong."

No time to fight it out now, thought Randall Williams. "What would it take to make orbit?" he asked Drake.

Paul Drake shook his head on the small video screen. "It would take several hours of hard decel and then a new approach path. Do we have six hours or better?"

They could have, Williams knew, the desire to make good on the original plan warring with his desire to continue on to the asteroid. In any other situation, he might have ordered a return trip to Earth in order to verify the anomaly. But this was not just any situation. "Bring us by close as you can, Captain. Coordinate with Lieutenant Boucher and head us on out to the asteroid. We will make all readings we can during the single pass."

With only video imagers pointing back toward Earth and on toward the system's solar body, Williams almost missed the changes. They were subtle at first, the barest fluctuation in the Maw's outline. The instruments warned him, catching his trained eye from one monitor. When he noticed an arm reach deeper into the Inner Circle, he shouted for an immediate shift of all instrumentation.

"The Eye, it's altering. Get the sensors realigned now!"

The planet was forgotten as the best imagers on the *Icarus* refocused toward the solar body. It pulsed in brightness, waving thick tendrils around as if alive. Lieutenant Boucher called out readings of increased gamma radiation, akin to the actions of solar flares. And anyone could see on the screens that light intensity was greater than before.

Several of the Maw's arms lengthened until Williams could only guess at the extent of their embrace. Two hundred million kilometers? Five hundred? There were planets in the Inner Ring, they knew that. What of them? One arm continued to extend. Could it be reaching out from the Central Ring? They still had no firm grasp of the Maw's size or distance, only the minimum expected based on two hundred years of data observing their old sun. Williams had a sinking feeling that none of the old rules would apply here.

"There is no shift in temperature," Brygan Nystolov announced quietly.

"What do you mean?" Williams asked. "We have a surge in radiation." For all the strangeness of the Maelstrom, basic physics remained basic physics. Didn't it? But Nystolov was a Mars explorer. With the red planet's thin excuse for an atmosphere, solar radiation had to be watched closely. He would not make such a declaration without evidence.

Williams walked over to Nystolov's station and looked at the numbers. Illumination was up, and the radiation graph spiked heavily on gamma counts. "That sensor cannot be functioning," Williams said. "Switch to another unit."

"I already have. All read same."

Williams switched them over himself, checking each one. Then he bent over a different console and checked them all again. That sinking feeling came over him again.

"You can't divorce heat from radiation," he argued. "It isn't possible." He tried to prove it, but the outcome never changed. It was while doing that, switching between the *Icarus*'s various sensing devices, that he caught the first telltale signs of a new anomaly. A small mass, almost in line between the *Icarus* and the Maw. He swept it with active sensors, and was rewarded with a reading and a weak pulse of energy back. Then another. A series of pulses.

"There's something else out there," he announced. And he thought he knew what it was.

Williams had guessed right. That initial, weak pulse was the largest of the three crystalline formations, reacting to his active sweep in the same way the smaller crystal forest on Luna had to their radio comms. It still pulsed steady, low-amplitude transmissions of the same frequency as the first formation. The other two remained dead, which puzzled Williams. He would have guessed that the pulses from one would trigger the others. He mentally filed that away as another in the growing list of mysteries to solve. He stared at the Maw, its physical activity becoming less comprehensible. Mysteries enough to keep him busy for the rest of his life, if it came to that.

"What do you think?" he asked his two companions.

Drake was quick to answer. "I don't like the idea of bringing any of that crystal aboard the *Icarus*."

Of course not. Williams had not forgotten Drake's initial reaction to the crystalline forest on Luna. "Would you like to register any particular objection?" he asked.

Drake stared at the screen, then said simply, "I don't trust it."

"We'll need more than instinct here, Captain Drake. Brygan?"

The bearlike Neo-Soviet took even longer than Paul Drake to answer. "I think I agree with Captain Drake," he said at last. "Still too many unknowns about crystals." Then he shrugged. "And these are moving on path near parallel to Terra. Recovery operations would be easy to accomplish at later date, while access to asteroid is only temporary."

Williams thought this response was out of character for Nystolov. It showed too much caution, not enough curiosity—even if his logic regarding accessibility of the various sites made good sense. Paul Drake did not react at all to the support thrown him by Nystolov. And neither of his companions had made particular note of the thickness of the smaller formation.

Williams now wondered if he might be able to recover large pieces from beneath the ruined landscape on Luna where Nystolov's ship had smashed the first formation. Most of it had shattered from the impact, but the team hadn't excavated more than ten meters before their departure.

He frowned, considering Nystolov's argument. He knew it wouldn't change his mind, but it still deserved consideration. In the end, he decided that the crystalline formations were the one phenomenon that had so far responded to proper scientific investigation. Apply test, recover consistent data. Some properties eluded him, but enough clues pointed him in the right direction that he was sure to discover their meaning. It was a mystery he stood a good chance of solving.

"I think I will insist on this, Captain Drake. I want to recover a sample while we have the chance." That certainly was true in most respects, but like Brygan Nystolov, Williams didn't have to name all his reasons.

Brygan Nystolov counted it a minor victory that he was included in the EVA party sent out to recover a large portion of the crystalline formation. He'd been sure that Paul Drake would override Williams's consent, especially when he learned that Drake himself would lead the team. It was only after the captain had Brygan tested on null-gravity maneuvers that he welcomed him to the team.

The null-grav competence came from years of experience in light-gravity operations, owing to the simple fact that Neo-Soviet spacecraft were not equipped with artificial gravity, as were Union vessels. Any spaceflight tended to require a great deal of zero-gravity time, unless they involved the high-velocity accel and decel runs that the Union exploration units seemed to enjoy so much.

Nystolov still had a hard time adjusting to the strange spacescape. Hardly any stars, though here in space one could make out more of the nontwinkling lights reflecting off the planets of the Maelstrom. And from inside the Styx Nebula, he saw its icy blue field spread over a large portion of the Terra-side heavens like some frozen cosmic storm waiting to be thawed and unleashed on the unsuspecting planets.

The space-walking crew swam out on long tethers that connected to the *Icarus*. The ship had moved in above the larger crystalline formation, matching its plane and helping to shield the walkers from the still-high radiation count. They moved about on tiny jets of air, then fastened on to the crystalline latticework and clambered to positions to begin cutting and hammering away.

Williams had wanted them to cut into the smallest of the three formations. Nystolov had calmly argued for the largest one, which was already pulsing out a signal. His reasons were easily put forward. The smallest formation was the only one Williams might hope eventually to capture and take back to Luna intact—though Nystolov hoped that did not happen. Also, by working on the active formation, they could study the effect of physical damage on the signal degradation, if any.

Williams had liked that idea, always one to go for maximum effect from minimal testing. It had appealed to Drake as well, though Nystolov guessed that had more to do with the man's discomfort over an active formation than a conscious decision.

Brygan Nystolov had held back from the expedition leaders his true reason for wanting to destroy the larger formation. The fact that he had an idea what these crystalline formations were.

The final clue had been seeing the three crystalline formations traveling along parallel tracks in what could only be termed a triangular configuration. No relative rotation between them. Silent, as no doubt the crystal forest on Luna had been before he smashed it. And then that weak pulse which started in a formation whenever subject to energy patterns that suggested a strong power source or modulated communications. It all spoke of a designed purpose.

It spoke of intelligence.

And that worried him.

"This is Captain Drake," he heard over the comms. "All units report in their progress." Drake's voice came in tinny and distant through the transmission. Almost like a distant echo came Williams reporting a surge in the formation's pulse.

Drake came on again. "You still with us, Nystolov?"

"At work, Captain Drake." And then some. Whenever possible, Brygan reached into the deep latticework and smashed as much crystal as he could. The shards spilling out around his position might look a bit odd next to the more precise work of the Union force, but then the Union judged the Neo-Soviets crude by their standards anyway. It was a risk worth taking.

He wanted that transmission stopped.

He knew Randall Williams would not spot the danger. Partly he could take credit for that. By trying to avoid the suspicion that he had any paramilitary background, he had continually tried to divert the major from the military implications of their investigations. Besides that he was sure Williams was being driven to distraction by the bizarre nature of the Maelstrom, which bothered even Brygan. Faced with a seemingly impossible phenomenon, Williams buried himself in the details of observation and experimentation.

These formations screamed of military function. Brygan knew Williams would ignore that in his pursuit of the scientific method. Drake, being a military man, might have seen it, if only he'd had *more* scientific curiosity. Again, it was a matter of being too focused on one side of the equation.

And now Brygan Nystolov was trapped in his own lie. If he tried to draw attention to military matters, he risked discovery. He didn't like withholding his suspicions, but he had to keep his secret if he wanted to maintain his cover story. So far the Union had accepted him, and had accepted him with full status as a staff member.

He didn't know if he owed them anything, if keeping silent was justified. If they hadn't scavenged the data from Sputnik-23, they wouldn't even be in this area of space. But then, he wouldn't either, gathering information he could share with the Neo-Soviet High Command. And that was his ultimate purpose here, wasn't it?

He'd never forgotten the day General Leonov *interviewed* the Mental, but his indignation had taken a backseat to the growing crisis of Terra's induction to the Maelstrom. Now he had to ask himself just how deep did those feelings of outrage run? Deep enough to question his purpose with Union forces, that much was certain.

While pulling himself out of a hole he had carved, Brygan suddenly noticed flaws in his tether in a number of places. A strange half-melted look. He tested the strength and found it adequate, but he still wasn't satisfied. He tried rubbing the spots on the edge of some nearby crystals, but they didn't cut.

He held the tether, thinking. It looked as though something had cut or nicked it. It was possible he just hadn't noticed it till now, but it was second nature for him to inspect his equipment. He looked at his tether again and found a new weakened spot where he had rested it against the edge without rubbing.

A cold sweat gripped Brygan. He found a fresh stretch and held it unmoving against an edge, double-checking the process. After thirty seconds he found it eaten half through. Now he checked his space suit, what he could see of it. Fortunately, they'd let him bring his own from the *Kolyma,* and by removing some insulation and reworking the air recyclers he had better range of motion than anyone in the average Union suit. Now he found several half-melted spots creasing his knees and shins, across his waist and chest, and over his arms. He had sealed chambers protecting a loss of atmosphere from a limb, but if his torso had lost pressure he would have died a quick and silent death.

Silent!

"All units report in *saechas*—at once!" he ordered, bypassing Paul Drake as he rushed to avert a possible catastrophe.

Whether from the urgency in his own voice, or their conditioning to respond, the Union force checked in by numbers. Three and Eight dropped from the rolls.

"Nystolov! What are you playing at?" Drake sounded distressed, though there was no way of saying whether because of Brygan's assumption of a command role or his men's following it.

"Three and Eight?" Brygan called. Silence. "You've lost two men, Captain. Everyone get away from the crystals. *Saechas!* Now!" He positioned himself on the flat facets of a large crystal growth, angling around to leap back for the *Icarus.*

"I'm loose! Help, Captain Drake!"

Finding the flailing man was not difficult. He tumbled around in a bizarre, twisting motion over the formation, venting a mist of crystals into space, the mist coming either from his suit or the container he used to power his movements. The man could still talk—and so still breathe—but the fact that he couldn't move told Brygan that the crystals had cut into his propulsion system. Several of his comrades leapt out for him, trying to catch him before he was lost beyond the range of their tethers.

Brygan leapt as well. That the man was Union military did not matter. His life had been devoted to scouting out dangers such as these, and in a manner timely enough to prevent losses. But he was used to having some advance time to check out an area, not working in the midst of others. He should have broadcast a warning before examining his own suit.

The man continued to tumble and scream for help. The transmission did not rob him of his panic, and light washed over the white suit as he slipped out of the *Icarus*'s shadow. Brygan was farther away and watched as first one man, then another was pulled up short by their tethers.

Drake cursed, and Brygan slapped his disconnect as he reached the end of his tether and flew free into space. He didn't bother to calculate his own chances. He'd damn himself before allowing another man to lose his life when it might have been prevented.

Jetting forward on small bursts from his suit, Brygan reached the flailing man, who now drifted dead in space—his propulsion reserve spent. Brygan grabbed him and hauled him around to look into his face. The man was alive and still jabbering in panic, though he calmed at another's touch and fell into a heavy-breathing silence when he was finally able to look at the reflective bowl of Brygan's helmet. Brygan grabbed the man's cut tether, and using longer bursts from his system, arrested their flight and moved them slowly back into the *Icarus*'s shadow.

Drake remained out at the very end of his own tether, holding position with his thrusters. He grabbed both men and ordered them hauled back to the vessel. In the airlock, the rescued man was quick to peel off his suit and regain the safety of the interior ship. It left Brygan and Drake alone for a moment, staring at each other with helmets removed and held under arms.

"That was fast thinking, Brygan Vassilyevich. Thank you," Drake said, then went to check on his man.

Brygan tried to dismiss the pleasure he felt at Drake's

using the familiar form of address. He was still riding an adrenaline surge and counting himself fortunate to have saved the lives he did. Yet, the respect the captain had shown him felt good. This simple recognition of a job well-done was something he'd never been given back on Mars.

It wasn't until much later that he wondered when exactly he had told anyone his middle name.

21

The plan had been straightforward. Small units of Vanguard and Union infantry pulled the Sleeper's symbiot army in several different directions, leaving it protected by a small number of offense-capable creatures. At a spot where a wide draw split off from the main canyon, the Sleeper would continue to follow the Kotuy River up into Gory Putorana or would detour into the dry canyons to the west. Several Neo-Soviet and Union squads waited there. When the creature turned, the off-side squads would hit it and try to confuse it while the others came in close.

That was the monstrous creature's weakness, small units coming in close. Armored vehicles it could deal with by generating a limited-range electromagnetic pulse. Large battle lines as well, relying on its monstrous size and at times spitting small quantities of plasma. But small numbers of infantry and support specialties, there it tended to rely on its symbiot force. The trick was to see if enough small units could work in close enough to do the damage necessary to kill the thing. Colonel Romilsky thought so, and Sainz had backed her. Even Rebecca Howard had signed on to the plan when she learned that the bulk of the Union force would guard the draw, and so would be the likely diversionary attack force rather than the up-close frontal assault.

No one had asked Sergeant Tousley, but he'd seen worse plans in his time. It wasn't complicated or so rigid that the smallest deviation would ruin it. It relied more on small units thinking on their feet and working together. Zyborgs and Cyclops were brought in as the hardest-hitting units the Neo-Soviets could field. The Union would try to work Draco launchers in close and Ares assault suits that could turn on a temporary field to shield themselves from the Sleeper's EMP defense. It should have worked fairly well.

Should was the operative word.

"It's turning!" Kelly Fitzpatrick called out, five seconds ahead of Colonel Sainz transmitting the same words from the top of some nearby cliffs, where the joint command units had taken post.

The Sleeper swung its cobra-hooded head around on its long, thick neck, hunching back and then thrusting its head into the draw so that the neck stretched to its greatest length. It let out the tortured scream that now gave Tousley nightmares—a long, shrill screech accompanied by a crackling sound of the thing's fangs rasping together. It was only here, staring down the Sleeper's throat, that Tousley finally found out where the weird crackling noise came from.

"Okay, we're live," he called out to his abbreviated

squad, chambering a grenade into the lower launcher of his Bulldog assault weapon. He intended to open with a bang once he was forced to fire.

"Kelly and Jim, take flank and knock down anything smaller than an APC that looks our direction. Nash, you and Johnson hold those Dracos as long as possible. Move out!"

His squad broke from cover just ahead of a Vanguard unit escorting one of the massively cyborged mutants known as Zyborgs. Several other Union squads moved in carefully from the other side of the draw, and more from deeper back. Tom threw his opposite number in the Vanguard unit a sketchy salute. The bow he got in return was just as lacking in sincerity. Tousley's fingers tightened on the trigger of his Bulldog. Given the choice, he might have flipped a coin over where he'd donate his first grenade.

Already the chattering reports of distant rifle fire echoed up the draw as what had been the primary assault force tried to play the part of a diversion. A single Draco missile arced up and impacted the side of the Sleeper's head, gouging into the ridged chitin that spread protectively to either side. A gray-green fluid seeped out to wash over its neck, and the alien shrieked its fury. It craned its long neck back around far enough to disgorge plasma at the offender. With its attention diverted, a pair of Ares assault suits ducked out from around one corner to lock on with a Harbinger rail gun and a Lucifer plasma cannon. One hammered explosive ingots into the Sleeper's carapace, cracking the thick chitin and drawing out a minor trickle of the translucent gobbets. The plasma ball tracked quickly down the magnetic chute but drifted wide. It exploded to one side, ripping free several of the pincer-legs and flash-burning the Sleeper's side.

The alien shrieked again, this time with a touch of what

Tousley hoped was pain, and rounded back against the draw defenders. The Ares suits pulled back to avoid any EM pulse from the Sleeper.

Concentrating on working his squad in close and watching for threats as Kelly and PFC Nicholas put down an ocher-hued Spitter at distance, Tousley had covered half the distance to the advancing alien when he noticed the lack of weapons fire echoing into the draw. Already the fire from Union forces this side of the Sleeper drowned out the supposed hard-punch diversion. A dome-bodied carapace shuffled out from behind some boulders, and Tousley stopped it cold with an M-81 twenty-millimeter grenade directly into one side. A Feeder swooped down, and Tousley wrote off the dome as finished now that the scavenger was arriving. He lagged back, trying to give the diverting force time enough to engage on the Sleeper's rear quarter, calling to his squad to pace themselves. Kelly was already too far out in front, leading Nash and Danielle Johnson on a dash to the Sleeper's side.

"Bravo forces, take care. We are having trouble coordinating your diversion," said Major Howard.

Tousley didn't get it. What trouble? The Neo-Soviets had several packs of Rad Troopers and a trio of Cyclops on the other side, not to mention a pair of Zyborgs and who knew how many Vanguard units supporting Typhoon missile platforms. They attack, the Sleeper is hurt, and the forces inside the draw move in for the big knockout. He heard the long, deep staccato chop of Vanguard Kalashnikovs now, but not so many as he'd have liked. Mostly Union weapons.

He increased his speed, grabbing Nicholas away from putting the final few rounds into a struggling spear-shaped flier. They were all approaching at an oblique angle to the Sleeper's head. It shrieked, twisting around to search out the larger threats. The creature's immense armored tail rose over its back, then smashed down hard. The ground trembled and Jim stumbled to his knees. Tousley left him to catch up. Kelly, Danielle, and Nash were too far in front of the main advance, especially considering the strange signals from 'Becca. He had a feeling they would need him up there.

The distinctive howl of a Wendigo's antigrav generator running full out challenged the Sleeper's intermittent shrieking. Tousley saw the armored tank speed in, flanked by Aztecs. He hadn't heard that order passed.

"Major Howard, we have an armored assault coming in. Should we clear?"

No answer. Had something happened to the command post? Lieutenant Landvoy would be senior officer on location until one of the column captains made contact. A chancy decision to mount an armored assault. One electromagnetic pulse from the Sleeper and those vehicles would be so much dead metal.

Kelly, Johnson, and Nash were at the creature's side now, dwarfed by its chitin-covered legs that tore at the ground to heave the monstrous bulk along. The bulk of the Vanguard had arrived as well, though the mutant handler and Zyborg lagged considerably.

Tousley tried again. "Major Howard, respond please!"

The antipersonnel round actually came from the flank, catching Tousley high in the left chest. It spun him to the ground and out of the path of another burst that cut the air over him with the whistle of hypersonic slugs. The Zyborg that had lagged behind its Vanguard escort spun about on augmented legs, tracking along to fire on Jim Nicholas. Jim took a full burst from hip to shoulder, throwing him back several meters.

Barely able to breathe, face against the cold dirt floor of the draw, Tousley suddenly knew what "trouble" the Union was facing.

Betrayal!

The Fifty-sixth Striker's Class F Cyclops mutants should have spearheaded the diversion after the Sleeper turned up the draw. Romilsky's orders were sent down at the same time as those of Colonel Sainz, though she noticed that confirmation of her order came back late. Her forces moved forward behind those of the Union, late. And the Vanguard engaged first without waiting for the suddenly lethargic mutants.

Too late.

Romilsky gave the colonel credit; he did try to hide his suspicions and growing anger. His Major Howard did not, though she seemed unable to decide between open hostility at the Neo-Soviets or wounded faith in her commanding officer. Romilsky concentrated instead on the battle raging below the bluff onto which her Zephyr command crawler had lifted them, trying to divine the reason behind her Striker's hesitancy to commit.

"Gregor—" she began.

"I am on it, Comrade Colonel." The lieutenant sprinted for the Zephyr, the thruster-modified command crawler they'd landed not twenty meters back. It was faster than passing communications through the sergeant stationed within.

"There has to be a reason for their delay," she said when Sainz rounded on her a few seconds later. They stood watching their carefully constructed battle plan fall to pieces because of the Neo-Soviets' lack of effort. It didn't matter that the Sleeper had chosen the draw. Her plans had taken that into account early on.

"Colonel Romilsky, we have a situation among the mutant handlers. You had better get in here." Gregor's transmission whispered in her ear with only the slightest burst of static. From the reactions of the Union officers and their bodyguard, he had sent it on a common frequency. "Colonel Sainz, I have a relay from your Station Freedom as well. Recommend you take it local, unless you'd like to give me your safe frequencies."

"Keep on things, Major," Sainz told his exec without a second thought. Again Romilsky wondered at such trust in a subordinate as she and Sainz stepped up into the Zephyr and the door rolled shut behind them.

Gregor Detchelov welcomed them into the crawler with a silenced Ledzya submachine gun. With one hand he flipped a row of toggles, shutting down power to the communications board. Now Major Howard was cut off from the ground forces as well. Romilsky's Sergeant Treyk lay on the floor behind the traitorous Gregor, thrown half into the Zephyr's forward compartment, his blood spreading over the floor.

"I *am* sorry, Comrade Colonel," Gregor said. "But I'm afraid I cannot allow you to endanger that creation out there. It holds too many secrets."

A cold flush gripped her flesh. "Detchelov, you have no idea what you are interfering with. Put that weapon away, and at least your family will not suffer for your treason."

Sainz was slightly faster putting it all together. "Like hell he will, Katya. He engineered your problems below, too." Then he shook his head in remorse, and said in English, "He'll play this through to the end."

Of course Gregor had set it up! Katya Romilsky wanted

to scream her rage. It was the mutants who were slowing things down and threatening the assault plans. Gregor had gotten to their handlers somehow. She had thought him more the *dagger in the night* kind of worry, not the orchestrator of such an elaborate charade as this. She had underestimated the depth of his resolve to preserve the Sleeper.

"I'll stamp your family with your betrayal for generations, Gregor Antoly Detchelov. No easy death for them, I promise you." She took a half step forward. "Give me that weapon and free up that comm board."

In the forward compartment, something moved!

"Collusion with the enemy. Failure to place concerns of the empire ahead of personal concerns. *Nyet*, Katya Olia, I am not the traitor here. Not even the Mental's testimony could have saved you anyway. I am merely hastening the process of your fall."

"Wait!" Romilsky damned Gregor for even mentioning a Mental in front of Sainz. She wanted to leap forward and rip Gregor's throat out with her own hands, but instead stalled for time. She couldn't be sure of what she'd seen. Except for the murdered sergeant, no one else should have been aboard the Zephyr today. It was a chance, though, and she grasped for anything that might draw his interest.

"Don't you even want to know how Colonel Sainz and I came to conspire together?" *Conspiracy*, the key word in most Neo-Soviet minds when it came to any talk with the enemy.

Most minds but Gregor Detchelov's. "Not really. I will make up my own story as I need it. *Dos vedanya*, Katya Romilsky."

The paired shots echoed loudly in the tight confines of the Zephyr. Romilsky jerked with each shot, thinking herself dead, and then remembered that Gregor's weapon had been silenced.

Gregor slumped to the floor, showing the two red wounds blown into his back. From behind him, Romilsky watched in awe mixed with shock as the Mental staggered forward under the weight of a heavy Nagant sidearm. "*Strasvicha, Tovarish* Katya Olia." His voice was reedy and laced with pain, as if it had cost almost as much to pull the trigger as it did to be on the other end.

"*Strasvicha, Tovarish.*" Romilsky stepped forward and gently removed the weapon from his frail hands. He winced and started, then clutched that hand to his side. She glanced toward Sainz, but then couldn't help reminding the Mental, "I ordered you to remain with the *Leonid.*"

"I had a feeling I would be needed." He glanced wearily at Sainz. "*Strasvi,* Colonel Sainz." And then the Mental fainted.

"*Strasvicha,*" Sainz returned to the unconscious man with due formality, then studied Romilsky for a bit. "Is this someone I want to know?" he asked.

A question that could be read many ways. So Raymond Sainz had not yet decided to throw away their truce. "It is not someone you are allowed to know," she said carefully.

Sainz nodded, and bent to the comm panel. "Then since it is only you and I in here, help me get this thing turned on. We have to pull out what's left of our troops before this defeat turns to complete disaster."

Tousley rose unsteadily to his hands and knees, feeling as if he'd been hit by one of the fast-moving Aztecs going full bore. His chest hurt, and that was good. Pain told him he was alive, and the dull aching that spread over his chest meant the flak vest had held up. Not that he could count on such good fortune if the Zyborg turned back against him, though it had other problems. The Wendigo clipped it with a high-explosive rail gun ingot, killing its handler and shredding one side of the large mutant. The Aztec SPEARs finished the job. The cycles broke off at hard angles, leaving the Wendigo to fight a slow turn away from the Sleeper.

Not soon enough. The monstrous, shovel-shaped head fell hard, caving down on the Wendigo and driving it into the rocky terrain. The field collapsed and the overload blew the flywheel power generators, and then the Wendigo disintegrated in a burst of released lightning.

The shock wave threw Tousley five meters to his side, new pain blossoming across his already-bruised chest. He rolled to a stop and again rose to unsteady feet. Kelly was halfway up the Sleeper's back, riding one of those ridges that could separate as an armored tentacle, sighting in on the creature's head. Nash let fly from below, his first Draco round missing in his haste. Danielle, made of sterner stuff, was clambering up after Kelly Fitzpatrick. The Neo-Soviet Vanguard milled about near the sharp-spike legs of the Sleeper, distracted by what was happening at their rear. Three other Union squads that Tousley could see were also staggering to a confused halt.

He waved his rifle at the Vanguard, then pointed at Kelly and Danielle. "Get up there and help them, damn you!" He staggered into a jog, still shaken by the sudden treachery but trying to catch up with his people.

The Vanguard didn't budge. They pumped grenade after grenade from their launchers at the Sleeper's head. Most connected, though the alien colossus simply shrugged off the damage as it crashed its head down against the Wendigo again for good measure. Tousley pumped a grenade directly into its open maw as it rose up again. Then Kelly cut loose on full automatic from the Sleeper's back, and Danielle launched a Draco missile at a joint in the chitinous plates protecting the neck.

Blue-tinged lightning crackled over the Sleeper's back in a display that made the exploding Wendigo look like child's play. The lightning showered down from the crown of bloated pustules and tentacles that waved atop the Sleeper's head, arcing and dancing over the carapace. Kelly shook as it caught her across the chest, spitting through her armor and cooking off some of her ammo. The Bulldog she carried blew out the breech and clip, taking her hands. Two spare clips shredded the front of her fatigues. Lower down, Danielle ceased to exist as at least one Draco round she carried detonated. On the ground one Vanguard had stood between two of the Sleeper's legs and as lightning crackled there, he also fell under the massive damage that erupted over his chest. His fellows left him there, retreating with PFC Nash in their midst.

Tousley slowed to a walk as he watched Kelly's body tumble down the mottled carapace. It bounced off the jointed leg below and rolled off to the side for several meters. The Vanguard retreated along his path of advance, keeping an eye on the monstrous head that swung about in search of greater threats. The Aztecs continued to fly around with reckless abandon, drawing the creature's attention for the time being. It gave them all a chance to escape. Tousley continued to walk forward.

"You come," a Vanguard sergeant said as the Neo-Soviet squad met him in the Sleeper's shadow. "Colonel Romilsky out. We retreat now." He held up a hand to grab Tousley by the arm.

Tousley shook him off rudely, then jabbed the lethal end

of his Bulldog into the stomach of the Vanguard sergeant. His finger was a hairbreadth from pulling the trigger.

"We go nowhere with you," he said coldly, eyes never breaking from the Vanguard's. "Nash, you're with me."

Then he stepped away and turned his back on the Vanguard, not giving a damn just then whether the man shot him in the back or not. He waited for that bullet with every step, but did not once look back or at the Sleeper. They didn't matter to him. He stooped over Kelly and picked up her lifeless body, slinging it over his shoulder.

He began the slow walk from the field with Nash his only shield against the appearance of any symbiot creatures. "We don't leave our people behind," he whispered to himself.

22

An air of nervous excitement gripped the bridge of the *Icarus* as the four men and two women stared fixated at the main screen. Computers held the Union vessel at a constant position relative to the asteroid, constantly engaging the drives and firing attitude thrusters to follow the large mass as it tumbled on three axes. The hum of electronics was the loudest noise except for one female corporal's heavy breathing and the methodical rapping of Captain Drake's knuckles against the armrest of his chair.

Randall Williams preferred not to think about the extra five hours the latest high-velocity burn had taken, as if the Maelstrom was trying to make up for its earlier gift on the approach to the gas giant. At the midway point, Darcie Boucher had noted a slight deviation in their projected time, and halfway through the decel burn Williams confirmed that the asteroid was not approaching as fast as it should given their speed. So began the process of decels and coasting, coming up on the asteroid much more slowly than initial calculations suggested.

Another affront to Williams's scientific demeanor, handled with frustrated calm this time as he focused instead on the approaching target. Though the forward science station had better equipment, he had chosen to watch the final approach from the bridge. Recorders were running, the data would be properly analyzed over weeks or months, possibly even years. This was a time to savor, the pinnacle of achievement dreamed of by any space-exploration specialist.

The proof of extraterrestrial life.

The asteroid might have qualified as a small moon had it been in orbit around any major planet. A great, dull brown-black rock drifting through space, a large portion of one side was covered with metal-faced buildings. Square and rectangular shapes seemed to be the basic building blocks, but arches were also common, with a heavy reliance on triangular supports. The metal had been treated to soft tints of blues and greens and pale yellows. Initial sampling via laser spectrometry indicated alloys unknown to mankind and the presence of a honeycomb structure in the walls. It took some searching to discover any heavy damage to the compound from an ages-old meteor strike. A tight video still of the broken wall showed a triangular honeycombing like small geodesic domes built into the wall.

Williams thought he should say something. Anything. Everyone seemed to expect it. Certainly the moment demanded it, but he could do nothing but stare in fascination.

He cupped his chin in his right hand, stroking his pointed sideburns. Finally, he said, "Now we know."

It was no great statement—no "one giant leap for mankind"—but it satisfied his scientific mind. No need for conjecture or speculation. The answer stared them boldly in the face. Mankind was not alone in the existence of sentient life.

Brygan Nystolov cleared his throat, the bearlike rumble demanding attention now that Williams had finally broken the silence. "Have you noticed," he asked, "there is no evidence of a dome, and all buildings are open to space?"

No, Williams hadn't noticed. Looking now, he saw it was true. Triangular windows and arched doorways seemed to beckon. "They must have generated an atmosphere." Though even the Union could not have done so under the minimal gravity the asteroid possessed. "Or didn't need one." The Maelstrom had certainly taught him never to take anything for granted, and it was a mind-set Williams hoped to hold on to in his studies. He filed away the questions at the top of the list, to be answered soonest.

"No evidence of a power source down there," Drake said, coming out of his own reverie. "No machinery even, at least out in the open. The abundance of metal in the construction could be blocking anything deeper into the asteroid." The dark-skinned man swung around to face Williams. "I'd like your science staff to verify that as much as possible, before I allow the *Icarus* in any closer or men on the surface."

When Williams started, shocked that he would not have to argue for the time to explore, the Marine grinned tightly. "I am not even going to argue that point. Go down there and set foot on it, Major. Make sure that it is real. But we will hold to our timetable—General Hayes was most adamant about that. This is an opening survey, not a full exploration party."

If ever there was a time when military protocol should be suspended! But Williams knew he could push Drake only so far before safety of the vessel and crew overrode everything else. Two men had already been lost. He didn't want to risk more lives either. "I'll want two-man search teams, we'll cover more ground that way. *Icarus* will be set down for easier access rather than waste time shuttling everyone down."

Drake frowned at that last, then nodded reluctantly. His brown eyes flickered toward Nystolov. "Anything else?"

"Brygan comes with me. I'll be responsible, but I want him down there."

The captain nodded to the Neo-Soviet rather than Williams. "Good choice. I'll trust Comrade Nystolov to watch out for you then."

The major bit back a reply that he could very well take care of himself, that this kind of work had consumed his earlier military career. But he had what he wanted from Drake, so arguing would accomplish nothing. Besides, clearly the military man was voicing his respect for the Neo-Soviet scout's abilities.

And that could not hurt anyone's agenda.

Brygan Vassilyevich Nystolov had hoped that once again walking the unknown might bring a joy back that he hadn't felt in some time. It was the purpose he had chosen for himself on Mars, setting his skills and natural talents against the red planet. The asteroid looked and felt nothing like Mars, but it offered its own challenges, protected its own secrets, and Brygan intended to set himself against them.

The gliding step he had perfected on Mars worked here, too, carrying him over large expanses with little effort. Inside buildings, he literally flew down corridors and dropped through shafts that might once have housed elevators or lifts. Major Williams could not have matched him if Brygan had intended to run off alone, though with admirable effort he did manage to keep up with Brygan's average pace.

"Magnificent," Williams said as they exited a corridor for another of what he had named a *grand hall.* Long and wide, with a vaulted ceiling, the corridor spilled into the room after a sharp dogleg. Three exits were set at the far end, beneath a balcony overhang. "Simplistic design, but almost regal in its execution."

Execution was just what Brygan had considered as well, though with a different meaning. This was a murderous trap, set by a military mind. Though not a true military man himself, he was comfortable enough with the concepts to recognize them. He looked back toward the corridor as the pair of them drifted forward. A sharp turn to prevent easy massing, and then a long run or glide across an empty expanse. Put a demisquad of four Vanguard infantry armed with Kalashnikovs up in that balcony, and they could easily slaughter or hold back ten times their own number. Maybe more.

This was the third such stretch they had found, which could mean they were approaching something of importance. Or something that used to be of importance, anyway. So far they'd found not a single clue about the former inhabitants. No tool or item of clothing. No writing—not even graffiti. No evidence of hard technology at all, though the excavation and metal fabrication must have required it. Williams was perplexed by the pristine condition, though no less fascinated for the discovery. He worked off the architecture alone, trying to divine anything at all about the aliens' physiology or culture. Brygan watched for evidence as to why they had abandoned the asteroid base.

"What you truly hope to find here, Major?" Brygan asked after they leapt up to check the balcony, which was empty. "Is not enough, the buildings above?" He looked over. Both men had raised the reflective shielding on their helmet bowls. Williams's brown eyes were still glowing with his enthusiasm.

"More than enough," the other man said, his voice hushed through the transmission. "But we have a few hours left on Drake's timetable, and I want to penetrate as deeply as we can. You know, if this asteroid has been honeycombed, we could be looking at thousands of kilometers of chambers. We'll do little more than scratch the surface this time."

To come back later in force and set up a permanent facility to search out every square centimeter, Brygan did not doubt. He knew it wouldn't matter if he took the same information back to his nation. The Union held a strong edge in space exploration. Always had. They weren't worried over the competition now, and to Brygan's surprise, neither was he. Since joining the *Icarus*'s staff, he had not thought much in terms of Neo-Soviet and Union. Holding back some information had been a result of personal interest rather than national loyalty—treasonous but true. Randall Williams so far had not delved too deeply into the military mind-set, and Brygan couldn't afford for him to. Not if he wanted to remain part of the expedition.

Part of the team.

Brygan stumbled his next gliding step as that thought

surfaced—that at some point he had welcomed being part of a group for perhaps the first time in his life. The Union praised individual achievement, yes, but they also worked together, relying on each other's strengths to balance their own weaknesses. As a nation the Union could still be as overbearing and self-righteous as the empire, but at this level, where Brygan preferred to live, the system worked. And he was adopting it, mostly thanks to the efforts of Randall Williams to make him feel accepted. His deception twinged at the back of his mind, reminding him that Williams accepted the persona Brygan lived, not the scout himself.

"And you, Brygan," Williams asked as the scout recovered his balance, the humor in his voice apparent at the faltered step. "What were you hoping to find?"

"Mars," Nystolov said simply, and refused to elaborate.

But Mars was dead to him now. Died, actually, the day he had stood witness to the struggle between the Mental and General Vladimir Leonov, watching Leonov's oppressive nature overbear the frail Mental. Even if they found a way back, would Brygan return to Mars? Could he? Chances were good that the Neo-Soviet empire would not even let him return *here* if he *did* give them the location of this asteroid. He was a rogue personality, never to be fully trusted with anything approaching delicate work.

Not in the empire.

"Vozle gorashix ogney!"

The old oath, *by the burning light,* slipped out before Brygan could help himself. He had sailed into a corner, kicked off a wall for the usual short dogleg into a hall, and launched himself into the ready arms of a massive alien creature.

Hunched down on lean but well-muscled legs, it still stood as tall as any man and at least three times as broad across the shoulders. A grimace of large fangs smiled at him. One hand rested on the floor, palm up to show a hand that could enfold Brygan's head—helmet and all—and was well armed with large claws. The other hand dug its claws into the side of the corridor, through the metal facing and into rock behind. Brygan counted himself a dead man. No way around it. By instinct he tucked himself into a tight ball and prayed that he might survive the first attack and so then escape.

He bounced into the alien as if he'd struck a wall, then rebounded back the way he'd come, holding his breath and ready for the stab of pain from teeth or claw. He hit the back wall again, and then spun down to the floor before vaulting back into the air.

Brygan opened his eyes, twisting about in the light gravity. The monster remained where it had been, a reddish blue wall of heavy muscle and threatening teeth that nearly blocked the corridor from wall to wall. Brygan caught himself against the ceiling and rebounded carefully back toward the floor. He turned on his magnetic soles, which grabbed the alien alloy as well as they might have man-made steel. He stood there, gazing at death.

The creature would have risen easily to three and a half meters, almost four, if it had stood on its thin legs. By strange comparison, the arms were better than four times as massive and looked long enough to drag the ground even if standing at such a height. Brygan moved in closer to the frozen creature, aware now that the blue tinge to it was a coating of iced flesh. The asteroid's thin atmosphere was one step from what might be called vacuum; this thing was dead.

It still frightened him. It had the look of pure predator, with fangs longer than the full spread of a man's hand and razor-sharp claws to match. A row of razored spines ran from the large horn cresting its skull back down its spine and the stub of a tail it owned. Tiny, wide-set black eyes suggested the creature could not rely too heavily on sight, though Brygan would not have bet his life on it. This was a hunter.

An alien.

"Brygan! Are you all right?"

The insistence of the voice finally broke through the spell, and he realized that Williams had been calling to him for several seconds. Since his involuntary outburst. Randall Williams was trapped several hundred meters back along the corridor by a cave-in. His bulky Union space suit had not been able to squeeze by the small entrance Brygan had made.

"I am fine, Major. A . . ."—he stammered a moment—"a portion of ceiling collapsed." A lead weight sank into his stomach with the lie. It was a poor trade for the comradeship he had been shown, and Randall Williams deserved better. But Brygan would not—could not—discuss such a find without first considering its import.

He had already withheld too many indications of alien intelligence, especially when it hinted at a military threat. Was he about to hand over such a hostile-looking creature? If they began to see aliens as a serious threat, what of the enemies the Union had fought for so many decades? They might look closer at Brygan's own nationality, fueling new doubts in Williams and raising again Drake's original suspicions. They might decide it in everyone's best interests to dissolve the team and confine Brygan to his quarters.

The very thought startled the Neo-Soviet scout.

"Come back, Brygan." The concern in the major's voice bled through the transmission. "We can search a different passage, *da, Tovarish*?"

Brygan shook, confused and upset as much for the other man's concern as the fact that Williams named him a close comrade. He tried to put off the latter to the scientist not knowing Russian well enough to realize the subtle differences in address. A difficulty when he remembered how both Williams and Drake seemed to follow the proper forms just fine.

"A moment, Major Williams." Then he looked past the obstructing creature—a sentry—and into the hall behind. He would need more than a moment, and had to tell Williams something before the scientist tried to claw his way past the obstruction and damaged his suit. "I may have a sample for you." He squeezed by the frozen sentry.

He only had to choose. The grand hall was filled with the monsters. Fourteen, he counted. Not a lot considering the size of the passage, but each one did an awful lot of filling. They were arranged in a semicircle around the largest of the pack, the bull-leader. An incredible creature better than four and a half meters if Brygan could judge from its crouched position, with three-fourths of its body weight concentrated in the upper half. The main horn jutting out between the eyes was broken at the tip, leaving it a serrated hook. It crouched amidst a pile of crushed and splintered bones.

"I found a few bones," he said, expanding the lie and feeling the worse for it. Damn his earlier precautions that now exacted such a price! "I'll gather them." A few of them. He picked three of the less damaged and slipped them into a zippered thigh pocket.

He also decided to take a tissue sample. Maybe he could explain away his reluctance to tell Williams over the radio what he had found. Give the scientist a good sample to study and keep him occupied without ever having to see these ferocious creatures. Standing in that chamber of horrors, it seemed like a good idea.

Removing the military knife from a sheath along his leg, Brygan approached the bull, but then shied away from that fierce visage to a smaller creature off to one side. Perhaps he would come clean with the major. Bare the entire charade in hopes that such a discovery, shared, would be enough to overshadow a deception that had merely been designed for his own protection. Never to harm. At least he should keep it as an option. It was something to consider carefully in the time remaining before their return to Luna.

He hacked down hard against one of the alien's arms, hoping to splinter off a large piece from the frozen flesh. Some of it did chip away as he'd expected, but not much. Then the blade bit deep, and a wisp of steam froze to a tiny crystalline mist and drifted up from the wound. Brygan yanked the knife free, and watched with dawning horror as the creature bled freely for a second until the wound iced over and staunched the flow.

It was still alive!

Blood flow meant a circulation system that had not shut down. It meant a warmth that still burned within the core of the creature, fighting off the encroaching cold. A hibernation of sorts, protecting the creatures for as long as possible. Could it draw its breath slowly from the thin atmosphere of the asteroid? Did it require breath? Brygan backed away, glancing frantically from one frozen statue to another as if they might come alive. The one he'd wounded obliged, shifting in its position. Muscles flexed, whether voluntarily or not, cracking the frozen flesh that encased its body.

That was enough for the scout. He turned and fled, all thoughts of redemption lost in his rush.

He had met the enemy, and he was terrified. And rightfully so.

23

With Luna's fence line smashed and an uncertain number of Neo-Soviet troops massing in Union territory, a large push against Union forces on the moon had been expected for some time. The Union had already lost three atmospheric processors and two bases before any strong reaction could be mustered. Two of their strongest commanders had been lost in battle, undercutting General Hayes's ability to respond. No one doubted that the empire would make one more bold grab. It became a matter of when, and where, not whether.

The diversionary assault against Tycho came while Corporal Phillipe Savoign was running a patrol with PFC Kevin Davidson, the two of them gliding over the lunar plains in a stripped-down Pegasus light-assault antigrav sled. They had volunteered for extra reconnaissance duty, with the understanding that Savoign would be recalled by Brevet-Major Olsen when it came time to task Freedom for operation support on Earth. The battle station had been moved into position, finally, not twelve hours before and reestablished contact with Colonel Sainz and the Seventy-first Assault Group in Siberia. Phillipe did not know much more than that as Sainz requested secure transmission to Earth and, when that was unavailable, prevailed upon the field-promoted major to carry his report straight to Hayes. Whatever had been in that report, and it did include video stills, had shaken Olsen to his core. Hayes had slapped a tight security clearance on the project and kept operators on a need to know basis. It would filter down sooner or later, especially to men like Savoign, who were currently critical to such things as weapons tasking for the battle stations. Savoign was one of those fortunate few who really loved his work.

"Prince Seven, have you estimated force strength of Neo-Sovs yet?"

Phillipe ignored the question that crackled over his headset, intent on raking a line of fire from his Rottweiler heavy-assault weapon over a pair of Vanguard infantry. Three hours of hit-and-run attacks left him in no mood to field repeated requests. The Hum-Vest made it difficult for comms anyway—a convenient excuse.

Not so for Davidson apparently. "TC&D wants our estimate of the attacking strength," he yelled, drifting the Pegasus along a parallel track to the Neo-Soviet rear lines.

"I heard," Savoign said, swinging the Rottweiler around to reach for another target. Missed. The Pegasus had been stripped of its light-missile system for use as a lunar messenger and scout sled. Savoign had welded a simple open bracket onto the crossbar and a post to the base of a

Rott. Insert post through bracket, and he had a bastardized turret weapon, good at least against unarmored targets. He popped the clip and grabbed another from the bag at his feet, thought better of it, and simply settled in for support. "Clear out!" he ordered.

Davidson turned into a hairpin, racing the Pegasus away from the Neo-Soviet return fire. A few bullets spanged off the vehicle. One skinned the air near Savoign's head. He waited for ten seconds after the bullets stopped skipping around them before he slapped off his own Hum-Vest. The experimental powered vest ceased the throbbing hum that gave it its name, and the temporary force field it generated collapsed. "How is she holding up?" he asked.

"We've blown a flywheel generator, but we're good to go still." Davidson turned off his own vest. "My Hum-Vest is heating up pretty bad. I think I'm about to lose the field." He glanced into the back as he swerved around to set up another run. "You want to answer Control?"

"Tell them we've seen no sign of their main force. Still. We'd call if we had, damn it."

"Tycho Control, this is Prince Seven. We have no estimate for you yet beyond original contact." Davidson left off the corporal's qualifier.

"Copy, Prince Seven. Keep us advised."

Savoign stood up, straddling the two passenger seats, and slapped the fresh clip home, chambering the first round. He waited until he saw the first puff of gray soil indicating a Kalashnikov pointed in their direction, and slapped his powered vest alive again. The hum rattled his back teeth and gave him the eerie feeling of a feathered touch crawling all over his skin. But it kept the bullets away for now. Only problem with the units was that they weren't extremely dependable. Still in prototype stage for the Union in general, on the moon such equipment was a bit more commonplace.

"I'm hit!" Davidson yelled only two minutes into the run, giving the stick a slight hitch that gave Savoign a shaking and almost threw him off. Davidson slapped a quick release and threw the smoking vest unit into the empty passenger seat. "Field collapsed. I'll give you another fifteen seconds."

Ducking himself back into the Pegasus carriage, Savoign shook his head. "You get us out of here now! Where are you hit?"

Not waiting to be told twice, Davidson leaned the sled hard over until the gyro deadened the stick and forced him into a slightly milder turn. "My leg. I took a ricochet off the front board." The blood drenched the leg of his gray uniform a dark red-black.

Savoign cut the long strap of Davidson's ruined Hum-Vest, wrapped it about his leg and twisted the loose ends together into a knot. "Use your free hand to hold pressure on this. Not too tight, though." The pair sped away, looping in a very wide arc that would bring them in at the back side of Tycho.

The commlinks built into their helmets crackled to life. "All units, break away. Assault suits and powered armor recover your equipment and rendezvous with Tango carriers two klicks at twenty-five degrees."

Evac of all augmentation suits? Savoign ignored Davidson's pointed look and opened his transmitter. "Tycho, we are en route with wounded. Request repeat."

"We found the main Neo-Soviet force, Prince Seven. They caught the general's support force heading out to our aid, then turned on Tranquillity. They are off the air. This was a diversion. We're going to button up on the defensive and send what we have to the general's aid."

Savoign bit back an outburst. No one had expected an overwhelming attack against Tranquillity Base itself, the center of control on Luna. Hayes maintained a large army there. It would be a suicide run, or near enough. Though with their recent string of successes, General Tamas Yorikev might have decided to make the gamble for a Neo-Soviet-dominated Luna. The corporal glanced over at Davidson, who was looking fairly pale. "We better get you in and looked at."

The PFC shook his head. "Ares first. You'll be needed at Tranquillity."

"The Freedom—"

"You can task it just as easily from Tranquillity if you have to. And they *do* have other weapons specialists on Luna, you know."

The corporal hesitated, his desire to be suited up again and wading in against the enemy warring with the more unique and curious task of helping to program a battle-station assault against ground targets. There was also Davidson to consider, but the kid was strong and had already voiced his vote. Savoign nodded, grabbed a fresh clip, and sidled back around to man the Rottweiler again. "Then you better punch through the Neo-Sov line. It's the only way we'll make the time." He shoved the new clip in, chambered a round.

"The Void take anyone who tries to stop us."

Sergeant Tom Tousley knew that, technically, he had committed a gross act of insubordination. The Union forces were placed on standby duties while Neo-Soviet Vanguard reconned the area. His particular orders were to stand down and wait for further orders. Crawling about in the darkness with what remained of his squad was not a choice he had been given.

The Sleeper had slipped into a dry canyon growing some strange black grasses amid the tumble of rocks and stretches of barren ground. It looked settled in for the evening, though the more dangerous symbiots prowled a wide perimeter. Its Feeders roamed the immediate area as well, bloated and waddling, not many of them airborne now. The few still in the air were flying a straight-line path up onto the nearby slopes of Gory Putorana, except fewer were coming back than went up, and finally they quit flying and grouped about the Sleeper.

Tousley had only seen the Sleeper dormant while it fed, the last time being over the site of the Irynutsk Facility. He wanted to know what had brought it here, to rest. He wanted to know how to kill it. He was tired of running.

Maria Carr guarded his back as the two held the upper slopes above the dormant Sleeper. In case things fell to hell, they guarded the way out. Nash and Private Nicholas formed a guard for CBR specialist Loveday, talked into joining them on this excursion. Well, tricked into it was closer to the truth. Nicholas was in bad shape from blood loss, though like the sergeant his body armor had protected him from the worst of the shots the Zyborg had hit him with. He refused to be left behind, and Tousley needed him. Their three-man team was working in as close as they dared to the symbiot force. Everyone wore night-vision specs, borrowed from one of the Trojan supply carriers, and silenced Pugs to accompany their assault rifles.

Tousley opened a channel. "Baker Team, what have you got?" He kept his voice low, not a whisper, but the next thing to it. The foul, acrid stench rising from the shallow canyon already told him something of what he wanted to know. Caustic, like flame-scorched earth or a diesel fire. He remembered the scent from Irynutsk.

Nash's transmission was breaking apart, but still the sergeant could hear his confidence. "You were right on the money, Sarge. Corporal Loveday is reading all sorts of contamination below. It's glowing off the scale."

"Is there a vector?"

"He says none he can see, and it should be glowing just as hot. It's either a dump or it's piped in." Tousley was betting on the latter. "He wants to work in closer—"

"Negative," Tousley interrupted. "We have half of what we came for. Fall back into position for stage two."

He uprooted some of the black grasses and shoved them into one of his many pockets. He then tapped Brevet-Corporal Carr on the shoulder and motioned upslope and in line with the path the Feeders had taken earlier. It was slow going at first, the way covered by loose rock. Then they hit a well-beaten trail, stamped by the prints of Neo-Soviet combat boots. More than a simple patrol of Vanguard could have made recently.

"Payday. We've got a trail." He came quickly upon two different forks. "An entire system of trails. Baker, when you hit them remember to angle up and to the left. I'll scratch an arrow at each fork I notice."

Midnight slowly crawled by. The sergeant took it as a positive sign that he had yet to be called over the Seventy-first's command freq. Across the canyon and above on a protected bluff, the lights of the encamped Union force could just be made out. Higher up still were the brighter lights of the Neo-Soviet Striker. Word was that Colonel Romilsky had wanted to attack earlier, but that Sainz had vetoed the plan to allow his people a period to recover from what had been a near rout. Tousley didn't buy the breakdown-in-communications act the upper echelon put on for the benefit of those who had found themselves unsupported at ground zero. Though even Major Howard was in on that one, so Tom had no recourse but to let it slide. For now.

He found the small but deadly battlefield higher up, around a ventilation exhaust camouflaged by fake trees and brush. The canyon had a crenellated look, and the small bluff guarded a second draw that ran back the other side. Three Feeders lay in immediate sight. Nash found two more *and* a dead Vanguard infantryman as he and Nicholas approached via a different path with the CBR specialist. They brought Tousley the dead Neo-Soviet's shoulder patches. The name and rank he cared little for, but the unit was not the Fifty-sixth Striker. Tousley couldn't read Russian, but the insignia was clear enough. Where the Fifty-sixth emblem was that of a silver-eyed hawk's head, this one was a shiny black peak.

Chernaya Gora. *Black Mountain.*

They were standing on it.

"Sergeant. Company."

Maria Carr's hissed warning came as a light flickered along the upper slope not fifty meters away, a group of figures sliding over the rise from the other side of the bluff, over the partially hidden draw. Through the night specs, the flash stood out like a white-hot beacon. The sergeant flicked the lenses up onto his forehead, but not before counting eight armed infantry.

"Ground and freeze," the sergeant ordered in a whisper. Five Union forms melted to the ground. He tried to breathe shallowly, the acrid scent natural to the black grass burning his sinuses.

There was a chance that this was an ordinary Vanguard

patrol sent by the Fifty-sixth. If so, the Union patrol could claim a duplication of orders to recon the area and bluff their way back to camp. That thought lasted all of the two seconds it took to complete it. Anyone allowed to patrol this bluff knew of the Black Mountain facility, and certainly was under orders to protect it at all costs. Escaping from this one clean would mean nothing less than the Neo-Soviets passing by and not spotting the Union force. The flash switched off, and Tousley shook his specs back into place. The eight figures were heading straight down into them.

"No such luck," he whispered, barely any breath behind the words. "Silenced Pugs on my order, and not before. Weapons free if they fire anything noisy. By rank take the targets in order. I have one and two." With complete surprise, the Neo-Soviet force would die as silent a death as the Feeders had earlier in the day.

A touch of luck which simply was not with them. Corporal Loveday sneezed, all the more loudly as he had tried to stifle it even to the last possible instant.

Ah, hell. Tousley cut loose with his Pug, the soft zipping noise of the silenced shots tearing through the calm night air and stitching into the forward-most Vanguard. He drew a line at helmet height, heard the cracking noise of bullets passing through either protective gear or skull. Skull, apparently, as one infantryman went down without so much as a gasp.

That was all the luck his squad could muster. Three Vanguard cut loose on full automatic at once. Though they were firing blind, these soldiers were no fools. Each took a safe line of fire and sprayed figure eights that would give maximum effect to their spread. Someone cried out to the sergeant's left—Nicholas or Nash—and the Kalashnikov barrage was answered with silent death and a single Pitbull now chopping away at the enemy. Two more Neo-Soviets fell, and the remaining four fell back at once. Another didn't make it two steps. The sixth fell in the final flurry of traded fire as the last two cleared the bluff and dropped from sight.

"After them?" Carr asked, rolling over to Tousley's side. "Jim took another round in the back of the leg, but he'll live."

The sergeant shook his head. "No. We lost the chance." He slammed a fist into the ground. "Go drag Loveday out of whatever hole he crawled into after that performance and help Nash with Jim. We're out of here."

"The colonel is going to step on us, isn't he?"

Kelly Fitzpatrick's death had dragged him out here and cost him a wounded man, and the sergeant would sleep well enough on that, but it was not the kind of action that endeared one to the chain of command. Tousley's first impulse was to agree with Carr. His second was to put off answering until later. He'd take the fall if there was one to take, that went without saying. But then he held up the shoulder patch of the man Nash had found and walked up hill to compare it to the identical one on each of the fallen Neo-Soviet Vanguard. He ripped a few more from sleeves.

"Maybe not," he finally said. "Just maybe not."

24

The Siberian early morning had a cold bite to it, dusting the ground white and frosting breath. Raymond Sainz had forgone his cold-weather jacket, meeting the predawn cold in regular combat fatigues and his Kevlar vest. His anger would keep him warm. He and Major Howard stood in the neutral ground between their Hades command transport and Romilsky's Zephyr. Sergeant Tousley's people backed the two Union officers as they faced off against Katya Romilsky and a full Vanguard squad. The dawn still hours away, the floodlights of both vehicles provided light.

Sainz rarely relied on his size for intimidation, but today would take every advantage he could get. He towered over Romilsky. She gave back a strong presence thanks to the broad, armored shoulders and torso of her officer's trench, though clearly Sainz's arrival ready for a fight had startled her for an instant. The Union commander had strapped on two Pug autopistols, one at his left shoulder and another riding his right hip, reversed for a cross-body draw. A pair of grenades dangled from the vest's front. The Vanguard had shifted into ready stances, and the tension was palpable as the two leaders squared off.

The Fifty-sixth's commander refused to look up at Sainz, and instead her icy gaze stared past him to bore into the hard-set face of Sergeant Tousley. "I find it insulting that you brought this man as your guard, *Colonel.*" No pretense of civility, snapping out her fury in Russian with the most basic form of address possible. "You know what he is responsible for."

And Romilsky was no doubt wondering exactly how much they knew. Classic Neo-Soviet confrontation would be to overtrump her right away, parading his knowledge of Chernaya Gora and escalating the stakes. He had no intention of playing the game her way. "Your *request* for a meeting interrupted our debrief, but I know the important details, yes." He spoke English, letting his displeasure show in his own lack of courtesy.

It also left vague whatever knowledge was in his possession, and Romilsky's eyes showed a flash of feral cunning before she managed to hide it. She ran a hand back through her short auburn hair in a delaying gesture, unconsciously tracing the silver streak in it. "Firing under a flag of truce is a crime the Union recognizes. You will turn him over to me."

He had expected that. The Neo-Soviets had always been good at playing the hypocrite. "No," he said simply.

Anger flared in Romilsky's face at the abrupt dismissal. Her voice was tight with barely controlled rage. "I want that man!" she demanded, stepping to one side and stabbing a finger at the sergeant.

Matching her step, Sainz blocked her from even being able to see Tousley. His tone was even and deadly calm. "You'll have to go through me to get him." He didn't look back at the sergeant. Tousley had been instructed on the role he would play—silent and confident of the Union's superiority, not much of a stretch for him. But if he showed one trace of fear or doubt in his commander, Colonel Sainz's play would be undermined. The Seventy-first's CO gambled on Tousley setting aside his prejudice for loyalty to the Union.

So far, by Romilsky's actions, Sainz had figured correctly. "This is your Union justice?" she asked. "Under a flag of truce your soldiers are allowed to make unsanctioned patrols and murder allies? *Temporary* allies." Her stressing of the informal arrangement made the qualifier an obvious threat.

Rebecca Howard turned back to the squad, leaving Sainz to remain in constant eye contact. "How about it, Tom? Do you have a defense?"

One he had already been coached on. "They shot first," he lied, a trace of smugness to his voice.

Katya Romilsky was at a loss for words for all of three seconds. Then, "That is a cold-blooded lie," she accused Tousley in English. "They ambushed a patrol of Neo-Soviet Vanguard without provocation."

It was the opening Raymond Sainz had been angling for. "Define *provocation,* Katya Olia," he said calmly, slipping into Russian for the benefit of her Vanguard. This was a confrontation he wanted passing around through the Neo-Soviet ranks. "I'd be interested in seeing if these fit under your definition." He produced the Black Mountain uniform insignia Tousley had brought back to him. A few straws of the black, bladed grass that grew on the contaminated slopes were twisted into the ripped cloth as well.

Instantly forgotten was Sergeant Tousley. The late display caught Romilsky with her flank exposed, and now Raymond Sainz intended to bury his teeth into her. "Vanguard guarding a facility that isn't supposed to exist? Bearing its insignia?" He let his disgust show. "All a hoax, meant to trap the Union. To discredit the Mexican Contribution Forces. Isn't that what you maintained? Not a bad lie, for all the fact that it was a lie. The posturing and petty games. You *knew* that monster would turn up the draw! You've known from the start where it was headed, and you put us right in its path. What do you call that, Katya?"

The Neo-Soviet colonel had seemed to recoil into herself. Now she sprang back with virile intensity. "Duty!" she nearly yelled. "Everything is about duty to the empire—duty above all! Your precious belief in honor on the field was a key to the Seventy-first. It would have destroyed you in the end. You are alive now only because I found it in the better interests of my nation to kill that monster out there rather than follow through on my original plans."

Sainz tried not to show that she had struck a nerve. "And the Neo-Soviet assaults on our moonbases? Tycho was heavily damaged and critical areas of Tranquillity are in Neo-Soviet control. A strong coincidence that just as we are planning a strike with Freedom against the Sleeper, your countrymen interrupt that operation. Do you want the creature dead or not? What game are we playing now, Katya Olia Romilsky?"

Her eyes narrowed as she digested the information given her. "Believe what you want, Colonel Sainz. I have not been in contact with the High Command, and I think you know this."

Her reaction suggested that she had not known of the moonbase assaults. But then she might not have been told. The question was whether she had passed the information to her superiors. Sainz didn't think so, but then she had surprised him too many times already. A shriek echoing up from the shallow canyon below shivered through all of them, and reminded all of the main problem. "We needed those bases to task Freedom's missiles for any accuracy," he said, then couldn't help slipping in his own oblique threat. "We would have to saturate this area now to hope for any effect."

That stiffened her spine. "Any attack that results in damage to the Fifty-sixth Striker or Chernaya Gora would be construed as a formal act of aggression and break our truce." The chill in her voice left no room for debate. "I would see both our commands smashed before allowing Chernaya Gora to be destroyed."

"Your Sleeper is stirring down below. Without the both of us, it would smash your weapons facility regardless and then continue on. Yslad Power Facility? The Tolsky spent-fuel dump? That heads it straight into the city of Igarka, doesn't it, Colonel? Perhaps then it turns toward Noril'sk." He left his ultimate point unspoken. That she couldn't be certain who else could be moved into position to stop the creature.

She obviously reached that conclusion on her own. The Union colonel could almost read her thoughts. That if Sainz were making a point of it, then he had not discarded the possibility of keeping to the truce and his bargain. Her frigid blue eyes narrowed to study both him and Rebecca Howard.

When she spoke, it was with a recaptured degree of control and calm. "What are your intentions?"

Howard fielded the question. "Being back in touch through Station Freedom is helpful," she said, reminding Romilsky that the Seventy-first *could* defer to a higher authority. "Union Command has *recommended* that the assault group break off and try to make a rendezvous for extraction, though they always leave such decision to the on-site commander." She shrugged with forced casualness. "My recommendation is to leave this fight in Neo-Soviet hands."

Sainz nodded. "I am tempted to leave you to your problems."

Romilsky's frustration could not be kept from her face. If the Seventy-first chose to pull back, she would be caught between engaging them or the Sleeper. In the former case, she might take the enemy with her but was guaranteed to lose Chernaya Gora. The latter would risk an empty death, but at least the possibility of saving the facility was there. "I spared your life and saved your command, Sainz," she said in a calm whisper. "You owe me."

Definitely *not* the way to win friends in this company. "I owe you nothing!" he stormed at her, letting the implication prick him where any demand or casual insult would have been ignored. One Vanguard flinched, and for a moment it seemed as if the tableau might erupt in wholesale slaughter, but the infantry managed to hold themselves in check.

"Nothing," he repeated, slipping back into Russian again. "Everything about you was a lie. You assisted my command to further your own goals, Romilsky. You think you can buy my loyalty, even with saved lives? Well, it isn't for sale. Whatever my command owed you, they paid back yesterday when your Lieutenant Detchelov's treachery cost unnecessary lives." That stung deeply, parading her lack of control over Detchelov in front of her Vanguard. "All you have to rely on now is my word that we would help."

"And that is of much less value today, is it?" she hissed, striking where she knew it would wound. "If your honor is conditional, then it has no absolute value. Then you are—just—like—me." She snapped off those last three words with a kind of ruthless pleasure.

Was that what he was? What every officer had to be? There was just enough truth in her words to make them sting, but not enough to convince. Sainz drew himself up proudly, knowing Tousley would despise him for it and that Rebecca would task him over his attitude later in private. But it was necessary to paint the image to Romilsky. "My word is just as good now as it has ever been," he promised. "Your lack of honor does not negate my own. *That* would take a much stronger purpose. We'll help you kill the Sleeper, Romilsky, obliterate it—if only to make sure the creature never falls into your hands for study. But we'll do it under my planning, this time, with your review and proposals for alteration afterward. But nonnegotiable is that your forces will buy us the time to task Freedom's weapons for a pinpoint strike."

"If one missile falls on Chernaya Gora—or if any of them are nuclear—"

"I think you are mistaking us for a Neo-Soviet unit." That comment earned him a hard glare, which Sainz shrugged off easily. "You have my word that we'll help you bring down the Sleeper. Now you can take it, or you can handle this problem yourself."

The Fifty-sixth's CO obviously did not care for the way the meeting had run, but in the end she had little choice. "Very well," she agreed, nodding abruptly. Then she spun around and stalked back toward the Zephyr. The Vanguard fell in around her, backing away to watch the Union forces until the last moment.

Sainz felt the hollowness claw at his insides—the struggle within him over for now and the vanquished fleeing. Duty and honor—yes, Romilsky had been right about that. But *everything* was conditional. Sainz had always known and respected that, and there Romilsky made her biggest mistake. His reputation that she counted on so much was built on a knife's edge of difference. He would have walked it forever if that had been possible.

But here, pressed by events that had spun so far beyond any one person's control, the edge ran too fine and it cut, bleeding out his personal honor in favor of his oath. Forsworn either way, and knowing that for the first time in a long career he would have to break his word.

25

On the bridge of the *Icarus,* Major Randall Williams sat down heavily in the nearest chair, feeling like his legs might give out. It was Captain Paul Drake's seat, but he wasn't using it. The captain was occupied at the ship's weapons station, making certain everything was primed and ready. Just in case.

The violent scene played out on the forward monitor in eerie silence. The crew said little as they went about their work, glancing now and then at the screen. This new revelation was phenomenal, more even than the discovery of the abandoned asteroid base. Only Paul Drake continued to speak in a normal voice, letting his people know their commander was not afraid, even if he was. Especially if he was, thought Williams, but even he had to admit it made him feel better.

On the monitor, two alien races faced each other in a nightmare battle between landed spacecraft. Detail was difficult to make out—the *Icarus*'s video-imaging array being thirty kilometers overhead—but it wasn't hard to recognize the tactics and weapons of warfare. Individuals moved as parts of smaller units, and the smaller units jockeyed for position against the enemy. Gouts of hellish energies—pulses and streams ranging from violent red to burnt orange—lashed out from one side to scour the other. Large pieces of land would suddenly geyser upward, scattering bodies and debris. Sometimes a body would seem simply to disintegrate.

Drake had uttered only one direct comment to Williams so far. "Now we know," he'd said, walking over to the weapons station. The same words Williams had spoken about the asteroid base. Williams nodded, knowing there was nothing more to say.

Now they knew that aliens were still alive in the Maelstrom.

Now they knew that the creatures were just as warlike as Earth-descended man.

The planet the *Icarus* orbited was the smaller of the pair the team had intended to survey on the return leg of their journey. It was the size of Mars, with no indication of breathable atmosphere. Not the world Williams would have chosen, except that one of the science staff had found a weak signal of ultrahigh-frequency pulses they now recognized as coming from the crystalline formations. The chance to observe a third specimen or group of specimens, and these existing on a much larger mass, was not an opportunity to be passed up lightly.

Brygan Nystolov and the captain had argued against it, however. Drake was obviously remembering the two men he'd already lost, but Brygan Nystolov did not state his reasons. Williams had observed Nystolov showing more and more agitation the further they got into the mission. Probably feeling the pressure of having to decide whether to remain with the Union or accept their offer to return him to the empire, he thought. Even Drake conceded that Brygan's skills were of value, and doubted they were put to full use by the Neo-Soviets.

Randall Williams had made the final call to survey this ruin of a planet. What they could see of the surface looked pummeled to a barren wasteland by asteroid strikes, as if the world had already made several orbits through the dense asteroid fields of the Maelstrom's Central Ring. Other spots reminded several of the scientists of large, strip-mined areas. There were the tailings of digging and massive earth movement, though on an impressive scale. The crystalline formation was one of the largest yet, sprawling over thirty square kilometers in interconnected patches. Its signal was weak, though, as if triggered from a low-power source or for only a short period of time. That might also be a function of size, Williams thought.

Then the ship's communications specialist picked up strange transmissions as the *Icarus*'s orbit reached halfway round the planet. A weak signal, but definitely modulated. A sign of intelligence.

They traced the transmission to an enormous crater on the planet's far side. Large enough to be easily measured from space and coming in at roughly the size of the Union's American District of Texas, it looked less the result of an impact than like something had ripped away a colossal chunk of the planet. The hole punched down into the planet's crust so deep that all atmosphere had drained into it, like water slowly draining down to the lowest point.

And in that small pocket they found the warring aliens.

The doors to the bridge slid apart, a diamond-shaped aperture growing until the final angles disappeared back into the wall. Brygan Nystolov stepped into the control room, escorted by one of the *Icarus*'s crewmen—a combat-rated Marine, not a technician specialist. Brygan seemed intent on the main monitor as he walked in. No doubt he'd been observing the battle back in the science stations. His expression showed a troubled, almost sorrowful frown rather than the shock other bridge members were displaying.

Williams rose from his seat at Brygan's entrance, borrowing from the other man's near-indomitable strength.

"The science probe is almost down," the comms specialist announced calmly. "We'll have a picture in ten." She waited several seconds, calling out the final, "three, two, one."

The video feed did not last long. The probe transmitted its last hundred meters as it swept low into the battlefield, trying for a close-up shot. It fell in behind a trio of humanoid combatants, wearing some kind of angular, blue-glowing armor. They seemed to move stiffly, though it was hard to tell because of an area of distortion that extended around each one. Then a carmine spray of pulsing light hit the forward-most of the three, and his form erupted in a cascade of blue-and-green-tinged lightning. The remaining two scattered, opening up a clear shot of the opposing force. Also humanoid and uniformed in gray, they wore a kind of metal armor of black and burnished bronze.

Then one of the two blue-armored aliens spun about

and pointed at the probe. The air shimmered, and the transmission cut to a static feed.

Drake strode over to communications and punched in a link to the main science station. "Isolate close-ups and route them to the bridge," he ordered. Drake shot Brygan a suspicious look that Williams thought was unwarranted. "I want to see faces."

The reply came back immediately. "Already have them, Captain. Best we can manage, anyway. The distortion makes detailed pictures of the first aliens impossible. But the second"—an awkward pause—"well, you're not going to get a face, sir. I don't think they've got much of one left."

The main monitor split off to one side, allowing the bridge occupants to keep tabs on the battle on the main screen while a still image was pasted up on the smaller one. Williams drew in a sharp breath at what he saw. The alien looked a cross between some rotted mummy of ancient Egypt and a technological nightmare not unlike a Neo-Soviet Class F mutant.

Gray bandages swathed its head and arms, though they'd unraveled enough about the face to show a bare skull and one eye socket set with some kind of black gem. The being wore a black robe clasped at the waist with an ornate skull buckle. A mass of hoses was strapped into an evacuated stomach region. Bronze metal had been plated on over the alien's left shoulder. A small bronze tank set with gems had been buried in the other shoulder and now stuck out awkwardly. That arm hung limp. Metal tubing ran from the tank to the side of the alien's head, and then again from the head to the stock of the rifle it carried in its left hand.

"Good Lord in heaven," the corporal sitting communications murmured loud enough to hear.

Her words seemed to break the spell holding Paul Drake in check. He rounded at once on Brygan. "How long have you known about these creatures?"

Williams first thought Drake was reacting out of his own fear and ignorance. Then he remembered Brygan's look of sorrowful acceptance—that lack of surprise. If there was any doubt, Brygan now gave himself away. He looked guilty.

"Never," he said. He stared at the creature still framed on the monitor, then looked a silent entreaty to Major Williams. "I never knew of these."

A half-truth, Williams felt certain.

Drake, too. "But you suspected, Brygan," he pressed. "You're observant, like all scouts have to be. How long?"

Brygan's eyes widened as Paul Drake tagged him a scout rather than a scientist. He was sharp enough to understand that it was no mistake. Drake wanted him to realize that they knew his true identity. Williams could hardly believe that Brygan had deceived them beyond his initial identity. They had tried so hard to make him feel accepted.

"How long have you suspected, Brygan Vassilyevich, that the aliens might be so hostile?" the major asked.

The man's voice was a deep whisper. "Two days." He started to speak again, but shied off.

Paul Drake turned away, not waiting to hear more. "We're getting out of here. Helm," he called out, "swing us out of orbit. Best speed for Luna, and watch for shifts in our approach vector." He looked over at Williams. "We should get this information back to Luna and Earth as soon as possible, don't you agree, Major?"

Williams swallowed dryly and nodded his assent. Brygan had been right, back at the beginning of the survey flight. Some things a person should never want to know. He had thought to reach the scout's loyalty—damn it, he had! He couldn't be wrong about that. But apparently not deeply enough.

Williams glanced to the warring aliens on the forward monitor, and then to the augmented corpse of the alien framed on the split screen. Were the Neo-Soviets so alien, too, that there was no reaching them? Was this what mankind had to look forward to, always fighting each other even as new threats appeared?

It was with no small measure of sorrow that Williams spoke to Brygan. "Go back to the science stations and help with the video analysis," he said.

Brygan looked from one officer to the other. "Maybe it better that I confine myself to room."

The Union scientist was not about to let Brygan retreat so easily. Especially now, while vulnerable. Williams thought he might still reach the Neo-Soviet scout, and even if not there was the matter of whatever information he had learned of two days before to point at warring alien races. And more since? The scientist frowned. This would take careful handling.

A caution which Paul Drake was ill inclined to give.

The Marine kept his back turned on the Neo-Soviet, studying the ongoing battle. "That has always been your choice, Nystolov, and apparently you made it two days ago." Williams thought he detected a trace of wounded sorrow in the Marine's tone, though it was cloaked by harsh words. The captain then paused, as if sensing too late the delicate moment. "The science stations are Major Williams's domain. If he allows you their use, I'll not override him. But you are no longer welcome on my bridge."

Williams watched it happen. Brygan's slow withdrawal

back into himself, which they had worked so hard to reverse. But now trust was shattered, though Williams could only guess at what service to the empire had forced the break. Maybe those wounds could be healed and the trust restored, but obviously not now. Not today.

And with a speedy return to Earth ordered, there wasn't much time left.

26

Katya Romilsky walked over and stood at the edge of a bluff above and far to the rear of the Sleeper. A bitter Siberian wind whistled up through the draw and over the ridge that also hid the Zephyr. The wind tugged at the ballistic cloth of her officer's trench and ran chill fingers through her hair. Accompanied by the Mental and her elite squad of Vanguard, she had brought her command transport here for a better vantage point. She raised her field glasses and peered through them, observing the main battle below.

At the head of a narrow defile, barely wide enough for two crawlers to travel apace with each other, the Sleeper looked larger and more frightening than ever. Its nerve-rending shriek sounded repeatedly through the shallow canyon, slicing through the roaring cacophony of the Union and Neo-Soviet combined assault. The maddened scream sounded more like a howl of frustration and rage than pain. And of hunger, so close to its goal.

The creature tore at the ground and the steep, rocky face, widening a passage for itself. Chitin-armored legs chewed up ground, and its immense head slammed repeatedly into the rocky face, dislodging small slides that slowly worked at a greater opening. Two spiny ridges now separated from the alien's back to become armored tentacles, sliding into the gap and anchoring themselves in protected crevices. They strained to pull its monstrous bulk through the gap.

On both sides of the defile, the Union and Neo-Soviet forces fought to keep that from happening. The roaring reports of better than a hundred assault rifles raised a din that echoed through Gory Putorana's labyrinth of canyons and draws, an artificial thunder occasionally answered by a natural rumble from the overcast, dark sky. The weapons fire faded for a time, as soldiers reloaded or worked themselves into what they hoped were more advantageous positions, but never ceased altogether. From the bellies of Neo-Soviet Avalanche carriers, Union Trojans, and Hydras, the supplies were brought forward and spent.

Katya Romilsky tried estimating the weight of ordnance already wasted on the creature. A metric ton? Two? Stronger than ever, the colossal alien shrugged off most of it while continuing to work its way toward Chernaya Gora.

Romilsky shifted the field glasses and let her gaze wander over the smoking wreckage of two Union Wendigos. They had managed a half kilometer before the Sleeper's electromagnetic pulse defense ruined their circuitry and the flywheel generators blew apart. Four Typhoons, her last missile carriers, still burned farther back on the ridge, taken out by some kind of new ability the Sleeper had unleashed that day.

"Not every effort has proven wasted," the Mental reminded her as if reading her thoughts. He pointed a trembling finger at the black grass-covered hillside, which showed the scars of their one minor victory.

Romilsky nodded. The Sleeper had first tried to go over the mountain, attempting to reach the draw and the opening to the no-longer-secret facility. Vanguard and Union infantry had slowed its advance, though Romilsky had been forced—*ordered*—to pull back her Chem Grunts.

The Sleeper reacted favorably to the mutagen they sprayed. Instead of the rapid-generation mutations that invariably proved so lethal to any Terran-based life-form, the Sleeper had simply grown another armored ridge on its carapace that quickly separated into a second tentacle. And when casualties mounted too high—Union casualties, she noted, not Vanguard—they fell back and blew the mountainside with explosives. That had hurt the creature, though not nearly enough.

"At least the charges convinced the Sleeper to abandon the mountainside route," she said, though without much enthusiasm.

The defile was the more difficult path, but better protected the Sleeper from the bulk of the two armies. The Seventy-first Assault Group dominated the lower canyon, striking at the creature's flanks and rear quarter, with only moderate help from the Neo-Soviets' Fifty-sixth Striker. A mere fifty meters of narrow passage separated the Sleeper's head from the open draw leading up to the Chernaya Gora compound.

Most of its remaining symbiots swarmed the ground

ahead of it, currently out of her line of sight. Occasionally a new batch of such creatures would slip out from between the folds in the alien's chitinous carapace, whether held in reserve or generated new, there was no way to tell. Major Howard had noted the complete disappearance of Feeder symbiots and suggested that they were being transformed back into offensive types.

Whatever their origin, Romilsky held the waves of symbiots in check by advancing line after line of her quickly depleting Rad Troopers and mutants. Behind that the bulk of her Vanguard forces stood a nervous, final line of defense. Soon she would bring the Zephyr around to join them.

It was the reverse of the assault plan she had devised the day before. This time her army stood in the creature's path. A few token squads of Union troops joined them beyond the defile, just enough that Romilsky could be certain that Sainz would not pull back and abandon her people. That troublesome sergeant was back there, too. She frowned. *He* would be taken care of—the meddling *oubluduk*—it was already arranged. A stray bullet would claim him once the Sleeper broke through and the fighting was heaviest.

She owed him that much.

The Sleeper worked its long neck far enough into the narrow passage for the shoulderlike bulges in its forward carapace to come into direct contact with the rock. A brilliant, near-blinding flash washed off the facing, and several meters of rock ran molten. The same thing occurred roughly every half hour. She averted her eyes from the flash, then turned completely away from the battle as the dedicated link Sainz had given her buzzed for attention.

"I still have no idea what that is," she said testily over

the link. Whatever allowed it to work through the rock was the same weapon that had destroyed her four Typhoons.

"Well, I do." Sainz's voice sounded strained. "My CBR specialists confirmed it. It's a low-yield nuclear pulse. Only it's very clean, leaving behind little radioactive debris."

She nodded to herself. "Of course. Why waste its food reserves?"

"If that thing burrows much farther into the defile—"

"*Da!* I know, I know. It escapes into the draw, and Chernaya Gora falls."

Sainz let the thought hang there for a moment. "Worse, Katya Romilsky. Those rocky cliffs will shield it from Freedom's missile barrage, providing we retake Tranquillity in time to task the weapons. We have an opportunity now, while it's in the open and on the other side of the defile before it begins to tunnel into your underground complex. After that, I cannot guarantee we can kill it."

"Then we do it without the battle station."

Even through the strains of transmission, she could hear Sainz's growing anger. "Are you watching the same battle I am? Our bullets do little more than annoy it. Grenades are slightly better, but again, we can't work enough soldiers in close for concentrated damage. That thing is twelve percent larger than this time yesterday, Colonel. And its defenses are much more efficient."

She had thought it looked bigger. Still, "If you are arguing for a saturation barrage from Freedom, the answer is still *nyet*. And I have your word that Chernaya Gora is to be protected. *Da?*"

"Yes, Romilsky. You have it." He sound grudging. "Besides, I don't have to worry about Chernaya Gora. If we can't task Freedom within the next few hours, or find a way to buy time, the Sleeper will do the job for me."

"Now there I might be able to do something. I have ordered forward new forces."

Sainz sound alarmed. "You did not clear this with me. I have men down there."

"These are not mutants," she assured him. He expected another fiasco such as her ill-fated *mertvaya sobaka* attack of this morning. A good plan in theory, running the last of her rad-hounds forward and detonating them at the base of the Sleeper's thick neck. Except three mutant handlers had harbored sentiments similar to Gregor Detchelov and turned their death dogs against Union squads. In the confusion others detonated their canine explosives early, and the remaining few did little more than wound the alien.

Fortunately, only one of Sainz's men had been injured, and not fatally. Had there been any deaths, the Union colonel likely would have pulled back and abandoned her. She wouldn't have blamed him, though it still fueled her rage that she now relied on his efforts so heavily.

"Not mutants," she said again. "My Chem Grunts will take my directions exactly. And before you worry overmuch, all mutagen has been replaced with toxic wash. We know *that* can hurt it." Or at least make it very angry, she recalled from the Vanguard report of first contact with the Sleeper. "You worry about your battle station. I will stand ready to buy you more time." She switched off the link with a hard slap, then looked to the nearby Mental. "Right?"

The frail man nodded carefully. "The toxic will hurt the Sleeper, *Tovarish.*"

She raised the field glasses back to her brow, sweeping her gaze over the canyon floor until finding the Chem Grunt squad as they came in against the Sleeper. "I don't want it hurt, I want it dead."

She let the glasses down, leaving them hanging from the strap around her neck. "Ironic, don't you think? To save Chernaya Gora, I must rely on the very forces that came to destroy it. If the battle is to be salvaged, it will be on the honor of a Union officer, and the ability of Union forces to secure their moonbase." She nodded down into the canyon. "We had better move into position. The Zephyr can get us to Chernaya Gora, where I will take up command at the final line of defense."

A soft *"Nyet,"* turned Romilsky around. The Mental was crouched down, knees pressed into his chest and arms wrapped about his legs. "I would prefer to remain here, far from that creature."

Now was no time to get overly squeamish or turn coward. Romilsky let a touch of steel creep into her voice. "I can leave you no protection. You would have to remain alone."

A shudder. His voice, when he spoke, was barely audible over the thunderous roll of weapons fire. "That is your prerogative, Comrade Romilsky."

As if she wouldn't have to answer later for leaving so valuable an asset unprotected. And the Mental knew it, of course. Romilsky shook her head in frustration, then pointed out two of her guard squad.

"You two, stay and protect the Mental," she ordered. "Above all else, keep him away from any Union forces." They nodded their understanding. Mentals were always protected to the final moment, but none could ever be allowed to be taken by the Union. She headed for the Zephyr, then paused for a final farewell. "I will see you after the battle."

"Yes," the Mental said, suddenly much stronger in voice. "You will."

Climbing into the Zephyr, Katya Romilsky knew a moment of doubt concerning the Mental's certainty that they would meet again on the other side of the battle. She dismissed it. No reason to believe that the Mental's preternatural sight was in doubt. But the VTOL-augmented command crawler was barely in the air before she realized why it had bothered her. The Mental had not spoken the statement in comfort.

He'd spoken in sorrow.

Corporal Phillipe Savoign marched the Ares assault suit in between barracks buildings and onto one of the parade grounds of Tranquillity Base. In contrast to the deadly terrain he had faced on the Solstice Plains, in this battle the Ares commanded the battlefield as it was meant to do. His augmented vision picked out enemy threats with ease, blinking through the various imaging systems and then visually locking weapons onto the target. A gentle touch to the trigger and the Neo-Soviet force suffered new losses. He stepped over the carnage of melted metal and burned corpses, grateful that the closed cockpit system protected him from the sickly charred scent.

Thrusting his jaw forward to open his general channel, Savoign scanned the virtual landscape painted over his visor. "Rifle squad eliminated, parade grounds. Moving toward command center."

In his wake, a pair of Pegasus reconnaissance sleds skimmed the ground looking for stragglers or traps his augmented senses might have missed. Power-armor infantry moved up a half a klick behind them, and gliding over the lunar plains toward the edge of Tranquillity came the unguarded trio of Hydra transports they were all responsible for protecting. To either flank, set so their fire could overlap, other heavy assault suits walked, fronting for other Hydras. Five Ares spearheaded this portion of the move to retake Tranquillity, their ability to deal damage in a discriminating fashion making them more valuable than armored vehicles. The goal was to retake the base intact.

A light patter against his armor and the slight tremor to his step warned him that he was taking assault-rifle fire even before his sensor-analysis package acknowledged that the hail of metal might actually be considered a threat. He pivoted around in the direction of a small red arrow at the corner of his vision. A warning bar highlighted the open doorway of a barracks where a pair of Vanguard infantrymen hammered away at him. One leaned out and launched a grenade, the explosive device clipping his lower arm and shattering the armor protecting his wrist joint.

"Natural selection at its finest," Savoign said to himself, raising the Ares' right arm and tracking in his antipersonnel "enforcer." The APE was enough to take care of a pair of infantry.

"Say again, Ares Twelve?"

He'd triggered his comm systems by moving his jaw, talking aloud. "Disregard," Phillipe said, triggering off a full burst from the APE. The eleven-millimeter enforcer chewed a stream of high-explosive slugs through the wall of the barracks, drawing a line of destruction chest high across the door. Dust billowed into the air, and both Kalashnikovs fell silent. "I had to take care of some pests."

"Copy, Twelve." The voice shifted over to general address. "Ares auxiliaries, General Hayes has moved against the eastern centers. Swing over for immediate support."

The Ares assault suit was an impressive piece of work, but it did very few things immediately. For covering large distances fast, they relied on specially adapted Trojan supply carriers. In extremely light gravity an experienced specialist might coax a bit of extra speed out of the suit, but this portion of Tranquillity Base was terrasimmed for three-fourths standard Earth gravity. Still, Savoign throttled up to his maximum speed at once and began to lengthen his stride to reach a blazing ten-klicks-per-hour speed. He moved off the parade grounds and onto the grass-covered soil transplanted from Earth.

And suddenly he was pressed down into his cockpit, the form-fitting shockguard feeling as if it suddenly wanted to squeeze the breath from him. The Ares staggered, but fortunately Savoign had not yet fully lengthened his stride, so the gyro was able to keep the assault suit upright. On the virtual landscape projected over his visor from the outside lens clusters, he saw two trees topple over in a light stand of woods off to his left. He flicked his eyes to his sensor-package indicators, blinking through several status bars until finding the screen he wanted.

"Gravity increase, two-point-five standard," he transmitted, reading the change on his status indicators.

"The Neo-Sovs are trying to use the gravity generators against us," the coordinator's voice said, obviously straining under the heavier gravity as well. "They may be trying to use it to cover their retreat or as a prelude to attack. Ares Twelve and Seven, you should have power relays coming up within range. Our technicians promise that by blowing those relays, gravity generators will shut down to shunt power to more critical systems."

Savoign found the station relay nearest him, a small metal shack nestled up against the back wall of an administration building. He'd replaced the Harbinger rail weapon on the shoulder mount with the Lucifer plasma cannon for this operation. Though shorter-ranged, the Lucifer was still not a precision weapon, but against the well-armored relay building it would serve well. He focused in on the relay, the Ares' targeting system reading off his vision and centering over the metal shack.

Then Savoign backed the reticle off five meters and fired. Even through the Ares' armor, he heard the high-pitched hum as the Lucifer quickly back-built energy. A magnetic tube stabbed out from the shoulder-riding cannon to be quickly filled by a compressed ball of plasma. It sailed out over the terraformed landscape, drawn down the tube which drifted off his mark by three meters. The field collapsed a second later and the superheated gas tore into the relay station and a good portion of the building wall beyond. Metal twisted and melted under the force, then began spitting electrical sparks. Bricks shattered and part of the admin building's wall caved in.

Not too bad, considering.

"Ares Seven, target eliminated." The announcement beat Phillipe's similar call by two seconds.

"Good work, Seven. Twelve. We have word from the general. The enemy is running."

Threat warnings flashed almost immediately, accompanied by the insistent drone of a cautionary alarm. The virtual imaging on his visor washed with red as multiple threats overlapped. Magnification dialed in automatically, recentering his screen to the lead Neo-Soviet crawler as it barreled in at him. A modified Typhoon, the first of five, running an arrowhead pattern of interference for what looked like a full column stretched out behind. Carefully drifting his gaze around, Savoign identified several Blizzard light-assault vehicles and what he thought might be a Zephyr, though even his Ares' targeting software had difficulty at this range.

"You might have mentioned that the enemy is running right for us!" Savoign said, thrusting his jaw forward to engage comms. "Ares auxiliary is moving to local coordination. Seven and Ten, pull in on my position. Two and Three, form square behind us. Protect the Pegasus vehicles and our power armor."

The Union formation took shape slowly. Too slowly to suit Savoign, who watched the range counter scroll down until a half kilometer separated the Ares unit from the Neo-Soviet advance vehicles. Well within range for the Harbingers carried by Ares Seven and Ten, and at the point where his own Lucifer might track in accurately enough. Still he waited. And just in case his companions thought to fire early on, or the coordinator decide to retake remote control in the silence, he whispered, "Wait for it. Let them in."

The Typhoons released one poorly coordinated wave of missiles, then another. The missile carriers bouncing nearly out of control in the now-light gravity contributed to a wide spread. Nothing an Ares had to worry about except for that freak chance of misfortune. The Earth-quality soil, transplanted at great expense, erupted in geysers of black dirt and shredded sod. One missile caught Savoign's heavy assault suit in the right leg, another just below the left-shoulder shield. He rocked backward, the hard-hitting punches threatening to topple him from his feet. The Ares' gyro and Savoign's own stubborn determination kept him on his feet.

"Center on the lead Typhoon," he said almost casually. "On my mark. Now!"

Two rail gun ingots slammed into the forward Typhoon,

peeling away armor and punching through to the internal carriage before detonating. The vehicle was already in the process of disintegrating when Savoign's plasma weapon detonated ten meters in front of it, the devastating eruption slamming into its front and stopping it as if it had hit an invisible wall. The nose crumpled inward even as the fireball from the explosive rail ingots bulged out the armored sides and then finally erupted out through the top-mounted missile launcher, the ammunition detonations adding to the fiery force.

Savoign had his reasons for the overkill, trading off what might have been at least two separate kills to shatter the nose of the Neo-Soviet formation. As the other Typhoons peeled away radically, none wishing to risk that kind of violent death, the backing Blizzards were thrown into a confused state as they scrambled to avoid hitting either a Typhoon or each other. On a direct charge, the Neo-Soviets might have ridden over the Ares formation and laid waste to the small Union force. Already in retreat, though, thoughts of self-preservation overrode any fanatical leanings, and the entire column broke apart.

And, as Savoign had hoped, exposed the Zephyr command transport at the center of the column.

"There's our target! Lock on to the Zephyr and fire."

He followed his own order, visually tracking in and caressing the trigger to send first one plasma discharge off down the middle and then bracketing it at twenty meters to either side with follow-up shots. The Lucifer's high-pitched hum shifted into a complaining drone at the rapid rate of fire. Savoign almost backed off, but his desire to bring down the enemy commander overrode safety concerns, and he fired another two shots in overhead paths.

Apparently, he was the only one who had considered

the fact that Zephyrs had VTOL and limited flight capability. When the first rail ingot tagged the command transport in its side, chewing away armor and ripping away a side door to expose the interior, its pilot threw open the thrusters and hopped the vehicle into the air. It sailed over the first plasma pulses with no more trouble than some light understructure damage.

It might have avoided the second pair as well, except that Ares Seven managed to correct its aim at the last instant to clip the Zephyr's tail thruster with another rail ingot. The explosion did little more than ruin the thruster port and throw the transport into a temporary aerial slide. It was enough. One of Savoign's plasma discharges caught it on the forward-right post, bursting in a shock that tore into the Zephyr with lethal effect, driving it back down toward the lunar surface. The crash finished the vehicle for good, breaking it into two major pieces, though it continued to bleed metal scraps over the landscape.

The loss of the Zephyr was the final straw. The Neo-Soviet column shattered beyond repair, each vehicle making its best speed in escape.

"Beautiful work, Ares Auxiliary." Not the coordinator from before, but a new voice. Calm and commanding. Savoign had heard Brigadier General Hayes's voice often enough to recognize it.

"Ten, Two, and Three, pursue to the edge of Tranquillity Base and take targets of opportunity. Seven and Twelve, if you're done playing, we could use your help getting weapon consoles up and running. There is also the small matter of tasking Station Freedom's weapons."

Watching the retreating Neo-Soviet forces on his virtual monitor, Corporal Savoign knew a moment of loss that he would not be able to pursue, a sensation quickly replaced by the pleasure of the general's request for assistance. An Ares might lend its pilot a titan's command of the battlefield, but there was also something to be said for tasking battle-station weapons against the Neo-Soviet empire.

"Copy, General Hayes. Heading in to Tranquillity Command."

Variety, after all, was the spice of life.

27

Sergeant Tousley found a perverse kind of satisfaction in watching the Neo-Soviets expend rank after rank of Rad Troopers and its larger mutants to hold back the Sleeper's symbiot army. They had replaced their uranium-tipped ammunition with stock ammo, as firing such bullets into the Sleeper or its symbiots fed the aliens' reserves as much as it damaged them.

With their ammunition weakened and their numbers near useless in the face of so strong an enemy, the Rad Troops seemed all the more pitiful wrecks of men and women now sacrificed to creatures better evolved to live with the effects of radioactive debris. Mutants, stronger and tougher than the massed shock troops, fared better, but the aliens held the advantage even against them. Symbiots returned to the Sleeper's protection, working their way into folds in the chitinous carapace, as fresh replacements took their place. Mutants and Troopers took their wounds and kept fighting until they finally dropped. No quarter asked and certainly none given.

The very way Neo-Soviets should be treated, in Tousley's opinion.

His own abbreviated squad and four other units from the Seventy-first Assault Group held a small rise just opposite the Chernaya Gora compound entrance, an immense tunnel cut back into the mountainside. A thick vault door had been dropped over the entrance, fronted by Colonel Romilsky's Zephyr. She stood in the midst of her remaining Vanguard and the disparate special forces left to her Striker. Tousley estimated that the door would stand up to maybe two of the Sleeper's nuclear-flash charges, but Romilsky and her Vanguard not at all, even with Union support.

First-column Brevet-Captain Matthew Dillahunty commanded the Seventy-first's forces placed this side of the defile. He had arranged the four assault squads into ranks that would take turns offering covering fire to the advancing Neo-Soviets, but otherwise held position, waiting for orders. Two full infantry squads, cobbled together from shattered units, an untouched Draco heavy-assault team, and Tom Tousley's makeshift unit. In the far back a trio of weapons specialists prepared a like number of *Dragon* automated defense drones, their flame-thrower turrets currently retracted and cold.

The call came, and Tousley moved his squad up. Nash and Maria Carr. Jim Nicholas, walking wounded but refusing to take a medical relief from the fight. Corporal Loveday, pressed into service with a Pitbull and also advising Captain Dillahunty on any CBR-related issues that cropped up.

Tousley sighted his Bulldog support rifle in on the Sleeper's head as it thrust all the way through the defile, its vertically slit maw shrieking out its rage and hunger. Tousley punched into it with one of his two launched grenades and a good forty rounds of eleven-millimeter ammunition. The bullets stitched small holes into one side of the Sleeper's cobra hood, ignored.

The grenade found the nest of bloated pustules and tentacles crowning its head—the organs responsible for its electrical defense. It exploded into the mass of yellow-green flesh, shredding and ruining them. The Sleeper screeched in pain. Lightning jumped around its head and flowed back over its carapace, arcing out into a Cyclops that had pressed through the symbiot line. The lumbering mutant fell over, the armored supports encasing its legs spot-welded into immobility. The immense hooded head pulled upward and back, but not before Tousley saw new tentacles growing up from the crown as the Sleeper regenerated its defenses. Its body remained solidly wedged into the defile.

"You hurt it," Maria Carr shouted over the din. It was easier to cry out to someone nearby than worry about opening a frequency.

He nodded, thinking how it still wasn't enough. Squeezing a figure-eight burst of fire into a slithering symbiot that had angled toward the Union contingent, he prepared to pull his squad back and let another up forward. It was never enough, and he tired of falling back.

Colonel Sainz surprised him, overriding all Union channels. "Station Freedom reports missiles tasked and launching," he announced with barely subdued excitement. "We need that thing out in the open. Captain Dillahunty, bloody its nose!"

The captain's voice rode in immediately on the back of

that order. "Third squad, advance. Four, load up and hold fire. Cover fire for the rest. Go, go, go!"

The Union detachment rose up and surged forward, Tousley's squad on point protecting the full Draco squad at their immediate back. Dillahunty advanced the rearward fire-support teams.

"Colonel Romilsky," he called. "We need those symbiots cleared. Let them through."

Rad Troopers fell back almost at once, the smaller alien creatures swarming after them back toward Chernaya Gora's last line of defense while the Seventy-first's squads and fire-caster ADDs forced a wedge between Sleeper and symbiots. It was a dangerous plan, sandwiching the Union contingent between the Sleeper and its symbiots, which were, in turn, trapped between the Union anvil and the Neo-Soviet hammer. A desperate plan. But to drive the Sleeper back into the open canyon beyond, the assault group squads had to get up close.

Just how close the Union soldiers learned seconds later as they reached the head of the defile. With another of its soul-grating shrieks, the Sleeper's head thrust back through the full defile and into the lower reach of the draw.

"Down," Tousley yelled, as the head swung over them, and he dived for a stretch of hard-packed dirt amid the tumble of broken rock scattered over the ground. The maw slit hovered over them, the high-pitched screech accompanied by the crackling of dry tentacles and chitinous plates rubbing together. A foul, acrid stench almost suffocated them. Tousley rolled over onto his back, firing up into that toothy darkness.

The Sleeper suddenly rocked back, its head high in the air and shrieking in what now sounded like pain. Tousley's squad clambered to their feet and moved forward. He noticed the creature's body twisting about, saw its flat-armored tail swing up over its back and come smashing down on forces behind it.

Something back there was disturbing the Sleeper, giving the Union force this side of the defile a chance to get into position. Dillahunty's fire teams were setting up to hold back the symbiots in a cross fire with the Neo-Soviets. Tousley rushed forward, the Bulldog bucking in his hands, firing a steady stream of bullets into the Sleeper's ridged neck.

Just then a pair of bullets caught him from behind, in the right hip and upper leg, slamming into him and spinning him roughly to the ground. Three more shots ricocheted off nearby rocks.

Though treacherous, the attack actually saved Tousley's life, coming as the Sleeper's head slammed back down from the defile and brought with it an avalanche of broken rock. Several big boulders landed in front of him. The next nearest soldier, PFC Nash, had remained on his feet to ready his Draco launcher. The tentacles whipping out from the Sleeper's gaping maw wrapped about the man's body, lifting him from the ground. He screamed in fright and pain.

"Fire! For the love of God, fire!" Tousley yelled back to the following Draco squad, one hand clapped over his bleeding wounds. Despite the pain, he swung his own Bulldog up. One-handed, he selected for a grenade and fired up into the dark mouth and saw the thirty-millimeter shell explode back inside the monstrous throat.

Brevet-Corporal Maria Carr had noticed her sergeant's fall, and now crabbed over with a first-aid kit to slap field compresses over the wounds. Over their heads, the Draco squad fired a concentrated salvo of eight missiles at the Sleeper's body. Three of them detonated early as a charge of lightning whipped the air, but half slammed home, cracking through the carapace and digging large chunks out of the base of the neck.

"Reload," ordered Draco squad Sergeant Hess.

With Carr tending to his injury, Tousley used both hands to continue pumping grenades into the Sleeper. When the chamber clicked dry, he switched back to automatic fire with the ten-millimeter assault rifle. He didn't bother looking back to see who had fired on him; he knew who'd ordered the attack. It was no surprise that Romilsky had lived up to his low expectations. But he had a larger enemy to defeat just now, and a man to save.

PFC Nash actually saved himself, regaining his courage just long enough to sight in his Draco rocket launcher against the underside of the Sleeper's cobralike hood. The heavy infantry weapon drew a short path of smoke upward, and a fiery explosion blossomed. The Sleeper thrashed about in pain-filled rage, its long neck whipping about violently and slamming the armored back of its hood against either side of the defile. Rocks tumbled down, and among them PFC Nash, who had been thrown free. A boulder smashed into two of the Draco squad, crushing them. Loveday also took a glancing blow against his shoulder and the side of his helmet, knocking him down and out of the battle.

"Loose!" Sergeant Hess ordered behind Tousley's position, and another brace of rockets screamed forward to bury their explosive heads in the Sleeper's bulk. Five of the six found the Sleeper, scattering a handful of destructive blossoms over its wide carapace.

The fleshy gobbets that made up the alien's radioactive blood poured out to pool on the rocky ground. Gray-green fluid leaked from a score of wounds as well as spitting from the Sleeper's mouth. Now it began to retreat, slowly, its body twisting about as if unable to decide which way to turn. The head pulled all the way back through the defile, tearing loose a new avalanche of rock.

Tousley fought his way back to his feet and limped forward with Maria Carr at his side, stopping only to eject one clip and slam home a new one. His leg flared with pain at each step, but he set his jaw against it, continuing to work at the spots where the armored carapace had been smashed by rockets. A new symbiot slid free to challenge the advancing infantry. A dedicated burst was enough to put it down.

Daylight once again intruded between the alien colossus and the sides of the defile, revealing the reason for the Sleeper's agitation and pain. A double-squad of Neo-Soviet Chem Grunts came at the Sleeper from its right flank, their chemsprayers releasing determined jets of green toxic wash. A few slid through the gap, placing themselves between the Sleeper and the safety of the defile. Their caustic streams worked in past broken and splintered chitin. The two large tentacles separated from the Sleeper's back and each wrapped about a Grunt. It tossed one a good hundred meters up into the air. The second one the Sleeper pulped against the cliff face.

But that also ruptured the Grunt's tanks, spilling a great gout of the toxins down the unarmored side of the tentacle. The exposed, creamy white flesh singed black in reaction, whiplike hairs curling back in as they died. The Sleeper shied off toward the other side, toward the main advance of the Seventy-first. And that gave Tousley an idea.

Sainz broke back in before he could follow up on his idea. "Missiles imminent. Canyon forces, fall back now. Captain Dillahunty, you hold that defile. Whatever it takes."

"As the colonel orders," Tousley whispered.

Grinning savagely, he hunkered down within the mess of rock and boulders now clogging the defile and sighted in at the back of a Chem Grunt that had made the lower defile. He triggered a short burst directly into its pressurized tanks. The Grunt ceased to exist as the metal tank ruptured with the force of several grenades. The putrid wash splashed over the lower defile, the other Chem Grunts, and the Sleeper, which shrieked further displeasure and retreated farther.

Maybe Sainz would have another stripe from him for this, but Tousley wasn't thinking about that. He was in the field against the enemy, which included more than just the Sleeper, as witnessed by the bullets fired into his right side.

Sighting in at another of the Grunts, this one flailing as the splashed chemicals from its companion worked their way past protective gear and bandages, he ended the Grunt's misery with another controlled burst to its chemical tanks. Behind him he heard Captain Dillahunty overriding Sergeant Hess and directly commanding the Dracos.

Through the pain in his leg and confusion of heavy fighting, Tousley made no sense of the orders. Then the warm rush of acrid wind swept over him, the backblast of a concerted rocket launch. It was several long seconds after the violent explosion before he noticed that the rockets had not passed him overhead. That same instant a shot ricocheted off a nearby rock, close enough that he heard the snap of its hypersonic passage just before the high-pitched *spang* of the deflection. He checked his latest burst and swung about.

Romilsky's Zephyr burned, the cockpit of the Neo-Soviet command vehicle smashed in and gutted. A Draco hit, no doubt about it—two, very likely. From smoking gouges in the blackened earth, the rest of the rockets had torn into the shrinking line of symbiots struggling to return to their mother colossus. It wasn't possible that a pair of rockets could misfire by so great a margin. The ruined

Zephyr was intentional. But what did that do for the battle except . . . make sure Romilsky did not escape!

The realization temporarily burned off the fog of pain in his brain, and Tousley took another look at the developing fight. The trio of flame-thrower defense drones had set up a wall of fire that held the symbiots back from the Seventy-first's detachment, but Dillahunty's fire squads were no longer hammering at them. They were exchanging fire with the forward-most Rad Troopers while back behind them the Vanguard milled about in some confusion. A few snapped off quick bursts toward the embattled Seventy-first's position, but most seemed unwilling to commit against these former allies—still in the midst of battle with the Sleeper, no less—without exact orders to that point.

Raymond Sainz had never intended to simply walk away from Chernaya Gora. The reality hit Tousley with the force of a hammerblow between the eyes.

"Whatever it takes." That had been the code to Captain Dillahunty. How appropriate. And if the timing meant anything—hard to believe it didn't, Sainz was no fool—Tousley knew what was to follow. This defile was the safest place to be, provided that Dillahunty held back any rush to take it. And the Sleeper did not move back in against them.

There was still work to be done, then. He settled back into the rocks, trying to put as much cover as possible between his back and the Neo-Soviets as he sighted back in against the nearest Chem Grunt. Another well-aimed burst and the violent explosion filled the lower end of the defile with a heavy mist of toxins.

No quarter asked. None given.

"Whatever it takes."

With the code phrase spoken, Major Rebecca Howard

ordered the final attack. She'd led the flanking assault against the Sleeper, trying to hurt it enough to force it back from the defile. The Neo-Soviet chemsprayers and Dillahunty's auxiliary force on the other side of the defile had done the bulk of that work, and except for a bad moment when the Sleeper's armored tail had smashed into and wiped out a full support squad, her casualties had been light. It left her in direct command of three Union squads and two of Neo-Soviet Vanguard. And not even that a moment later.

"Fall back ten meters and reload fresh clips," she ordered, working her way back through the broken terrain and out of the Sleeper's shadow.

If the Vanguard found anything odd in the order for a coordinated ammo change that meant discarding good clips, they gave no sign of it. Union battle tactics had never made much sense to the average Neo-Soviet soldier anyway, or so Colonel Sainz had promised her. A few of them took the opportunity to burn out the rest of their ammunition and then began to change out their own empty clips.

The armored tail slammed the ground again not twenty meters behind, shaking the ground with a false quake. Several Vanguard looked that way with looks of apprehension. The faces of Howard's Union infantry showed the same expression, but for another reason. The last clip was slapped home and the first rounds all chambered. The air was tinged acrid from all the ordnance spent this day, and it caught in her throat as she drew breath for the final order. "Auxiliary targets. Fire!"

Her Pitbull twisted in her grip as she sprayed fire on full automatic, stitching red splashes in a line across the chests of two nearby Vanguard. Her people were all careful not to shoot through a Neo-Soviet soldier and into their own. The betrayed infantry jerked and stumbled, then fell to the ground lifeless. Two Vanguard were fast enough to hurl themselves behind the protection of other bodies, slapping at comms to alert their colonel. One managed, "Taking Union fire—" before the final burst from an assault rifle silenced him for good.

Howard cursed silently. Colonel Sainz had wanted no warning back to Katya Romilsky. But the Vanguard were tough soldiers all.

"Operation Sting completed," she said over her private link to Sainz. With a beckoning gesture she led her forces on a run across the side of a hill, trying to put the curve of its slope between them and the Sleeper.

"Thirty seconds, Rebecca," Sainz warned her. "Get out of there."

She kept a silent count to twenty-five, and then threw herself to the ground into the lee of a boulder. Her people followed her example and also grounded for cover—no need to tell them. Craning around the edge of the boulder, she noticed that the Sleeper had been driven farther out into the canyon. The first missile actually tunneled into the ground between it and the defile, throwing up a heavy curtain of scorched earth and burning wisps of grass.

The ground trembled in protest as another of Freedom's precision missiles framed the Sleeper on its other side and a third fell almost immediately on top of it. It detonated in an aerial burst, as if it had hit some kind of field, but the raw force of the explosion hammered down and flattened the titanic alien against the ground. The armoring of several of its legs bent and cracked under the pressures. The monstrous head was rudely slammed down flat. It sprang back up almost at once, whipping about to stare up into the sky as if it could see the offending battle station or its incoming death. Its long neck at full extension, the Sleeper shrieked once more its earsplitting, high-pitched scream as the missiles began to fall fast and furious.

Twenty missiles all told, smashing down within a quarter-klick diameter centered just off of the Sleeper's position. A few impacted the upper slopes over the defile, but most fell into the canyon as target-identification software and tracking data pulsed out in the final split second so that better than half hit or fell near the Sleeper. The thunderous tumult died away as quickly as it had begun, and as a breeze cleared away the dust, Rebecca Howard nodded her satisfaction.

The Sleeper was dead.

Its head severed from the body, the entire creature mangled into a mess of ocher tissue, grayish green chitin, and pools of black-specked white fleshy gobbets. Pieces of the carapace lay about like broken bits of an armored shell, steaming thin wisps of black smoke. Large streams of bloated gobbets and black fluid poured from deep within its body, staining the ground. A caustic stench rose over the canyon, but apparently nothing more harmful than the stench of death.

Then, as she watched, something deep within stirred and struggled to the surface of the mess of internal fluids and meat. First one, then a half dozen, and finally a full score or better of new creatures unlike any they'd seen before. Bloated, ocher-colored sacks of flesh ringed with thin but strong tentacles that pulled and pushed their way out from the inner cavity. Clear of the body, they vibrated and shook the slime and fluid from their skin. Feathery antennae rose to sample the air and then continued to vibrate as the fleshy sacks rose into the air, trailing the tentacles behind them. At the same height, the tentacles dropped away like useless shedding, and the final birthing of symbiots rose quickly into the sky, always upward. Rebecca Howard followed them until they were lost from sight, bidding them a hearty good riddance.

"Colonel Sainz! This is Colonel Katya Olia Romilsky of the Neo-Soviet empire's Fifty-sixth Striker, demanding the attention of Colonel Raymond Sainz!"

Colonel Romilsky sounded less than pleased, and Rebecca Howard walked her gaze from the dead Sleeper back to the sky where she'd seen the final symbiots disappear, waiting. Watching.

"Yes, Colonel Romilsky." No measure of respect or courtesy decorated Sainz's voice now. Flat and emotionless, he simply recognized her demand in the simplest way possible.

"I demand an explanation for the lack of contact with my auxiliary force attached to Major Howard's command. They do not answer any calls. And your people in the defile have violated our truce by destroying my Zephyr and firing on several of my units. I had your *word,* Sainz."

"*Duty above all,* Katya Romilsky. Isn't that what you argued to me?" His voice never rose beyond a casual tone. To Major Howard he sounded almost resigned. She knew how hard this was for him, but that fate had left him no choice. He had his orders, his sworn duty. He had given his word. One of them had to give.

"I am sorry, Katya, but you lose."

"I will bury you for this! You and your entire command, beginning with the snakes cowering in the defile."

Howard saw it then, the trail of vapor condensation that marked the first missile of a new set, arrowing down from space. It slammed into the ground just beyond the bluff, over Chernaya Gora, transmitting target-correction data back to all those which followed.

"No," Sainz said in the few seconds' lull that followed. "I don't think so."

And the missiles began striking in earnest against the Black Mountain.

28

Brygan Nystolov shivered, but the chill wasn't one of temperature. It was the cold silence that greeted his arrival in the science station and then followed him as he set about his chore.

His requests were met with silent compliance, no words. The consoles to either side of him stayed empty, and the only scientist who would meet his gaze was Randall Williams. And even Williams didn't speak as he watched Brygan collect his copies of all the data to date; everything to which he had been a party, which Colonel Allister had promised him. Watched with a wary eye.

It was near time for him to depart, but he knew that meant leaving something precious behind. In the fragile trust he'd built with Major Williams, Brygan had felt for the first time in his life that he belonged to something bigger than just himself. That he was valued, respected by his comrades even as he respected them. Staring at the *Icarus*'s stark metal bulkheads, he had never felt more alone than just then.

The Neo-Soviets spoke of such a camaraderie, promised it to each other constantly in their varied forms of careful address. It took the Union to show it to him, though, no doubt hoping he would return it. Hoping he would defect? Probably. But on the bridge he'd seen the disappointment in Major Williams's eyes. What the major had offered, he'd given freely for its own sake.

Brygan had wanted to believe that from the start, from the first offer to join the exploration mission. Yet he lived behind the wall of his carefully crafted identity. He'd never trusted enough to come clean as lie piled on top of lie, all the while postponing his return to the empire, drawn by the lure of mutual respect. Devoting his skills to the service of the empire, the years spent challenging Mars on its own terms, all that had been merely a method of existence. No one had truly valued his efforts. Not until he became part of a Union team. Not until these last few short days.

All lost.

Pausing at Randall Williams's console on his way out, Brygan held the computer file copies of the survey's work in his two large hands. Williams paused in his scrutiny of the *Icarus*'s approach to Terra, the imminent slingshot pass that would lead to the final decel burn for Luna. The scout wanted there to be something he could say, something he could do. Give up the data and deny it to the empire? *That* would make him a defector and a traitor besides. The Sputnik data belonged to the Neo-Soviets, as did the research based on it. Didn't he owe that much to Mother Russia? Did he owe her anything? These were questions with no easy answers. If there was a line he could walk without feeling the betrayer, likely he had already stumbled across it. And there was no going back.

"You could stay," Williams said slowly, preempting whatever the Neo-Soviet might decide to say. "We've days of work ahead of us at Luna, reviewing and analyzing the information collected by the survey." His dark eyes flickered for an instant to a few of the nearby scientists. "The offer still stands."

From Williams, likely it did. But that brief glance revealed his concern for the shattered trust between Brygan and the other team members. And, by implication, between Brygan and Paul Drake, who would make his own report to Colonel Allister. Perhaps Drake would balance the lives Brygan had saved against the minor deceit. Perhaps not. But it wasn't fear of Colonel Allister's response that kept Brygan from accepting. Not truly.

"All you ever asked of me," he said softly, his voice pitched for Williams's ears only, "was that I give to team as much as I take." He shook his head. "I failed that trust."

That was not an easy admission for the man known as the Bear to make.

Williams cupped one hand under his chin, stroking his sideburns. For an instant the wariness fled his eyes, replaced by frank evaluation. Another problem to which he could set his mind. "But are you avoiding the problem now, or turning to face it?" he asked.

Williams had put his finger on the heart of Brygan's trouble. He had never thought his leave-taking would be easy, given that his impromptu escape might look to Williams—and certainly would seem so to Drake—like he'd never planned a return to Luna. They would never know how close he had come.

"There are several problems, Randall Williams. One of the first I must deal with is the loyalty I owe Mother Russia.

That exists whether the empire . . ."—he paused—"values it or not." He had almost said whether the empire wanted to claim him, or not.

"This isn't about politics," Williams said.

"It should not have been," Brygan agreed. "Your Union, my empire." He shook his head sadly. "But I brought politics into it. Me. That means I am not ready."

Placing one hand on either side of his console station, Williams stared down at the screen for several long seconds. Finally, he exhaled deeply, and said, "I see. I can't say I agree with your decision, Brygan Nystolov, but I understand it."

Yes, he would. It was the major's nature to probe something until he understood, though Brygan might wish that Williams were not so tenacious in that respect. It made him a dangerous man, both personally and professionally. It also made for an open and curious nature that Brygan would miss.

He sketched a light bow to the major, leaning forward slightly at the waist and dipping his head. "Good-bye, Randall Williams."

Williams smiled thinly, eyes guarded as he returned the courtesy. "*Dos vedanya,* Brygan Vassilyevich."

Brygan nodded again, this time more abruptly, then walked quickly from the science station. Once in the corridor, he leaned back against one of the bulkheads until his uneasiness passed. He'd steeled himself against this moment, but receiving a Russian farewell only deepened his self-inflicted wound. It would be a long time closing, if it ever did.

It was almost as if Williams had known those would be the last words he'd ever speak to Brygan Nystolov.

Phillipe Savoign continued to track the emergency escape shuttle, which had separated from the *Icarus* as the spacecraft approached its slingshot around Earth. It was currently locked into a rapidly decaying orbit, decelerating at better than five standard gravities as it swung over the Laptev Sea. He checked the approach vector again, and it cut straight across Siberia and the southern Urals. He knew enough of orbital mechanics to program ballistic and orbital missiles, such as the space-to-earth weapons he'd helped Freedom task. If his calculations were right, the shuttle was making for the landing fields outside Volgograd or Zhdanov.

"Say again, Major Williams." Savoign adjusted the link nestled into his ear, thinking he hadn't heard correctly.

"The shuttle we launched is to be given clear passage," the major said. "Pass along the authorization to any battle platform it passes near."

Actually, the shuttle would pass almost directly under Station Freedom on its current course. Not that Savoign had to pass along the authorization codes, though. Freedom's targeting was still slaved to his console, its own abilities not yet back to full capacity. He glanced at the video feed showing the twenty-three small figures rising through the upper atmosphere. A decision had yet to come back down from the general about those. Now he had this new problem.

Savoign switched back over to the video link as if wanting to verify that Williams was who he claimed to be. It was the major, right enough. Savoign also checked out Williams's bona fides, just in case the video images were falsified. If this was a trick, it was a well-prepared one.

"Sir, do you know where that shuttle is coming down?" he asked.

"Somewhere over the Neo-Soviet empire, I'm sure." Was that a touch of resignation to the major's voice? "Phillipe, do you remember that Neo-Soviet we had in custody at Tycho?"

"I heard about him, Major." He'd been out on constant sorties then, trying to control the Neo-Soviet rush over the smashed fence line. "He's the one Colonel Allister sent up with you on the *Icarus*."

"Well, we've released him back to his own nation, as part of an agreement I arranged with the colonel. Now if you need to, get General Hayes's direct consent. But clear that shuttle."

Easier said than done. Tranquillity's central control was still a bedlam of activity, with the general coordinating a battle to secure the western plains in hopes of reestablishing part of the fence line. Not even Savoign's report of aliens rising up toward Freedom had garnered much more than a curt, "I'll be there in a moment!"

That had been over an hour ago.

With the general indisposed, no one else had the authority to second-guess Major Williams. Especially as he stood in line to take over Tycho Base. What was left of it. And Savoign knew the major. That counted for something as well.

"The shuttle is flying through a sensitive area," he said carefully.

"How sensitive?"

So sensitive that Phillipe Savoign had not believed the target profile General Hayes ordered him to program for Freedom's first missile launch. He'd thought the whole thing some poorly timed joke and the video stills a hoax. But Hayes wasn't known for a sense of humor when it came to military priorities. The fact that he'd stood over Savoign's shoulder, ignoring the battle he was now commanding, proved that the general considered this no light matter. It was true, then—mankind had made its first alien contact. An event Savoign was sure every spacefaring Union rank had considered at least once in passing thought.

And they had killed it.

Knowing the major's propensity to ask questions first—lots of questions—and shoot later, he could well imagine Williams's reaction to that event. Fortunately for Savoign, the event was classified as "need to know" and currently could only be briefed by hard copy. No transmitted data. He wouldn't be the one to inform Randall Williams that he'd been deprived of studying what might be the only alien contact in his lifetime.

Savoign checked the shuttle's progress and followed its proposed course within a hundred kilometers of the rising aliens. A close pass when one considered the normally vast distances associated with space travel.

"*Very* sensitive," he promised. He glanced to the other side of Tranquillity Control, at the officers running their battle by remote. "I'll take care of it."

The major didn't press. "Good enough. *Icarus* out."

The first of the bloated creatures had actually escaped the atmosphere, though how they managed that at such a slow rise Savoign had no way of knowing. Freedom's imaging systems showed them drifting out on a trail of frozen flesh and small crystals of expended gasses.

The creatures were fairly large now, twenty meters across, though the Seventy-first had gauged them at no bigger than two meters each when first they'd lifted into the sky. They were sloughing flesh and blood as they moved away from Earth, as if cannibalizing themselves and spitting out the detritus as a minor form of propulsion. Nearly disintegrated, the lead creature was barely recognizable.

A quick check of the numbers told Savoign all he needed to know. Most would hit the vacuum of space and likely die in a similar manner before the shuttle passed near. His only concern would be for the last two or three. They just might interfere with the shuttle's passage.

Maybe the Neo-Soviet officer shouldn't be allowed to see them. Or maybe he was looking for an excuse for target practice with more of Freedom's weapons. Savoign smiled at the hit. Well, General Hayes had already authorized the use of deadly force against the alien, which could extend to any offspring, and Major Williams wanted the shuttle's path "cleared." It was a judgment call. That was enough.

Besides, what could it really hurt?

The trailing three seed-bearers burned the last of their reserves to strain against the hold of the planet below. Their antennae continued to generate lift against gravity, now completely taking over for the initial rise provided by a lighter-than-air mixture of gases. The plasma spark that fueled all necessary functions dimmed within them, ready to convert over to the time of consumption. Then their bloated bodies would begin to eat away at themselves in order to provide that final thrust into space. And as that plasma core snapped from existence, the Sleeper seeds would spread to the solar winds.

The tight beam of coherent light that speared them one by one lasted no more than a millisecond. It disrupted flesh and burned away the antennae providing its lift. The touch of plasma inside two seed-bearers flashed out of control, consuming them. The third managed an instinctual override of such a useless death, snapping the plasma from existence as it drained away its final strength to seed early. Deep inside, thousands of tiny motes, no larger than dust specks, erupted from their organ. Most were destroyed in the searing heat of the laser. But not all.

The seeds drifted out into the Earth's upper atmosphere, already growing as radiation penetrated the shell to feed the life within. A Sleeper, every one.

And they slowly fell back toward Earth.

29

All said and done, the Seventy-first Assault Group was mauled but still alive. Still a functioning command.

The overcast haze above Gory Putorana had finally burned away by late afternoon, revealing the pale wash of a Siberian sky and the large, radiant scar that now commanded the day. A stiff breeze had risen, sweeping the smoke from the battlefield but unable to scrub the gagging scent of the dead Sleeper from the air. The occasional rifle shot punctured the stillness, the dying echo finally giving way to the sound of soldiers and vehicles on the move.

Colonel Raymond Jaquin Sainz made a rough head count as the unit slowly formed up into two short columns. Captains Searcy and Dillahunty had reassigned men as necessary to fill vehicles and maintain their subcommands at a rough parity. Matthew Dillahunty was functioning with a broken leg and four bullets pulled from his left arm and shoulder, but he refused medical relief.

Sainz knew that the Seventy-first was down to forty percent in equipment, most of which consisted of the Hydra troop transports so rarely fielded in direct combat. No Wendigo ag tanks had survived the final battle. Of the eight Aztecs, three would ride out under their own power, and the scraps of two more would be loaded aboard a Trojan supply carrier.

But Colonel Raymond Sainz would bring out better than sixty percent of his command, if just barely. Considering the unthinkable events of the last few days, that was better than anyone might have dreamed. He could live with that, and the personal price it had exacted.

His people massed in force at the lower end of the canyon draw, where the Sleeper had turned for Chernaya Gora in the face of the first Union and Neo-Soviet combined assault. This kept them away from the radioactive disasters of the colossal decaying corpse of the Sleeper and the now-smashed facility of Chernaya Gora. Only CBR specialists and their recruited help were allowed back into the area to search for any last survivors, be they Union or Neo-Soviet. Major Rebecca Howard was heading up those efforts, and now sought him out.

"We found them," she said. "Coming down the draw." There was no need to say who "they" were. Sergeant Tom Tousley was the only junior unaccounted for, and one of two left on the list of those for whom the colonel had demanded immediate notification. The other was Colonel Romilsky.

"Let's see how Tousley is first," Sainz said.

The sergeant lay on a stretcher, at the edge of the cordoned-off area the Seventy-first's medics had appropriated for the triage. He was still covered with the lead-shielded blankets the CBR specialists had used in recovering him from the defile. Sainz and Howard knelt at Tousley's side.

"They tell me you're going to live," Sainz said by way of greeting.

Tousley didn't look well, his face pale with shock. He'd lost a lot of blood and had at least three busted ribs to go with a broken collarbone and possible concussion. The scrapes and cuts covering his exposed skin were too numerous to count. Despite the fog of pain, a hard intelligence showed behind his eyes. Sainz felt more than a little awkward trying to offer comfort to this man who'd made a habit of opposing his command of the Seventy-first, but it came with the job. And as Tousley had proved again, he, too, was a man who knew how to get *his* job done.

"You came through a tough spot, Tom."

To Tousley's credit, his question was not for himself. "My . . . squad?" he asked, the effort at speech seriously taxing him.

Sainz glanced over at Howard and nodded for her to field the question. "They're alive," she assured the sergeant. "Nash was broken up pretty bad, and Loveday took a heavy dose of radiation, but they'll make it. Most everyone from the defile survived."

Another medic stepped in and knelt at Tousley's head, where the man couldn't see him. He shook his head lightly, warning them off.

"Get some rest," Sainz said evenly. "You did well, Tom." He got up to leave, as did Howard.

"Colonel," Tousley said weakly, and the two officers turned to look at him. His pain-shrouded eyes flicked up toward the head of the draw, toward the dead Sleeper and what was left of Chernaya Gora. "So . . . did you," he said, just before his eyes drifted shut.

Sainz smiled sadly, finding solace in the words. He still ached for all he had lost in this fight, an almost unbearable feeling of emptiness. He nodded to Howard that they were done there, and the two continued their tour of the camp.

Union medics had set up a separate triage area for wounded Neo-Soviets, with a guard of several infantry squads. It was next to the section roped off to receive the few unwounded infantry they'd recovered.

"First and second columns are nearly manned and ready," Captain Ryan Searcy reported as Sainz and Howard entered the area.

Rebecca Howard acknowledged for them both. "Search teams have three more bodies to recover from the men lost in the defile. Then we head out." She looked to her commander. "Do we post Landvoy's Aztecs as outriders?"

Sainz nodded his approval, and Searcy sketched a quick salute before returning to preparations for the Seventy-first's departure.

By comparison with Tom Tousley, Colonel Katya Romilsky had come out of the upper draw both better and worse off. Her right arm was heavily bandaged up to the elbow. Two deep gashes on her left side were sewn together with butterfly sutures, while the compress covering her left eye was soaked with blood and fluid. Despite her injuries, she'd gotten off lightly, considering that she'd stood at ground zero during Freedom's missile strike. She was probably in a lot of pain, but what showed in her open eye was anger.

"And here the great warriors come to gloat over the defeated," she said in English, obviously for Rebecca

Howard's sake. Strapped into a stretcher, the closest thing the Seventy-first had to security restraints, she still refused to accept an inferior position.

"What is it to be, Sainz? Summary execution, or do the remnants of your *honor* demand a mock trial first?"

The colonel met her sarcasm with stony silence. Her words should have hurt, but Romilsky now seemed more a pitiful creature than the dedicated enemy officer whose opinion had once mattered to him. That person never really existed, though. She had been an illusion concealing a devious and vicious attack.

"Neither," he finally said. "We'll leave you with food and medical supplies so you can be recovered by whatever force your empire sends to investigate the destruction of Chernaya Gora."

"And my Striker?" She glanced at the limited triage area and the even smaller holding site. "What's left of it?"

Rebecca Howard pointed to a large stack of supplies protected by a rocky overhang. "Enough for you all," she promised. "We've been assured you will be found within two days."

Romilsky missed the implication, perhaps because of the single rifle shot that suddenly echoed down the draw. Then another. With a feral grin, she lapsed back into Russian.

"Some of my Vanguard resisting your roundup efforts?" she taunted. "I'd rather they went down fighting, so long as they take at least one of yours with them."

Sainz shook his head sadly. "No, Katya Romilsky. Those are mercy shots."

"Mercy shots?" The split second of doubt in her eye was quickly replaced by rage.

Major Howard nodded. "We are not recovering Rad

Troopers or mutants of any type. Or any Vanguard who have obviously taken too much radiation. Colonel's orders—they're all being"—she paused for emphasis—"*put down* for their own good."

Romilsky twisted under her restraints, glaring at Sainz. "*Vnebrachney,*" she cursed, but then returned to English. "But you'll never get away. At least I have that. How can you expect to escape the empire's borders alive?"

Raymond Sainz's opinion of Romilsky's cunning rose another notch. Even in defeat she had the presence of mind to try to ferret out intelligence of military value.

"I think it would be most unwise to tell you any specifics, Colonel Romilsky. Let's just say we have a native guide."

"A prisoner? You said you would leave my people behind to be rescued!"

"Not a prisoner. He requested to accompany us, not shocked at all that we carried the day here. But then that probably doesn't surprise you." Sainz nodded toward his Hades command transport, which was grounded off to one side of the formed columns. In its shadow a frail, stoop-shouldered man waited, huddled against the cold metal, his arms wrapped around his body as if he were freezing.

The Neo-Soviet Mental.

"*Nyet,*" Romilsky whispered, more to herself than Sainz. Then, more forceful, "*Nyet!* I forbid this."

She struggled violently against the stretcher restraints. The two Union officers backed off a step, watching dispassionately. "You cannot afford to leave me alive. I will hunt you at every step—strike at you in any way I can. Sainz, release me from this and face me on the field, damn you! If you have any honor left!"

He smiled sadly. "I have honor enough left, but not to be spent further on you. My mission was to facilitate the destruction of Chernaya Gora and return. And as you taught me so readily, Katya, duty rises above all else. Learning that cost me dearly, but I still accomplished half my mission. Teaching me that lesson cost you your command. That's a net victory I'll have to settle for."

He nodded to end the interview. "*Dos vedanya,* Katya Olia Romilsky." Sainz turned and walked away, and Rebecca Howard fell into step beside him.

"*Mojet nekogda ne uvidesh dom snova*!" Romilsky shouted at his back, mad with fury.

Sainz stopped short. He understood the words of her curse. He even knew its origin. Rebecca Howard looked at him strangely, but she let him be. A moment later he resumed walking, still lost in thought.

Mojet nekogda ne uvidesh dom snova . . . The curse came out of the Second World War, when the Soviets had faced the German war juggernaut. All of European Russia ravaged, all the way to the Volga. Leningrad besieged for two years. The cruelest thing to wish on a fellow soldier then: *May you never see home again!*

Not that he expected any superstition to prevent his forces from reaching rendezvous with the Leviathans. He could elude Neo-Soviet patrols, if they mounted any. A full day of hard travel would give them the coast of the Laptev Sea, just off Ust'-Olenek, and there they would meet up with Captain Fredriksson.

But a shiver of fear ran down his spine as he glanced up into the alien sky and that brilliant scar staring down on them. That they had survived the unthinkable over the last few days was wonder enough. If he could live through all that, no curse could keep Raymond Sainz from returning home.

If there was a curse, he knew it had nothing to do with getting home, only with what he might find when he got there.

EPILOGUE

Brygan Nystolov stood at the edge of a third-floor balcony in the Military Sciences and Technology Building in Moskva. He barely felt the freezing night of the Neo-Soviet capital, though his breath frosted in the air and rimed his beard with ice. Light traffic moved along Gor'kogo below. From his vantage he could see the Kremlin to the north, on the other side of Red Square. He stared south, ignoring the Taman Guards sentry who stood back along the wall. Instead he watched the thick sliver of moon as it hung over the Intourist Hotel.

There were no longer many stars to compete with the bright crescent's dominance of Terra's nighttime sky. The Styx Nebula would not be up for hours. Brygan knew that Randall Williams was up there, too, likely back to work at Tycho Base. Did he spare a thought now and then for the

Neo-Soviet who had fled his offer of friendship? Brygan hoped so.

It was one of a dozen thoughts or more that he kept private. His debriefings were mercilessly repetitive, held every four hours to keep him at the edge of exhaustion. Still he was getting quite good at managing a system of half-truths and omissions, giving his countrymen everything they needed for the sake of Mother Russia and the empire, but refusing to let them dissect his thoughts.

If they had no direct use for Brygan Nystolov, what did it matter if they understood him?

By the second night of debriefings, Brygan knew he would not be among the group that would return to the rogue asteroid. He saw it in the way the MST directors behaved toward him, at turns suspicious or completely indifferent. They seemed to care more about his observations of Union positions and procedures on Luna than his work on Sputnik 23's data or his observations and discoveries on the Union survey flight. The raw data from *Icarus*'s exploration flight they simply turned over to their own experts. And they fielded Brygan's own questions with only vague replies. Would there be a mission to return to the asteroid and investigate the frozen aliens? Possibly. What about the battle he had witnessed? It was being investigated.

If Brygan had to guess, he'd say that a mission had already been launched to the asteroid base and its possible storehouse of treasures. Perhaps the hibernating aliens were it. Perhaps not. But the suspicious absence of key military operators these last twenty-four hours suggested that a mission was under way.

With one final look at Moskva's skyline, Brygan turned his eyes toward the moon just long enough to whisper, *"Dos vedanya, comrades."* Then he turned abruptly for the door leading back inside. He had made his decision, and now stood by it. No regrets; not this time anyway. And if it wasn't a full life, it was an existence with purpose. In the empire, one could rarely expect more.

If Brygan Nystolov could hope anything, for now it would be that his sacrifice had bought the empire enough time to prepare.

Never enough time, Randall Williams decided, moving down the corridor of Tycho Base, in between labs and projects. With so much to oversee and accomplish in the two days since the *Icarus*'s return, he'd grown ever more annoyed with every wasted moment spent in tactical meetings and conferences with the Union military leaders of Luna. Even though Union Command had finally reestablished itself at Cheyenne Mountain down on Earth, there seemed to be no end to the nonscientific demands on his time.

Still, as he recognized the man waiting for him outside the next lab, this was one meeting he wouldn't mind taking. Besides which, he trusted the captain to keep it brief.

Paul Drake stood leaning against the wall, arms folded over his chest. "I wanted to say good-bye," he said as Williams came up to him. "The *Icarus* has been ordered to the Styx Nebula. Weapons R&D wants a closer look at its strange properties. I leave within the hour."

Williams nodded. "Not back to the asteroid then?" He tried to keep the disappointment from his voice. The abandoned base they had surveyed could hold countless treasures, not the least of which was more information on the alien races they'd witnessed in combat.

"Nothing will keep the Neo-Soviets from reaching the base first. They're burning in at four Gs. And Luna can't spare the military assets to take the base by force." Drake pursed his lips in thought, then admitted, "I have the *impression* that the *Prometheus* is being outfitted at Station Independence for just such a mission, though."

"You still regret allowing Brygan to reach the empire with the data," Williams said, making it a statement rather than a question. That had been a hard call for him to make, even though he was far from being military-minded.

"It might have been better for the Union if Nystolov had been intercepted."

Intercepted. A thinly veiled euphemism for the destruction of the shuttle that Drake had recommended. Even now, knowing that the Neo-Soviet empire might beat them to a major discovery, Williams could not find it in himself to condemn the scout.

"How many lives did he save, Paul, when we were bringing aboard the crystalline formation sample? Maybe even yours?"

Drake shrugged uneasily. "Maybe," he admitted. "I guess there's no disgrace in learning from the enemy."

"Not unless you want to make all the mistakes yourself," Williams said. He offered Drake his hand. "Good luck, Paul."

"Thank you, Major. I'm sure to see you when I get back." The Marine broke the handshake with one final pump, then turned on his heel and walked with purpose down the corridor as Williams keyed his security code into the lab's lock.

Passing inside, all thoughts of Drake and the *Icarus*'s next flight were forgotten. Randall Williams spared a final thought for Brygan Nystolov and the scout's assertion that some things were better left undiscovered. Ultimately, the scientist in Williams had decided to disagree. The potential alien threat existed and would have found them sooner or later. Now the Union had time to prepare, to unlock as many secrets of the Maelstrom as possible. It was the same motive that had driven Nystolov to abandon the Union team.

A group of four technicians worked around the large crystalline fragment, which took up better than half the large room. Two worked up close with delicate instruments, and another pair on consoles monitoring its signal pulses. Randall Williams walked along its side, one hand trailing over the smooth emerald facets and occasionally lingering on the new fracture growths.

He nodded a greeting to Lieutenant Theresa Dupras, assigned as his direct aide once again and the scientist in charge of this particular experiment. She made room at her console, its screen dedicated to a baseline trace over which the pulse would strobe like some alien heartbeat.

"Okay, everyone." Williams waved their attention toward the formation. "We're going to vary the top-end amplitude of a frequency-modulated carrier wave and see what that does to the crystals' output. Let's try and find the regenerative signal feedback this time." He nodded once to Dupras. "Give me a signal."

And then Major Randall Williams began to wrestle with a new problem, losing himself in the challenge.

The nanite cores sensed a nearby varying signal. Strong magnitude. The modulation suggested intelligence rather than background noise—an intelligence technologically advanced enough to be manipulating energy for the purpose of communication, power, or weaponry. It was what the probe was designed to recognize, and call attention to.

The incoming energy patterns were re-formed to elevate the power of the signal pulse already in progress. The strengthened signal radiated out from the crystals, to be sampled and recorded by the Union scientists' equipment. It passed through walls and out over the surface of the moon, above the Tycho Crater Base. Passing up through the thin atmosphere cost it less than three seconds and a small measure of strength as a portion of the signal reflected back off the moon's thin ionosphere. Then the signal was freed into the Maelstrom.

It reached and passed by the Earth. Stations Independence and Freedom might have detected it except for the repairs still to be made on their electronics capabilities. A Neo-Soviet ground-based installation did detect the ultrahigh-frequency pulses, but as the invariable signals seemed to convey no actual intelligence, the event was labeled one of several thousand anomalies.

Beyond the Earth, the signal found little except vacuum and minor debris for some time. The icy blue nebula eventually fell into its wake, as did a few of the planets that could be seen decorating Earth's night skies in place of stars. The signal passed through the space recently inhabited by a large portion of a long-dead planetoid, and it would pass by that same island ninety-three million kilometers later where it had temporarily fused into the surface of an airless planet. Asteroid belts. Rogue suns. Derelict spacecraft. World after world.

The beacon swept the alien sky of the Maelstrom, always searching.

About the Author

Into the Maelstrom is Loren Coleman's fifth published novel. His previous novels were all set in the BattleTech® universe. He has also written game fiction and source material for such companies as FASA, TSR, and Wizards of the Coast.

Loren currently resides in Washington State with his wife, Heather Joy, two sons, Talon LaRon and Connery Rhys Monroe, and a new daughter, Alexia Joy. He works in the company of three Siamese cats.

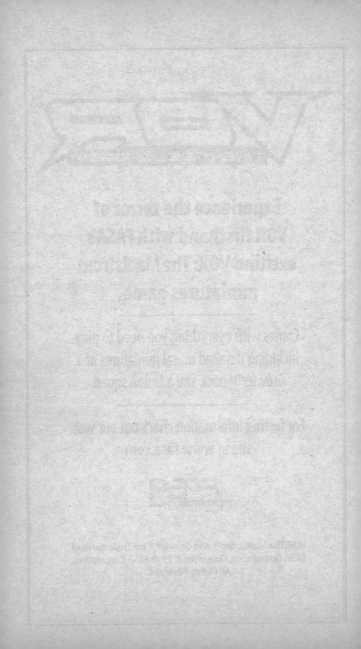